MAGNIFICENCE

MAGNIFICENCE

a novel

LYDIA MILLET

W. W. Norton & Company

New York • London

The author thanks Maria Massie, Tom Mayer, Jess Purcell, Ryan Harrington, Denise Scarfi, Amy Robbins, Nancy Palmquist, Don Rifkin, Tara Powers, Louise Mattarelliano, Steve Colca, Ingsu Liu, David High, Bill Rusin, Dan Christiaens, and David Goldberg for all that they have done.

Copyright © 2013 by Lydia Millet

Printed in the United States of America

First Edition

For information about permission to reproduce selections from this book, write to Permissions, W. W. Norton & Company, Inc., 500 Fifth Avenue, New York, NY 10110

For information about special discounts for bulk purchases, please contact W. W. Norton Special Sales at specialsales@wwnorton.com or 800-233-4830

Manufacturing by Courier Westford

Book design by Chris Welch

Production manager: Louise Mattarelliano

Library of Congress Cataloging-in-Publication Data

Millet, Lydia, 1968–
Magnificence : a novel / Lydia Millet. — 1st ed.
p. cm.
ISBN 978-0-393-08170-1
1. Widows—Fiction. 2. Taxidermy—Fiction. 3. Life change events—Fiction. 4. Inheritance and succession—California—Fiction. 5. Shared housing—Fiction. I. Title.
PS3563.I42175M34 2012
813'.54—dc23
2012015145

W. W. Norton & Company, Inc.
500 Fifth Avenue, New York, N.Y. 10110
www.wwnorton.com

W. W. Norton & Company Ltd.
Castle House, 75/76 Wells Street, London W1T 3QT

1 2 3 4 5 6 7 8 9 0

MAGNIFICENCE

1

It was a stricken love, but still love. It was the kind of love that gazed up at you from the bare white flood of your headlights— a wide-eyed love with the meekness of grass-eaters. Soft fur, pink tongue, and if you got too close a whiff of mulch on the breath. This was the love she cherished for her husband.

The love had other moments. Of course it did. But its everyday form was vegetarian.

She suspected it was the love of most wives for their husbands, after some time had passed. Not for the newlyweds—that was the nature of the condition—but for the seasoned, the ones who had seniority. When she thought of conjugal love she saw a field of husbands stretched out in front of her—a broad, wide field. Possibly a rice paddy. They were bent over, hoeing. Did you hoe rice? Well, whatever. The way she saw them, the husbands had a Chinese thing going on. They toiled like billions of peasants.

Technically, historically, and at this very moment in most of the world it was the wives who toiled. The wives toiled for their livelihoods, for the husbands and the little children. Sure; those were the facts. It was the wives, historically and factually—in that limited historical, factual sense—that were the beasts of burden. Even in the richer places, it was the women who shortened their life expectancy by marrying, whereas the husbands lived longer than their freewheeling bachelor counterparts.

Still, there was something about the essence of husbands that made them seem like sturdy toilers. Husband, housebound. It might be the wives who were bound to the houses, materially speaking, but the husbands were bound to them. This was because of the narrow focus of most men, how they tended to have few intimates, in emotional terms. They left the social bonding to the wives, so they were bound to them.

And she was ready to tell him all the details, if that was what he wanted. She was prepared to come clean. But a toiler could so easily be hurt. A toiler was chronically exhausted from his long days of labor. What labor, you might ask? The labor of being a man, of course. It was hard to be a man. The men were all insane, basically, due to testosterone. You could see it in them, roiling under the surface. The few exceptions proved the rule, and the smart men were big enough to admit it. For instance, steroids made you more of a man, chemically, and also—not a coincidence—made you insane. She'd read that autism was thought by scientists to be an exaggerated form of maleness. So there was that. The latent madness and retardation of men was compounded by the fact that most of them didn't get to kill their own prey anymore, stalk living things and slay them in a savage bloodletting.

The men, even when they didn't know it, were frustrated by this. They were unfit to live in civilized society.

Of course, women were also subject to hormonal madness—famously so. The estrogen or whatever, so-called premenstrual syndrome: the chemicals that, in excess, made them into caricatures of women. Hysteria, for instance, as Freud had called it. Neurosis. That time of the month. Of course Freud had been largely discredited. He had been a philosopher more than a scientist and Americans did not trust philosophers. Far from it. Also he did cocaine.

Still: no question, the fairer sex was more changeable than the unfair one. In practice this meant that the women's madness sometimes receded. But with the men it was constant. When it came to insanity, women were indecisive while men never let up. Oddly the chronic insanity of men was often referred to as stability; the men, being permanent sociopaths, got credit for consistency. Whereas the women, being mere part-time neurotics, were typecast as flighty. Essentially, the female bouts of sanity were used as weapons against them. Sociopaths v. neurotics. It was a nontrivial distinction since many men took the thing a bit too far, frankly, becoming serial killers, wife beaters, dirty cops, or boy soldiers in roving gangs; war criminals, tyrants, and demagogues.

Not so much the women.

In one sense, though, she didn't blame the men. That would be blaming the victim. They were hobbled by their repressed rage and Asperger syndrome, variations on which were lavishly spread throughout the male population, but so what? Far from blaming them she had always loved them, loved them for their sad flaws. The men were tragic heroes. To be a tragic hero, all that was needed was manhood.

She loved them. Yes she did.

Casey was driving her to the airport, down La Cienega at rush hour. There was a comfortable silence between them. Susan gazed out the window at traffic. The traffic was full of men, most of whom were tragic. The tragic men sat in their cars, driving. Some played with radio dials, others picked their noses while staring glassily at nothing. In many cases, completely unaware of their tragic identity. Women were also driving, of course—her own daughter, for one; Casey enjoyed driving and drove with speed and a certain measure of abandon—and yet these women, including Casey who was in a wheelchair, were less tragic per se than the men. The women might be unfortunate—take Casey, for instance—but few of them were Ophelia. No, when it came to tragedy the men had slyly cornered the market.

Driving gave Casey a feeling of mastery she didn't have in the chair, since she was higher up when she drove. In the driver's seat she was on the same plane with everyone else: the playing field was level. She was excited now, drumming her fingers on the wheel. Susan felt exhilarated herself. Her husband and her employer, both returning from the tropics. It was a homecoming, a heroes' welcome. Though come to think of it, the hero role, like tragedy, was unfairly, readily available to men. When she herself stepped off an airplane, no one would ever shriek in joy, jump up and down and hurl themselves into her arms.

Neither she nor Casey usually smoked but impulsively they had bummed Marlboro Reds off a burly biker at a bar, a guy covered in colorful tattoos with eagles feathering his biceps. The only reason they hadn't progressed to hard liquor, in a further festive gesture, was that the hour wasn't advanced. If Susan drank before sunset she tended to nod off. Her middle age began to show. They would wait, Casey had said, and have their drinks with Hal and T. They would meet the two men at the airport and take them out to celebrate.

"Maybe move into the right lane?" she asked Casey.

"Oh yeah? Huh. Who's driving?"

"You are."

"Exactly."

"It'd be smoother sailing, though. Look!"

"Mother?"

"OK, OK."

"Relax. It's not so bad. We could be on the 405."

Anyway: she would tell him whatever he wanted to know, he had the right to such knowledge, but all in all it would be far better for him if he never asked.

Of course she would never describe the exact dimensions of her affection to him. Those microscopic inclinations were a best-kept secret—out of protectiveness for the other, more than anything—a secret she kept to herself, as everyone guarded their shameful, shrugged-in shadings of instinct. No one told the smallest increments of their feelings to their dearly beloveds. No one revealed the minute singularities—the slack of an ass, say, how it could cause disgust. The response was involuntary.

There might be those, on second thought, who did reveal

such things in times of anger, but mostly those people were not women. She would keep the hurting elements to herself, those subtle insults to a man's self-worth. In certain moments, for instance, his sex could seem a forlorn, pugnacious servant, a servant that bowed its head and had a humble, comic quality. Anyway you could pity something, pity it as a brute and still want to use it: a brute part of a half-child, half-ape. Their handle, their use, their eagerness a panting hound. The metaphor was mixed, she knew that. Her love for husbands was like a love of deer, but then the men themselves were other animals, half-apes, and finally their sexes were doglike. Quite the menagerie, all told.

She condescended to the sexes of men, but it wasn't personal. Clearly they also condescended to hers. They had their own opinions about the sex of a woman, and those opinions were not all positive. That much was obvious—from, say, pornography, which almost every man loved, from the purest young boy to the jaded defiler. In other words small secrets were also held against her, and she did not need to know them.

Pornography, she thought. Degradation and debasement. A man liked to degrade a woman, in pornography. It made perfect sense. If she were male, she'd like it too. Because a man might not know he was tragic, but he often suspected it. On a subconscious level, a man suspected himself of pathos. A man walked around bearing that half-aware, weary load; it was more stressful to suspect than to know for certain. Women were oppressed from the outside, via the patriarchy—girls raped in various African cultures, for instance, then put to death for their trouble. But men were oppressed from inside their own skin. She saw it this way: the testosterone was a constant barrage, not unlike an artillery shelling. They had doubtless needed it, in, say, prehistory, to run around spearing meat, build up muscles that impressed the breeding-age females, etc., much as baboons made their loud wahoo calls or sported shocking pink anuses.

But now that the men were deprived of the endorphins of the chase and the butchering, the hormones were a call with no response, a ceaseless, useless siege upon the male psyche. Naturally the men, held hostage in bunkers of flesh, sought refuge in pornography and violence. It was just self-expression.

At the airport she would see T., who had disappeared in the jungle and then, a miracle, been found again. She had thought he was gone and then he rose up like Lazarus—her employer, a real estate developer who fetishized his Mercedes and wore no suits retailing at less than 5K, had been discovered a few weeks ago living on a tropical island with poor hygiene, ribs showing, and a hut made of twigs. Despite these choices her husband, who had found him, somehow claimed he was in robust mental health.

Admittedly it had been generous of Hal to fly down to Central America to search for T., a man he barely knew. Admittedly she was grateful. Even if the trip had been an excuse to get away from her, even if it was his answer to an unpleasant discovery, namely her having sex with a coworker on the floor of her office. (She was still mystified as to exactly how he'd been a witness to that encounter: the front door to the office had been locked, the blinds, she was almost sure, closed tight?) Anyway a hard conversation was pending between them re: infidelity.

And his evaluation of the situation with T. could not be taken at face value. He had no history with the man. According to Hal her employer had reevaluated his life while he was wandering,

starved and exhausted, in the rainforest, and this no doubt careful and rational appraisal had resulted in a decision to reside, for
a time, as a hermit on a remote island with no indoor plumbing.
Which Hal had tried to justify, over the phone, as a moment
of growth, a sort of premature midlife crisis that headed in the
monklike/whole grains/meditation direction instead of the more
popular red sportscar/divorce/trophy wife. He harked back to his
sixties roots: in his view T. had been seeking enlightenment.

But T. had lost a girlfriend recently, lost her to sudden death.
And Hal was not perceptive, when it came to human interactions.
Susan's husband was not what, in job interviews, you called a
people person. Herself she thought T.'s condition resembled a
schizoaffective disorder. She was no shrink, but she'd done some
reading in the DSM-IV. She liked the Case Studies.

Casey's excitement was simple. T. was her friend and to her
all that mattered was that he was rescued. If he was unfit for
business that meant nothing to her. And it should mean nothing to Susan either; she should be thinking first of his long-term
welfare. After all she and T. were also friends, beyond the work
arrangement, and no matter what there was no risk for her: he
would cover her salary.

But stress had worn her down, making financial decisions
without him. She had never intended to sign up for a job that
required actual thought. She'd become a secretary, after decades
of thankless teaching in the L.A. Unified School District, in a
half-relaxed and half-perverse gesture—purely for the anonymity
it offered and the straightness. She had put her energy into other
pursuits until recently, with a sleek and methodical urgency.
T.'s disappearance had obstructed that. She needed relief. She

needed him to come in and issue directions. "Do this. Do that." She longed to be absolved of agency. For all she knew she'd made bad decisions already, decisions that were draining his coffers. But if he was insane he could not effect her rescue. He would lack the power to reassure.

"So hey, when Daddy settles in? He's probably going to want to talk to you about something," said Casey.

Susan hadn't talked to Hal for two nights now. It was T. who had called and left their flight number on her machine—sounding even farther away than he was, over their staticky connection, farther away than the tropics. Likely exhausted by his mania.

T., who had always seemed the most solid of young men. It went to show you. The madness lurked in all of them. Smack a man down in nature and he returned to his Cro-Magnon roots.

Casey was looking at her sidelong, waiting.

"What something?"

Could she know what Hal knew, could Hal have told her? He wouldn't. He would *not*.

"My job."

Relief.

"The telemarketing thing?"

"Yeah. The deal is, it's phone sex."

Susan's head jerked to the left. Her neck hurt, it was so sudden. Past Casey's profile the side of a moving truck read STARVING STUDENTS.

"Case, please. You almost gave me whiplash. Can people get, like, sideways whiplash?"

"I'm serious, it's a 900 number."

The set of her lips was the confirmation: the lips and the chin, its slight lift. Even as a toddler she had lifted her chin like that when she was being stubborn.

"You actually mean it."

"Sleazy, yeah. That's what I like about it. I wanted to give you a heads-up, is all."

"Tell me you just connect the calls, or something."

"Come on. That wouldn't be any fun."

She found her eyes were watering annoyingly—couldn't she even take a joke? Damn it. Big deal. Laugh it off.

She turned away and looked out her window.

"And your father already knows this?" she asked, her gaze still steadily averted. Another truck; they were boxed in. This one was yellow and read PURITAN.

She looked to her left again, then back to the right: STARVING STUDENTS. PURITAN. STARVING STUDENTS. PURITAN. And here they were, between the two. It was a clear rebuke. A rebuke from the world, which knew them both and knew everything. Oh how the world reflected you in its unending streams of atoms, churning atoms out of which significance beamed—significance, but not purpose. The great collective knowingness of the world was a library of the hidden, a vast repository. But it was not meaning. It was the sum of an infinitude of parts, was all. There was the paint on the sides of trucks, the trucks themselves, which commerce and roads had brought beside her like this . . . in Casey's car, the car between the trucks, they were neither starving students nor puritans. They were sluts.

She was a bad mother and a slut; her daughter was a bad daughter and a slut. Two sluts.

The traffic started to move again.

Of course, personally she wanted to be a slut. She rejoiced in it. It was the sole creative gesture of her life. "Shit," said Casey, and swerved around a pothole.

It was the private room in her house, it was Bluebeard's locked closet—the only space, since the accident, where she was not only a dutiful mother or wife. Say what you liked about husbands: mother, now there was a role that typecast you for the rest of your days . . . being a slut was a survival tactic. No more, no less—that sly, indulgent freedom, that liberty in its rotten deceit, the sweetness in the rot. It had saved her from despair more than once.

When she was young she'd been pedantic on the subject: monogamy was authoritarian, a form of property law. On occasion she'd even tried to convince Hal, who had a more conventional mindset. There had been long earnest nights of conversation, now blurred in retrospect—one ego struggling to free itself from the encumbrance of another. Since then she'd dropped all that as a series of rationalizations. Arguments could be made, but at its base sleeping with many men who were not her husband was a pure satisfaction, an expression of greed and vanity, a glorification of herself. She could freely admit it; she did. In those spans of time, sleeping with other men, she emerged from obscurity into the light. She was the subject of the biopic: the camera followed her face, thus slowing time, and a score accompanied her movements. She liked to see herself with others; she wanted to be known.

And Casey, in the wheelchair, how could she make that gesture? It was the wrong kind of freedom for Casey, it was a category error. Yet here was Casey, willful as always, stubbornly ignoring the fact that her gesture was compromised. Yes, yes, this was the manner of her revolt—it was parallel—Susan saw that now. The two of them were the same in this, though Casey had no idea.

But Casey could not walk. She could not walk and had no legs that moved.

Poor darling, poor sweetie.

Possibly this 1-900 thing was a way of keeping her legless-ness private. Callers would never know that she was in a chair, so Casey could be pure voice—could gratify them in the warm and electronic darkness, the dark that bristled with mystery. Their private and dirty handmaiden.

Casey was always, always breaking her mother's heart—Susan had learned to withstand the familiar, crushing pressure. She'd been forced to. This was only the newest and latest erosion of her hopes and dreams. Now she was forced to see a stark out-line: her daughter as a phone-sex drone. Well, yes. Of course. It was the logical next step. Casey had already done the rest—done the apathy, done the rebellion, done the resentment and the self-loathing. Now, apparently, it was high time for the paraplegic sex work.

Susan could squint and make out the stereotypes of those outlines—archetypes, stereotypes that shone with depressing implications.

Gooseflesh crept up her arms.

"You told your father this?' she pressed after a minute, shak-ing her head. "And you didn't tell me?"

"I didn't tell him, actually," said Casey. "He figured it out. He just knew."

"He just *knew*?" It was embarrassing. She hated to get teary in front of her daughter, who would shoot her a familiar filial look that neatly blended compassion with contempt. "But it's *Hal*. He never *just knows* anything."

"Don't be a bitch."

Susan shook her head. Her throat was closing.

The car was a cage—how did people not always think so? Cages on the assembly line, metal cages with bars and glass, cages along the roads by the billions with their tailpipes shooting out poisons. After the accident she thought of all cars as her enemies, thought viciously that she hated all of them for what they'd done to Casey, hated them like animate creatures, maggots or weevils or scorpions, and she would kill them all if she could. Not KILL YOUR TELEVISION; kill the cars. But of course, she also had one of her own and drove it all the time.

Cars were the life, here in L.A. Cars were the smallest and most portable of all homes. Even Casey, almost killed by a car, still lived in them without obvious reflection.

She felt for the vinyl shelf along the side of the door, pressing down with her elbow. There was a narrow well, half lined with lint, on the blue armrest, and she looked into it studiously. The lint blurred. What did they make these oddly shaped holes in the armrests for? What was supposed to fit there? Nothing fit. Or if it did, it was unknown, illusive, and not part of life at all.

The holes were useless, and these useless holes were irritants, ever-present, inexplicable, angering.

"He heard something, is all," said Casey, more kindly. "He overheard me talking to a friend."

"You wanted to be a professor," said Susan. "Remember?"

She was still shaking her head, minutely. It was almost involuntary. She wiped the corner of one eye quickly with the heel of her right hand and insisted on staring out the window.

"You wanted to get a Ph.D," she went on.

"Now, that was just stupid of me," said Casey.

They were on the road into LAX now. Taxis and cars lined up at the curb to their right.

"You were going to improve your French."

"I was i-di-*o*-tic."

"You were going to go to *graduate* school."

"I was eighteen! And now I'm not anymore. And I don't *want* to be some boring academic. Even if I could. It's not the chair, Mother. It's just me. It's like, a natural evolution."

"So you *evolved* from a Ph.D. candidate into a phone-sex worker?"

"I evolved from a teenager to a grownup."

"But you're more," said Susan.

"Jesus. It's not the end of the world, OK?" said Casey. "Chill out. Take a deep breath. It's just a job."

She spun the wheel into the parking structure.

•

At the baggage claim carousel they waited awkwardly. Susan watched her daughter's face, the lashes shading the cheekbones. She had not always been so slight and wan. Before the chair she had often been tanned, cheeks flushed, hair lightened by the sun. She had a boyfriend who surfed and then one who was a skateboarder; on weekends they disappeared down the beach in sneakers and ratty, faded shorts and came home with peeling noses and salt tangling their hair.

Now she was always pale. But she was still beautiful. In her mind's eye Susan saw baby pictures.

God damn it. Stay presentable.

"You actually choose to do this?" she started, over the background murmur punctuated by loudspeaker announcements. "Because if it's money—"

"I choose," said Casey firmly.

Susan stared past her at a poster of a hotel: a white high-rise with looming palms in the foreground. She stared at the highrise. She stared at the palms.

Casey caught sight of him first, coming toward them in ragged pants and shirtsleeves. He was thin and too darkly tanned, like a Florida retiree, but lacking the beard Hal had described. A recent shave had left the sides of his face paler than the rest, the lower cheeks and the chin.

But what alarmed her was his expression—heavy, anxious. He bent over Casey first, knelt down at the chair and took her face in his hands. Susan saw how she looked at him, noticed it fleetingly, but then already—in the shock of this—the recognition faded as he stood up straight again, still holding Casey's wrist.

"I'm sorry, but I couldn't tell you this over the phone. I have very bad news," he said.

In an instant the whole of existence could go from familiar to alien; all it took was one event in your personal life. You might think you were only a mass of particles in the rest of everything, a mass exchanging itself, bit by bit, with other masses, but then you were blindsided and all you knew was the numbness of separation.

Casey clung to T.'s hand and Susan stood beside her with her own hand on Casey's other shoulder. She was pinching the shoulder, she realized slowly, quite hard though she did not intend to—out of anxiety, out of tension, pressing the hard ridge of the collarbone between her thumb and forefinger. She made herself relax her hold and the sensation melted into others, unnamed and nonspecific, hazy and suffocating as they stood there in a kind of dumbness. She felt buzzing around her from some unknown source. Was it electric? Was it imagined?

Casey did not seem to have felt the pinch. Her eyes were forward, fixed on the dark wood.

"Sorry if it's not—there weren't that many choices," said T.

The scene was theatrical, three people presiding stiffly at a glass airport wall as coffins were lowered from the belly of the plane and rolled across the tarmac. More than one coffin, she thought, looked like an army of them.

"There are bodies on most commercial flights," said T.

Often, when you flew, bodies flying beneath you, yet the proposition that on this flight one of them had been Hal's—that Hal's body had come in on this flight with T.—was absurd. The plane might have begun its descent just as Susan was leaning along the counter with her cleavage showing to ask the tattooed man for a couple of Marlboros—trying to picture, as she always did, whether he would be a strainer and heaver or a graceful thick beast. Whether his tongue would be stubby and awkward or pointed and cunning. Certainly, as a smoker, he would taste bad.

Hal's body slim and tall, compared to the big man's. And now also dead, compared to the big man's.

It was almost her own body. Or it was hers without being her own, hers in the way that a home was, those spaces where you spent your time—as much hers as another body could be. By that token she too was almost dead. Wasn't she? She had been with him forever, through all of it. Since the goddamn sixties. Three decades. He was hers and there were only two years between them; he had been fifty and she was forty-eight. She liked the smell and feel of his skin, she had always liked those things in him: his strangely delicate smell and the way he felt when she touched him. It was the skin that bound you most, the contact of two skins.

At that moment, because Casey had asked him, T. revealed quietly—trying to hedge at first but then, since there was clearly no way to dull the blow, said it outright—*He was killed, killed with a knife in a mugging.*

"Stabbed," said Casey, inflectionless. "You're saying my father was stabbed."

When she forced him to it he went on, persevered with the dutiful exposure of facts: Hal had lain alone in a gutter and bled till he died. He had died where he fell. A crowded city and no one found him in time.

Susan asked when and then computed the hours: it had happened only half an hour after the last time they talked. Stabbed to death for a wallet that might have held nothing but forty dollars total, the rest in traveler's checks. The cops had found it close by, in the trash.

Hal, hers. Thoughtful, sad, getting old. But not now. He would never be an old man.

The thought of him as he walked down the street, and then the sudden impact of the knife—maybe they threw him against the wall, maybe they knocked him down before they did it . . . she almost cringed as she stood there, thinking of pain, but then again it was nothing like real pain or shock, she recognized, nothing like them at all. The mere idea of a cringe, the projection of it—an anticipation of impact. She tried to feel it and not feel it at once. Pain and suffering, they said, were not the same, but stabbed in the stomach—it happened in war movies: gut-shot, the soldiers shivered and said plaintively, "I can't feel my legs, man." She'd seen it more than once. The same scene must occur in dozens of movies. She strained toward an intuition of bleeding, of an opened-up stomach, but failed miserably because the insides of her arms were against her own ribs, feeling her own stomach: regular stomach, enclosed and protected. Regular arms, smooth and unbloody. She moved her hands across the skin.

Dictators, killers, they had no capacity for empathy or no interest in it . . . but she, most people—you tried and you failed. Your efforts were inadequate. Pain was beyond simulation. Like sickness, it divided the population into haves and have-nots of pain. At the same time she wanted to be close to him and needed to be far away. Yet only one wish was granted.

He was utterly distant: here she was, and there was he. Gone.

The coffins disappeared beneath them, into the terminal

basement, but neither she nor Casey moved. Down on the paved surface the blocky carts went on beelining in between planes— baggage carts and catering trucks pulled up for loading and unloading. Between all this bustling activity and the group of them—her, Casey, and T.—was only the filmy and gray-streaked glass. Between them were the membranes. She stood staring forward and not looking at all.

Once Hal had been beautiful. It was the fading that made him a subject of sorrow, how you could barely see the vestiges of his old beauty. He had never been vain, and because of his lack of vanity he failed to notice what he was losing. In that way a virtue became a liability—he was blind to his own looks vanishing. Only five minutes before she had said something cruel about him— what was it? already forgotten—and Casey had called her a bitch. Richly deserved, no doubt. Casey defended Hal, always. For Hal alone she had a tender love, and in rejecting pity on her own behalf she also rejected it for him. To her his fade was charming.

The moment was worse for Casey than for her, even. She knelt, holding the arm of the chair. She almost never did that, had learned to steady herself on other things when she knelt—to squat without touching the ground, without needing to. One of the first things she'd learned. Not to infringe.

"I'm sorry," she whispered.

Casey's eyes were red but her cheeks were dry, unlike Susan's. She was in shock, Susan thought.

"Let's get out of here," said Casey.

"They're taking him to Forest Lawn," said T. "I'm sorry. It was the only one I could think of. At the time."

"Anywhere," said Casey, shaking her head.

Susan said nothing, following behind them. T. looked down at Casey often as they made their way to the elevators, put his hand on her shoulder more than once. Susan felt she was floating or being pulled: she barely saw anything but the carpet and the chair, the back of T.'s shirt and his pant legs. They had left Hal behind them; Hal was by himself. Lacking his faculties of perception, he could not know this, of course. He could not know he was alone. The saddest thing: he could not know he was alone. Or was it not sad? Not sad at all? He did not know where he was. He had become an object. She thought of him among the luggage—was it dark or fluorescent down where he lay? The rest of space lay against him.

A short time past she had only been thinking of T., but now T., standing beside Casey in the elevator, might as well be invisible. He was commonplace, by contrast with the killed. Stabbed and robbed, robbed and stabbed. Her husband had been killed.

She blinked rapidly, stood looking down in a daze at Casey as they moved into the elevator, passengers shuffling with their suitcases between their feet, crowding in. Casey hated it when elevators were full, her face forced into people's asses and groins—usually said something loudly so that they'd give her a wide berth. But at the moment she was saying nothing. Her eyes were on the floor in front of her, her shoulders bent. Susan stood over her in a shroud of self-absorption: she was a pillar of salt, Lot's wife.

She would be, from now on, that woman with the robbed and stabbed husband—from now until she died herself, till she herself was personally dead.

The woman with the stabbed husband: a kind, faded, betrayed

man, if they knew him as she did. The one who bled to death in a gutter, bled out by himself, with no one there who loved him or even knew who he was—only a body to them. A body in a slum, a gutter, another country. Her epitaph, since it was her actions that had driven him there, wasn't it? Without that particular adultery, that passing and mundane instance, he would never have flown out in the first place: without it he would still be here. He would be driving to work, he would be coming home as he always did, regular as clockwork, in the late afternoon.

She felt sickened—glancing through her was a nauseating unease, a dreadful suspicion. She tried not to feel it, talked to herself instead to cover the noise of her own thoughts, a stream of silent chatter doggedly opposed to both the sickness and the suspicion. It was fully trivial next to death, but her own identity had also been spirited away when the thief took the wallet, which had, it turned out, almost nothing in it. A mistake in judgment, an instantaneous mistake. If only someone had told the thief there were only traveler's checks in that wallet, if someone had taken him aside . . . her own identity, a side effect, was sunk and submerged in this new description, the stabbed-husband woman. As Hal lost his life she lost her own, as Hal was a murder victim she was an extension of him. That slut, that slut with the husband who got stabbed to death.

It made her feel better to think selfishly. She should think steadily of herself, not of Hal. Then she would not feel sickened, there would be less of an ache because she herself was a safe and mundane subject. There was no pain in thinking of herself. Though—maybe it *was* her, maybe she had done it, made a victim of him in the same way, in a slasher movie, the woman of low morals was doomed from the start, the buxom blonde in tight clothes good for nothing but ogling and murdering, her future blank save for the pending role as punished dead harlot.

Until this moment, she realized as the doors dinged open, she had been Casey's mother, but now she was Hal's killer. That was where her suspicion led.

She wanted to cry but her eyes were dry.

OK. Somehow, maintain composure. Her daughter was here, after all. Not to break down, not to. She would have another cigarette if she could, even a pack of them. Get Robert to buy them for her, call him and basically order them. Make him come to the house and be her servant. Or at least her waiter. A glass of wine. A highball.

She saw that Casey's eyes were filling as she rolled out of the elevator and she tried to keep close to her daughter, confused, forgetting where to walk, where the car should be parked. Casey's cheeks were damp and her mouth was clamped tightly closed, likely to keep her chin from trembling. Who could remember where they had left the car? Would they find it again?

But here it was. The car was beside them.

She stayed in Casey's apartment till after T. had left and all of Casey's friends were gone, into the small hours. Casey shrank inward, huddled under the blankets on her bed, and Susan sat on a chair beside it. After a while she lay down parallel, her arm around the thin shoulders, propping herself up on an elbow now and then to smooth the hair back from her daughter's wet face. Under normal conditions Casey had a bravado that passed for strength, but she had crumpled like paper. It was impossible for anyone to console her, and yet at first Susan tried, until she gave up and was willing not to try anymore. She had no choice beyond the effort of endurance—it was all you could do, lie with misery till it waned. She made the gesture, she yielded up her resistance to the forward pull of time, but the gesture had no content.

After Casey fell asleep Susan tucked her in as though her daughter were eight again, the covers up around her small sharp chin, and walked through the quiet rooms with a ringing in her ears. Aimless, she found a place to sit—on the edge of the couch in the living room, still, cupping both hands around the coolness of her beer bottle. She felt herself moving, in the inward hollow, between resentment and desolation. For a while she stared at the chair across from her, at the mantelpiece, a branch in a red vase, a small, enameled wooden box. She closed her eyes. But the eyelids were no help: what could she see from here? A black and burned-out place, an empty lot stretching ahead.

She realized she'd been convinced, in a deep unconscious presumption, that they were safe now—sure they were off the field, confident lightning would not strike again. The steep hills were supposed to be behind them, the rest a slow coast, the rest a relief. A feeling of security had descended once the worst was over, covering them both, her and Hal, once they recovered from the hit. There had been a plateau, a level of shelter. Now the roof was off, the shelter was gone.

Still, when she drove away from Casey's apartment in T.'s

company car, she was wide awake. It was dark out, dark for hours now. She saw young couples staggering and falling on each other on the sidewalk, laughing as they righted themselves. It reminded her of sex and drinking. She picked up the car phone and dialed.

Robert answered, groggy.

"Come to my place," she said. "OK? And bring me Camel Lights and something strong to drink."

"But you don't smoke, Susie."

"I do at times like this."

"Like what?"

Susie was not her name. No one had ever called her that; no one had been invited to, though Hal had fondly called her Suze, on occasion. She had been planning to stop seeing Robert since even before Hal found out, kept meaning to—the breakup was like an item on a grocery list, something to cross out, but then she kept forgetting it and pushing it back the way you'd forget to buy something and tell yourself: big deal, no cereal this week. But now she needed someone neutral, someone unimportant. She needed someone who had no ties to Hal, whose feelings were irrelevant. It was insulting to Hal that the very least of her encounters, the most purely trivial of them all, was the one that killed him. Because Robert was a lightweight, a person almost completely devoid of substance. The guy played fantasy baseball, and worse, lacked the discernment to kid about the subject.

Play fantasy baseball: fine. But at least have the wit to make a joke out of it.

His selling points were a taut, muscular stomach and well-built shoulders. Also he was submissive in a way that was almost dutiful, as though he was honoring an obligation—civic or military. There was something twisted in his simplicity.

"Times of mourning," she said.

*

When she told him, in the entryway of the house, he was mildly surprised. Not floored even. At this lackluster response a part of her was incredulous. And then, as the moment expanded quietly between them, infuriated. Apparently he was too insensitive to be shocked even by sudden death. A human block of wood. On the other hand, he was easy to shock with sex. The news of Hal's death barely moved him, but when she indicated that they could proceed from that sound bite to having sex he was uncomfortable. She relished his discomfort. She led the dog into the backyard and closed the door behind it.

A dog was not sexy. Also it was T.'s dog, which she and Hal had been taking care of after T. disappeared—practically a proxy for T. and thus also for Hal, for both of them conflated.

Then, in the dining room, she made Robert remove his clothes while she took a cigarette from the pack he'd brought in, lit it and poured herself a drink. He wore a half-wary expression and she knew exactly why: he was disgusted by the smoking, being a tan, buff, fantasy-baseball type. But not disgusted enough by the smoking to say no to the sex. He was neither shocked nor disgusted enough to say no to the cigarette-tainted sex. Rather he said yes. In fact he said yes speedily.

Most men were like that, when it came to sex. Their own desires came first, before whatever scruples, even revulsion they professed. Most women also. That was the definition of a scruple: something you consciously ignored to do whatever you wanted. Hell, what did he care. For him, no one had died.

And for herself, on this specific point—the timing of the sex—she did not feel guilt. She knew she should, likely. She felt anger, but it had no target beyond herself. As far as she went, she had ended Hal already. That black deed was done. Hal was over. Nothing could bring him back, nothing she did—no virgin purity, no nuns. Everything she did now was irrelevant, irrelevant to Hal, and though she would always be unredeemed Hal was not here to see. Hal did not care and Hal would never care again.

She closed her eyes, swaying with the drinking she'd done, and felt, uncalled-for, the edge of things, the brittle, slicing edge—the yellowing edge of old bone . . . she pushed it away by bringing Robert down. They were a warm mass against the woolen throw rug, which she and Hal had bought long ago at Ikea. Blocks of warm red, brown and beige. At the time they had thought the rug was a temporary measure, but then the rug from Ikea had stayed. As it turned out, she thought while Robert went down on her, the cheap rug from Ikea had stayed with them forever.

Robert was not particularly skilled despite the pointers she'd given him over time—had a robotic technique, in fact. In any case her mind wandered. What made her pull him off her after a couple of minutes and ask him to finish was a decision that arrived inappropriately: she had to see Hal's body. His body was in her mind, suddenly.

She had never seen a body, she didn't come from an open-casket culture. Her family had been more or less Protestant, uptight anyway and not given to sordid spectacles, and as a result to this day she had never been to a funeral where you saw the deceased. But she needed to see Hal. She needed to touch the seam.

"Sorry, not in the mood," she said, when Robert asked why she had stopped him.

"No kidding," he said, and got up, sticky and dangling, to get Kleenex for her stomach. He had slight rug burns on his knees. Most other men she'd been with wouldn't have asked, would have realized the effort was futile from the start. A failed comfort. It was where she went, but of course it was a dismal failure. So what.

Lying on her back, she looked up at the chandelier, whose dimmer had been turned down so that the filaments of the bulbs glowed a deep, warm orange. That was, in a sense, the benefit of Robert, whose critical capacity was low. He did not examine past a point, and was therefore unobtrusive. Almost streamlined, in fact. He was not hindered by complexity. Whereas Stellan, for instance, from about four months ago, had been overly given to psychoanalysis. Sex with Stellan, who hailed from some cerebral northern land like Finland or Sweden, was an extended therapy session. Nothing could be more annoying. Still, for a while she had relished her annoyance. Stellan, whose habit it was to sit naked afterward, smoking pot and discussing the quote-unquote relationship, was like a persistent itch—aggravating, but satisfying to scratch.

Was she relieved, slut that she was? Was there something in her that was relieved by any of this? If anyone could admit to such a thing, she should be able to. She was not only a slut but a killer.

But no. She was not relieved: she was robbed and it had left her empty. Hal had been robbed and she was robbed too, robbed of him, and now she was missing something and she always would be. That was all she had now: the freedom of nothing.

Nothing.

She realized she wanted Robert to stay, wanted it with a rare desperation despite the bad-sex episode and the fantasy-baseball element. She would smoke the cigarettes he had brought and drink his booze and talk to him: she would use Robert as a sounding board. That was what she would do, talk, smoke and drink, pretend she had velocity. Robert would be her shield against slowness and the loneliness that came from it, the morbid tranquillity. She would keep him here until morning, until the sun came up and the birds were in the trees and she could take him out to breakfast. Scrambled eggs did not remind you of death. (Did they? Yellow eggs on a blue plate. A warm feeling, farms or home, the morning sun, a nook with folded cotton napkins. Unless you thought instead about the beginning of eggs and then you went from beginning to end—eggs found in an autopsy— eggs themselves in their sensuousness or sterility—once, when she was pregnant with Casey, she had found a red fleck in an egg and thrown up.)

Whatever, she didn't have to have eggs.

Toast maybe. A waffle. A waffle could not remind you of death.

Could it?

What she didn't want above all, she knew—watching him as

he knelt down beside her with a tissue bunched in his hand to wipe the cleft of her belly button—was to lie there in the half-empty bed waiting to fall asleep. She was afraid of the certainty of those minutes, the cold night shining through the window onto the threads of her white cotton sheets.

2

The complex was manicured and bland, a sprawling suburb for the dead. Susan had taken a backseat and let Casey and T. handle the arrangements, so this was her first visit: for the coffin, the funeral service, the burial, all of it, Hal couldn't have cared less and she followed his lead.

Once she'd asked him to make a will—she'd read a magazine article in a dentist's waiting room that ridiculed people for dying intestate—and he had said absentmindedly that he would, but then he never bothered. She'd asked once if he had a preference for his body, in terms of being dead. She asked that mainly because she panicked one night about claustrophobia and beetles and wanted to tell him her own preference (cremation). But he had shrugged and said only yes, his preference would be not to be dead. On the subject of disposal he had no strong opinion; overall he was an agnostic, with a secular, institutional orientation and a general lack of interest in matters of the spirit. So-called matters of the spirit, he would have said, so-called spiritual matters. T. had already seen his body, long before it was embalmed. He had seen it in Belize City when it lay on the ground, seen it there in the street, seen it right where he fell. When Hal failed to meet him he'd flagged down a rattletrap taxi and told the driver the name of Hal's hotel. He had described this part to both of them, under duress, after Casey badgered him.

From the half-open window of the taxi, breathing the fumes as it sat idling in stopped traffic, he had noticed rubbernecking crowds gathered curbside. Without a clear motivation he had paid the driver and got out. The crowds had nothing to do with him, for all he knew, but still he found himself walking across the street and peering over the heads of bystanders. People were shorter there, he added.

And then he'd seen Hal on the ground, dying—already dead or maybe still dying, he never found out which. He pushed his way through and fell down on his knees beside him, soaked the kneecaps of his pants in the warm pool of blood, but Hal's eyes were closed and he lay unmoving. T. felt no pulse, felt no breath. Finally the ambulance came.

When given the opportunity to see the body herself, Casey had shaken her head and said no, she preferred not to remember her father that way. Susan thought she was right, Susan was glad. But herself she had to see him, so she was going alone. They had insisted on laying him out formally in a private room. A young man in a gray suit escorted her to the door of the room and then left.

She went in with a feeling of duty, trying to carry herself well. The walls were a placid beige and there were flower arrangements on a sideboard and the cloying smell of a deodorizer: a bouquet called orange blossom, she suspected, or tangerine breeze or mango blush. Its chemical sweetness conjured industrial parks along the Jersey Turnpike where scents were manufactured for cosmetics, malls, fast food. And here was the coffin, its lid propped up to show a white satiny liner. She approached with her breath held—half-frightened, she realized, her hands shaking. She thought of crime shows on TV, procedurals with all manner of corpses. They used real actors first, then dummies for the grisly autopsy scenes—she recalled a bright crimson, the flaps of chests spread out like butterfly wings. Her parents had died and she had never seen them; Hal's mother and father had died too, years since, and she had not seen their bodies either.

There he was.

She had expected waxy and limp—that was her expectation—but he was not. Like T. he was tanned, and his graying hair had lightened to blond at the temples. What shocked her was how good he looked—better than the last time she'd seen him alive. He almost looked young again. And it wasn't makeup but the effect of real sun. With the contrast of light hair against the bronze skin he looked, in fact, healthy.

Briefly she entertained the notion of laughing. But the room was airless and resisted sound.

On the other hand, it might not be Hal at all. Where was Hal? This was a dummy, after all—the real actor was gone. They'd dressed it in a suit and tie, a dark suit she'd never seen before and a discreet tie over a white shirt. T. must have bought it and brought it to them. He had not mentioned this. Maybe, on the other hand, the suit was one of T.'s own. She could check, if she dared to reach for the tags, touch the back of the dead, still neck. She knew T.'s size and she knew that if it was his it would have to be Prada or Armani, since that was all he owned. Or all he used to own before he appeared at LAX in the threadbare garb of a street person, with Hal as his luggage.

She stood there beside the casket. Particles of air were touching both of them, touching Hal's skin and then her own. His skin wasn't living, she knew that all too well, but maybe energy subsisted there. Maybe there was silent movement within, particles sweeping down over the planes of her cheeks, the streams, the rivers of atoms, sweeping down over all of her and sweeping over him. This was the last time they would share a space, the last time their skins would be close. After this they would always be separate, on and on past the end of time, until the sun burned out and everything dissolved. And yet even if they were apart from now on, there must be others like them, shadows or mimics, unconscious reflections. People were not unique, surely: there were no anomalies in nature, were there? Individuals were permutations of longing, moments, tendencies. They were variations. So other shades of Hal and her, their many versions, crossed each other's paths elsewhere, crossed over and merged, their cells swimming among the billions . . . Except for Casey. In Casey they were together. If Casey were to have children, if Casey could—possible, in theory; at least, no doctor had said otherwise—they would remain together there, the molecules of Hal and her, diminishing as time went on but never entirely gone.

Impossibly he was putting her to shame—complete, reposing there calmly while she was still amidst the chaos of growth and change, the mess of life, the stew and whirl of microorganisms. Although death too was disorderly, she conceded—simply delayed by chemicals as she stood here. Only the deathless were neat.

She thought of the stone biers of saints, of relics lying in state in ancient churches. They had seen one in Europe, a saint. Oh not the saint, but his image—graven in stone while his bones lay beneath. The church had been built over his dead body. Where was it? France? A church built over the laid-out saint, to house his sanctified remains. After you left that ancient church, in retrospect, you somehow confused the two, you thought the saint was in the stone—the saint was the figure itself, its contours smooth and pristine. A stone man, a stone virgin: people were always less beautiful than the images of them.

Hal was not stone. No one would build a church to him.

But *everyone* deserved a church, she thought, feeling naïve, feeling twelve again: all the tragic heroes that were dead men, once infants—each hobbled soul that wished and was undone. Maybe that was how someone had thought of mausoleums. Personal churches, skyward-pointing buildings. There were whole cemeteries of them. In some places it had to do with flooding, she knew, low cities like New Orleans or Buenos Aires, but here at Forest Lawn the mausoleums appeared ostentatious, the opposite of holy.

It was in the lying-down figure of a man that holiness arrived. If a saint were interred standing up, his stone image vertical like a statue, there would be no grace in that. A man had to be lying down or he was not even an offering.

She had tears on her cheeks, felt the wet streaks cool the skin, but did not feel them in her eyes. She wondered how she had missed her own crying.

Hal had not given himself up, but someone else had offered him. The thieves, she thought at first, but they were only a proximate cause: the root cause was still and always her. The death might technically be a random event, sure, but she couldn't stop there, the shape of her responsibility was too clear. She felt the struggle of trying to make death describe a single point, mean one thing that could be understood, but at the same time she knew she was spinning a tale out of physics, out of atoms. A bus lurching to a stop, a tree branch swaying and bobbing in the moving air, why, that was all that death was—a shifting of microscopic parts through time. The parts shifted and left you alone.

Hal might look good now but he would not stay good for long. From now on he was the property of the dirt and the water beneath the surface, the property of gnarled tree roots, grasses and microbes, larvae and slugs, rats, beetles, putrefaction, fermentation and dry decay. That was the allure of cremation, of course: when you thought of your body in future time you did not have to see it decomposing. Better to see yourself as ashes, ashes and rising smoke. But she had never liked ovens either. They had it right in India, where they wrapped them in white and lifted them onto pyres.

Hal had been good. Good friend, kind father and kind man.

And yet she had to think of herself. She always went back to her. Not even this dedicated moment could be selfless. Damn it! You had to see yourself there, where the loved one was, you couldn't help it: because finally you too would be forced out, would have to let it all go. Finally she would be a dummy in someone else's eyes, the living would look upon her from above. She would cease to be and *join him*, as was said. *Join him* in the sense of not joining him at all, in the sense of a parallel but utterly separate annihilation; *join him* in the sense of an eternal nonexistence that contained nothing.

Still they said *join*, they said *join* as though there was a throng there waiting, because that was their desperate hope, there was a throng there waiting with arms spread wide to embrace you— there they all were, all the ones you had known, cavorting on the alpine meadows green in stately, shining ballrooms.

It was unbearable that he should look so perfect, with what was coming to him next. Obscene. She leaned over the coffin and jerked his shirt up from under the pant waist.

The shirt cleared the belt line and she saw his stomach, a shade lighter than his face but still tan. What had he done there, down in the tropics? He must have been on the beach! She saw him walking into the surf, surveying the vast beyond. And there was the wound, the means of this ending. A small line. She reached out with fingers shaking and felt the bump of its lips against her finger pads. Life was a skin.

She would tell him she was sorry. Or no: too late. The body would not listen. It was a corpse, not him—but then it *was* him, it was. Wasn't it? The last him she would know—the trace of him, the path he left. The raw materials. Or possibly all there was, all there had ever been. It was not hers to know; no one would let her in. The door of knowledge kept her out, her and legions, the masses of the undecided—the living ones, the ones who had been living and were not anymore—try as they might to look through the windows, they could not get in. You knew nothing of death, then you died.

People intended to make you feel better when they said the body was not the person, you or themselves, at least, but those were the ones who believed in the fields of hereafter, those who believed in cherubim. Their words presumed an independent mind, moving, roaming freely. If that were true, who knew how it might be, Hal's mind floating untethered in this sterile room. Only herself for company. His mind and its murderer, her own. Maybe his mind was touching hers, in those infinite molecules of the air.

She willed her hands to rise, her arms to lift up, as though to feel the last of him going.

The cut was small. The cut was hardly there.

She pulled the shirt down after a while. She stood and looked and looked at him, the line of his nose and forehead, the eyebrows. But he would not say anything, and there was only so much looking she could do.

Though technically it was winter it felt like a mild spring day on the cemetery grounds. The service would be held in a steepled chapel called the Little Church of the Flowers, a name both quaint and faintly reminiscent of pederasty. Susan sat waiting in the first pew with Casey beside her at the end.

The venue had to be expensive, she thought—T. was paying, saying the funeral would be his responsibility—because it was an imitation of a church from Europe, an imitation of an English village church slapped down in the sunny, falsely green lake of Los Angeles County. Hal would have shaken his head at the pretension of it, but herself she found it pleasant enough. She didn't mind the fake quaintness. She was not a snob when it came to authenticity. Whatever works, was the way she saw it. Whereas Hal had a tendency to mock his fellow Americans. He looked down from a high place on his countrymen, as he called them.

In his way Hal was an idealist. Had been. He had lofty ideas, where she only had pragmatism. She wondered if that made him more European. Also he had believed in taxes. Yes: though he'd grown up right here, though he had visited Europe only once, and even then in a bus full of low-budget tourists who yearned for nothing more than to step out of the bus in Paris and find the nearest McDonald's, there were European aspects to Hal.

Sunlight filled the place with an excessive whiteness that made her blink when she looked up. Mourners were filing through the doors in surprising number but she didn't know most of them—her own friends, her friends from college days, were far away and most hadn't even heard the news. These were probably IRS employees, their equally unknown families in tow. Some were large, she noticed. Hal had never said his office was mostly overweight people, yet so it appeared to be. She'd never made a habit of dropping into his office, nor had she attended many office functions. And when she told Casey she would speak she hadn't considered these mourners or their expectations. For their benefit she would have liked to be eloquent, but in the end she would not be. Of that much she was certain.

An arm's length away Casey sat in her chair, head bowed. She did not wish to be spoken to. A few feet past her T. stood by a side door talking to a small man in black, the man who would officiate, Susan suspected—clerical-looking, nodding as T. spoke to him in a low murmur.

He did not say much—either that or Susan forgot to listen—and then Casey had intended to speak but could not, became choked up and had to roll back to her position at the end of the pew. Watching her made Susan wince but she had to get over it, she was up next herself, and she would have noticed her own nervousness if she had not been lost in feeling for Casey and the whine and the buzz. She had heard it from the moment T. told them Hal was dead: her life was full of background noise, a dull and droning clamor behind the voices or a ringing, a dreadful ringing like tinnitus that only diminished when she drank or smoked. Then things quieted and drew into focus.

It was not that she regretted all of it, only that she regretted this specific instance—that Hal had found out, that because of her carelessness he had seen. From that she'd failed to save him. This failure had driven him far away, and from far away came the man with the knife and slit his belly open.

She stood at the lectern with her eyes wide, as though shocked. As though she was stupid. She had an impression of clumps of flowers around her, wreaths and bouquets, white and purple and red, their cloudy colors on the margins, and wondered how she looked as the words flowed out of her, as she gazed down at her paper, which trembled slightly beneath her fingers. She held the paper and read the words, but the words did not say what she meant. She might look aged, widowed, dull, sharp, or blurred by grief. She felt suddenly like a vague being, a form without definition. She smoothed the paper on the lectern and glanced up from it—imprecise words—and out at the crowd, curious for a moment as to whether an ex had come. She hoped none had, of course. Robert, at least, was not here. She had told him it was over and he barely cared, she suspected, though he had seemed slightly annoyed. Inconvenienced, anyway. She cared even less than he did and wondered idly if T. would lay him off. T. had hardly dealt with him, didn't know him at all.

She could barely discern the faces. She saw their pinkness or brownness and their sympathy, an unsmiling sympathy but sympathy all the same. They sympathized because they had no clue that she herself was the murderer. They did not know Hal had been murdered. Or not, at least, by her. They knew of the stabbing but not the real culprit.

Not one of them had the least idea who she was.

Luckily.

Afterward, in their stiff dress clothes, they drank. She did, and so did Casey and even, she thought, T., though he could apparently hold his liquor better than either of them. There was an open bar. People came up to her and she was conscious of feeling better the more she drank—magnanimous even. She would be intimate, she would confide in them. When if not now? She went out in a radius from Casey, made forays into the passing crowds from a station at Casey's elbow. T. was drinking whiskey, a lock of his hair fallen over his forehead, his shirt unbuttoned. He was wearing a suit for the first time since he'd come back and had a debonair way about him, Susan thought, like a man from the roaring twenties.

She left them together to join a smokers' circle outside, near an angel statue. It seemed to be office people. A woman with frizzy hair and outsize earrings spoke to her.

"He was a special person," she said.

Susan took the cigarette that was offered and let someone light it for her, surprised at how bad it tasted. The first one always did.

"If there's anything we can do," said a man.

"This is a good beginning," she told him, raising the cigarette, and took a drag.

"Hal talked about you all the time," said another woman. Bookish-looking and gangly.

"He did?" asked Susan.

"He was devoted to you. And Casey."

"Casey, definitely," agreed Susan. She had put her plastic wine cup down near the angel's stone toes; now she reached for it and sipped. "He lived for Casey."

"He had a way with people," said the earrings.

"Really? I used to kid him about not having one."

There was a shocked silence at this.

"One time," went on the big earrings, as though to politely cover the transgression, "there was a crazy, you know, a hostage taker? Did he tell you that story?"

Beyond the woman the hedges were carefully trimmed into long boxes. If they grew wild, she thought, they would be far more lovely. Did people want to be buried beneath topiary?

". . . turned out it wasn't a real gun. It was a water pistol! But there was real, I mean, fear, you know? People were freaking out. And Hal, you know, he totally defused the whole situation."

"Mmm, yeah," said Susan. "The squirt-gun thing."

She did remember, or almost. The anecdote had a punch line, if she recalled correctly: the squirt gun had been green. Hal liked to tell stories, when he was in the right mood—mostly about his coworkers, their foibles and idiosyncrasies.

"The guy was a legend," said a young Hispanic man earnestly. He had a pathetic pencil mustache, a concave chest, and his pants were too long. Or no: they were belted just below the rib cage. "Name's Arlo, by the way."

"Oh," said Susan.

Rodriguez, Hal had called him. The pants were the tip-off. She shook his hand.

"Pleased to meet you. Again."

Surely she had met him.

"Yeah, Christmas party, right?"

"Right," she agreed. One of the few she'd attended.

"I'm serious. He was a legend. Old-school. Last of the Titans, man."

"Hal Lindley, last of the Titans," she repeated wistfully.

"Man, you know what? I gotta tell someone this," said Rodriguez, and bent forward as though pained. "I totally offered to go with him. I woulda had his back. I told him that. He told me he was going down there. I go, Take me with. Seriously! I hadda gone, you know, maybe this wouldna . . ."

He trailed off. He looked lost.

"You can't think like that," said Susan gently. "He didn't want company. It was his choice, Arlo."

"Yeah, but."

"It was his adventure," she said. As she said it she felt its accuracy: Arlo was comforting her, not the other way round. It was not that she denied her part in it—it was still murder she had done, at least manslaughter. But she remembered Hal's voice on the phone. A tensile strength, an alertness she had missed for a long time before that. How he had looked in the casket: curiously alive.

Her adventure had been without him, his without her. A last freedom.

The bookish woman was crying; the one with large earrings sidled close and put a fleshy arm around her, pulled her in. Susan rested her eyes on the woman's blouse, a pattern of wine-red and dark-blue leaves. Flesh was always a consolation—flesh, not beauty. Beauty was social, flesh was private. These days Susan consoled no one. When Casey was a baby and Susan still had weight from the pregnancy, baby Casey had nestled against her. She had kneaded the flesh and buried her face in it. Later when Casey was a toddler and the weight was gone, Casey had not liked the change or trusted it. She even complained. Susan remembered now: the toddler Casey had said her mother's stomach was no longer beautiful. She bemoaned its absence. To her consolation was beauty; small Casey had not thought of forms or majesty. She wanted body all around.

Susan felt a rush of affection for the earrings woman, as if by putting her arm around the other she had put it around her too. A common mother, a small mothering for all. Susan thought of her own mother. Then how rarely she thought of her. As though her mother had been a mother in another life, a life long past, a faint image or pattern of a mother.

And yet—at least when she was a baby, a small child—her mother must have felt for her, as she herself did for Casey, a deep and wrenching love.

But they hadn't been close; the love had been squandered. Somehow along the way Susan had squandered it.

A terrible remorse threatened.

She would go inside now to see Casey again.

"Let me get some more drinks," she said, for an exit. "Drinks? Anyone?"

•

A first cousin was in attendance, the only one she still knew. He was a consultant, something to do with computers. He wore a metallic gray jacket and a violet tie and was balding. She hadn't seen him for years; they'd never had much in common. They collided at the buffet table, near a vegetable platter.

"So how've you been," she asked, after condolences. She picked up a piece of celery. It seemed like days since she'd eaten.

"Oh, you know," he said. His hand made a gesture of dismissal.

"I don't," she said. "I don't at all. Tell me."

"Well, Deb left," he said.

The wife, must be.

"Oh. I'm really sorry."

He shrugged.

"Nah, it's for the best."

"And how are the kids?" She thought there were two of them. Both boys.

"College."

"Uh-huh? They liking it?"

"Engineering. That's Tommy. He's gonna be an earner. Gil's doing something useless. Art history."

Now she remembered. The guy was a tool.

"Hardly useless."

"Whatever. No money in it."

"Better than phone sex," said Casey.

There she was, drunk and flushed. Less pale than usual. She reached for a cherry tomato.

"You remember Casey. Casey, your second cousin. Steven."

"I remember Gil. And Tommy. We played with a soccer ball in the street. He did that thing where you head-butt it."

It struck her that Steven might not have seen Casey since the accident. He must have known; it could not be new information. But he looked mildly embarrassed.

"Casey, good to see you."

No, he had seen her once in the chair, that was right, a birthday thing for his own kid.

"Thanks for coming," said Casey.

She probably meant it, but there was something in the tone. She'd never liked him, Susan thought. She chewed her tomato and squinted up.

"Kids would have too. But they're busy."

"Studying art history."

"Gil's back East. Tommy's at USC."

"Mmm. Good for him," said Casey.

"I'm really sorry about your dad," said Steven.

Casey nodded. There was silence.

"Freak thing," said Steven. "You get a lot of freak . . ."

He trailed off, his gaze lingering on her chair.

"Huh," said Casey, and popped another tomato into her mouth. "Better quit while you're ahead."

She spun and wheeled off.

". . . accidents in your family," he finished, lamely.

"Uh, yeah," said Susan.

"Hoo," he said after a moment, with awkward jocularity, and shook his head. "Sensitive."

"Well. Her father was just stabbed to death," said Susan.

She left him groping a zucchini flower.

She called a real estate agent and put the house up for sale. Casey issued a grudging invitation to stay at her apartment but Susan was afraid of grating on her. Meanwhile T. was forcing her to stay home from work for a while. She was ambivalent about this: the office was somewhere to go, a location in which to exist. But he insisted she take a leave of absence, and she had no strength left to argue.

She established a simple pattern of avoiding the spaces where she and Hal had spent most of their time, moving out of the master bedroom into a smaller room that had once been Casey's.

But even trying to sleep in that room—a room she'd thought might be safe because it held almost no specific memory of Hal—she was preyed upon as soon as she lay motionless. Apprehension crept over her, a fringe of blackness she could almost see rising slowly from the foot of the bed, covering her feet, her legs, her chest, her shoulders, coming to smother her chin and her mouth like earth. Hal's death and her own were gathered wretchedly in the shadows, hunched down with teeth showing, sharp teeth and the talons of bony fingers. A heaviness made her heart beat hard with fear—a leaden certainty that her selfishness had killed him. There was no buoyancy at all, no river to drift on.

She shifted onto the living room couch for several nights and during the daytime moved the bedroom's furniture around, trying to find a configuration that would ease the weight. If it were different enough, she thought, it wouldn't cause pain like this, so she removed the shades from the windows and hastily painted the walls an eggshell blue. She made forays to housewares stores and returned with items that spoke to her of freshness—blue and white linens, cushions, a screen, a wall hanging, a cloudy glass vase full of pussy willows. She wanted it to feel like a replacement room, a surprise. But the change was so slight, after all that, as to be unnoticeable.

So she considered, every night after twilight, whether to go to a hotel. She thought of lobbies, their carpeting and warm lights and the people milling. But in the end she did not go to a hotel. In the end she stayed home. She went out for as long as she could, to bars or the promenade or the Santa Monica Pier, sitting and smoking and drinking and idly watching the movement of crowds. But then she came home to sleep, or to lie there trying. Maybe it was apathy or maybe it was penance. She couldn't decide.

Daytime was better. She went out with first light and walked T.'s dog around the neighborhood; she got coffee in the morning and took her lunches in restaurants or diners. Sometimes she drove around in a daze. Other times she asked friends over, made sure there were people in the house to lift its grimness. When she had to be there by herself she kept to the sunporch and Casey's room, venturing into the kitchen only when she had to. The two of them had spent years in the kitchen.

His car was still in the shop, having bodywork done after a fender bender, so she asked the man there to sell it for her. He said no at first, but when she told him why he relented and said yes. Then she began looking for a new place to live. It took her out of the house, it distracted her, it pushed her forward . . . she thought maybe a small one-room condo near the beach. That was the benefit of being alone: she needed little square footage, could buy for location, could afford, possibly, a clear view of the ocean. She tried to picture a new life and when she did so—putting it neatly into a frame as though the future was visible through a porthole—she saw the blue ocean.

She visited Casey as often as she could, sought her out for meals or trips to the grocery store and did not press her about the phone-sex job. She would not dream of asking. The job was irrelevant now, its triviality complete. One afternoon they sat for hours at the end of the Santa Monica Pier, where Casey also liked to go, barely speaking. They listened to the screeching gulls and watched the pier's small population of anglers, a few stubborn old curmudgeons who didn't mind pollution in their fish.

•

After a week T. came to the house to reclaim his pet. He had wanted to do it sooner but he knew she had grown fond of the dog. No doubt he was being considerate.

"So," he said, kneeling in the kitchen, his hands in the dog's fur, rubbing. "When you come back we can start the next project. But no hurry. None at all. Take all the time you need."

"A new project?" she asked.

She'd been doing preliminary research for him on a parcel in Tahoe when he disappeared, something about Whispering Pines.

"We're going to disincorporate," he said.

He'd said something about that, on the phone from Belize. Back when she thought he was crazy. She'd blocked it out, she guessed.

She realized she had a headache, thought it might be dehydration, and went to get ice for a glass of water.

"It can be a complicated process," he continued. "The lawyer will handle most of the details. I'd like you to stay on with me, though. If you're interested."

"I don't really get it," she said dumbly, and turned from the open freezer to stare.

"I'm going to do something else. You'll still be needed."

"Something else?"

"A foundation."

"Foundation? You mean, for giving away money?"

"A 501(c)3."

"Are you kidding?"

"Dead serious. But like I say, no rush. We can talk more when you're feeling up to it."

They were leaving then, he and the dog, with little acknowledgment, the dog's nails clicking across the kitchen floor. She noticed its bowls were still beside the trash can—one with a few kibbles remaining, the other with water. She and Hal had never had a dog. She thought vaguely that Hal might not have liked them very much, might have preferred cats such as the one he bought for Casey. Though he had always said he liked dogs, this might have been a white lie of sorts, she thought. Why had they never had a dog, if in fact they both liked dogs?

But it was true what he had told her about T.—her employer was sane, though certainly changed. Apparently it was straightforward: he'd turned liberal Democrat from fiscal Republican. Of course she did not know how he voted. For all she knew he never voted at all. But clearly he had some notion of being a do-gooder. (Why was the term so bitter, so resentful?) Anyway he was newly bent on charity. Such reversals were not uncommon, almost cliché, in fact: it was only the certainty with which he'd proceeded, before, the certainty of his commitment that made it seem absurd. Then again the kid was only in his twenties, barely older than Casey. She'd given him too much credit for being fully formed. He had always had a veneer of maturity.

She heard his car back out of the driveway and walked with her glass of water into the living room, past a bookshelf where there was a picture of Hal and her. It was before they had Casey, when they were young, and Casey had had it framed and set it up there. They were two young hippies, long-haired and smiling. Well, she was long-haired. Hal had never gone that way. But he did sport a mustache and the obligatory beard, which Casey always found amusing. True to its era the picture was sun-bleached and faded; they stood holding hands in front of a silver Airstream. Susan wore what appeared to be a striped muumuu, Hal a flowery tunic. She had picked out his clothes for him back then.

An offer came in for the house and she began to sort Hal's things into boxes to give away, boxes to move with, boxes for Casey. Into Casey's boxes she put a model horse, toy soldiers, a sailboat with peeling blue paint. That was easy; it was the half-broken objects that were hard, the ones too slight or old to keep—a slingshot made crudely out of twigs and rubber bands, Boy Scout badges, worn baseball cards from the fifties. There were report cards. In second grade Hal had received an A in Deportment; in fifth he'd gotten a B– and the remark, in a slanted, loopy hand, *At times, Hal can be boisterous.*

Her own items were the bulk of it. She'd kept more than Hal had and the worst was something she'd thought she'd gotten rid of, a book of lists. It was a bound journal from years ago, from a few months after the accident, when she first started sleeping around. Mainly it was a list of men. She'd been incautious then, maybe half hoping Hal would catch her and she would be confronted, but he had never suspected, as far as she knew, and her desire for exposure had slowly waned. The book was a juvenile collection—the names, physical descriptions, the events of their meetings. She barely remembered all of them now, and looking at it felt ashamed by the childishness. It had always been about knowing and being known, about experience and diversity, but here it was clearly teenage games. Now that she was a murderer, now that she had homicide under her belt, it looked to her like evidence.

She crammed it down into the kitchen garbage, then cleaned out the refrigerator and rained down old vegetables on it—rubbery carrots, yellowing celery, a torrent of moldy beets.

She had spent her morning on real estate—showings on the beach, slick modern condos the realtor picked out with wide windows that looked out over the Pacific, balconies that gave a view of the headlands to the north—when the lawyer's call came. Her great-uncle Albert, who had died a few months back, had named her in his will. She'd barely noticed the death when it happened; she had never known the great-uncle, had met him only once, as a child, when her parents took her over to his house on a weekend. Odd that she remembered it at all; the only reason was his player piano. The piano had stuck with her. He pressed a button and showed her how the white keys moved under the weight of invisible fingers. There was one other fragment too—a thin arm in a plaid shirtsleeve as it bent down and stuck a rusty wire hoop into the grass. That was all she recalled.

She drove to the lawyer's office in Century City, a tall shining building with valet parking, and sat across from his desk with her right leg vibrating restlessly. The lawyer talked on the phone while she waited. He was a stubby man with a gleaming nose and ruddy cheeks and she wondered idly what he would say if she told him her husband had been stabbed to death. She considered blurting it out. Behind his head was a Chagall print. The décor in the office matched the colors in the print, down to the blue curtains and the flowers on the desk. Chagall had always irritated her. There was an obnoxiousness to the painting, a repugnantly coy quality, like a grown man talking baby talk to other grown men.

"There's no cash to speak of," said the lawyer when he hung up, cutting right to the chase and handing her a thick file. "The bulk of the estate is the house itself. The house and the contents. Those are yours. You're the nearest next of kin, or at least the only one he bothered to name. Himself—as I'm sure you're aware—he died without issue."

"A house," she repeated. The one with the player piano? She would inherit a player piano: a murderer, a black widow, the proud owner of a player piano.

If she suppressed the murder part, the thought gave her a lift of pleasure.

"Where is it, again? The Valley?"

"Pasadena," he said. "The will, the title, the records he left are in the folder. Review them at your leisure. You may take possession at any time or of course you may also sell. Estate taxes are basically covered for you under the terms of a somewhat complicated trust. All in the file. Feel free to consult your tax preparer."

She took a minute to shuffle through the file, the documents that were impervious to her scrutiny.

"It's all there," said the lawyer, apparently impatient. "Feel free to consult your accountant."

"It's such a coincidence," she said, flustered. "It's one of those things. Because I'm selling my own home right now."

The lawyer nodded and took another call.

When she left she felt thrilled. She paid the valet and pulled out onto the street, her accordion folder on the passenger seat, then found a side street and parked to rifle through the papers till she found the address. It was unfamiliar—she barely knew Pasadena—so she dug in the glove compartment for her dog-eared Thomas Guide and flipped through it.

There were keys stashed, the lawyer had said.

*

She did not let her hopes rise as she drove, expended effort to tamp them down. A derelict bungalow that was two-thirds garage, a trailer with fruit stencils decorating the kitchen walls . . . thick-walled refrigerators from the fifties strewn across a dry lawn, their rounded edges speckled with rust. With sagging roof and umbrella clotheslines, it would sit hunkered down on cinderblocks on a grim street where the lots were separated by chainlink and pit bulls jumped at you when you passed, backed up to a fast-food chicken joint or a video store or freeway.

But the nearer she got the smoother the pavement beneath

her tires, the deeper and older the covering trees. Their shade moved over her car, dappling the windshield. Soaring limbs, velvet green leaves—even the bark looked soft. There were white flowers, opened up at the throat like trumpets, and then she passed a row of tall gates that reminded her of Bel Air. Hedges enclosed mansions.

"No fucking way," she said, leaning forward and clutching the steering wheel. Hal should have been here. He had always been middle-class and had never had, as she did, rich relatives in the hazy distance, perennially blurred figures. And there was the number from her paper, on a wrought-iron gate. At the top of the gate there was something else written—the name of the estate? She squinted to make it out: a rusty script with flourishes, letters missing, obscured by branches and leaves.

She was out of place here. Even her car, with its fading paint job, seemed like an insult to the street.

The drive was cobblestone and the gate was locked. She reversed and parked on the street to look for the keys. They were under a rock near the gate, the lawyer had said, so she knelt and pulled back branches until she found it, tipped it up and got her fingers dirty. That part felt right: grubbing in the dirt, squatting. She thought: *The murderer squatted.* She thought along those lines daily. The murderer poured a cup of coffee. The murderer went to sleep. The murderer disassociated.

After a while she realized she had the wrong rock. The fake rock was beside it, hollow. Underneath was a set of keys.

Once she'd pushed one side of the gate open and driven through, the car bumping and shaking over the cobbles, she could peer around at her leisure: a wide lawn with long, leaf-littered grass. There was a fountain off to the left and on her right a pool enclosure. The house, straight ahead, was sprawling and off-white and was surmounted by a green dome, probably oxidized copper. She saw archways over a slate terrace, white metal tables and chairs and parasols with scalloped edges that fluttered. The key stuck at first in the front door, which was intricately carved—some kind of nature scene with odd flat-topped trees—but finally the door opened. No alarm.

Inside it was dim, streaks of light through a window some-where, and smelled of mothballs. She slid her hand along the wall, feeling for a light switch. Instead it hit something strange—both smooth and furry, bulbous. She snatched her hand away, heartbeat quickened, and tried another wall as her eyes adjusted. She stood in an entryway painted deep red, deer gathered on the walls. Their antlers protruded, their glass eyes stared.

The murderer inherited a house full of deer. My deer, my deer. The universe showed off its symbolic perfection; the atoms bragged.

"Jesus," she said.

She moved forward. The next room was spacious, opened up to the dome above. A weak daylight filtered down and she could make out a wide staircase that circled up into a bristling dimness and still more deer heads, mounted on walls, sideboards, above doorways. Maybe not all deer, she thought: some were delicate and unfamiliar, striped or with elaborate curling horns—antelope or gazelle, maybe. There was a huge bull moose.

The ceilings were high and vaulted. Beneath the dead herds the place was startling in its elegance, though oddly decorated: purple curtains grayed by age and dust, crystal sconces on the walls, thick swoops of gold brocade—a magician's stage, a goth bordello. She pulled the curtains open as she passed them, turned on lights and moved past the staircase, into a living room with more animals still. Here there were cats. Cheetahs or leopards maybe, she didn't know the difference—not tigers, anyway. More than just heads, there were whole bodies posed leaping, posed stalking, streamlined with huge, round eyes and fur that seemed less their own than the coats of the rich black ovals on one, black rings with golden centers on another, the trappings of starlets. She looked closely into a face—the golden eyes, the fangs—then turned away.

The cats were captured forever in the seventies: stone fireplace, sunken lounge area, shag carpet and an L-shaped leather couch. Over the sofa was a lion rampant: its great mane flaring, it reared up, held its front paws in the air as if ready to box. It was either foolish or majestic. She gazed, trying to decide, but her eyes watered as she gazed. *The murderer's eyes watered.*

It was the dust, no doubt. They said dust was composed of human epidermal cells, but in this house it was the dust of Africa, she thought. The dust of the flesh of the veldt, the aged, slowly dispersing brawn of the Serengeti.

In a cavernous dining room with dark ceilings, wild dogs and foxes lurked. Here some of the animals had labels, ranging from finely etched brass plaques to a kind of dark-red tape with raised white letters on it that she remembered from the seventies. She leaned in close to read them: a timber wolf in a cabinet with sliding glass doors, an American mink on a sideboard. The teeth were sharp. She hadn't known minks had such sharp teeth. She kept on into the hallway with a shiver, where she found birds at her shoulders. Birds of prey—hawks, owls, eagles. An owl perched on a branch, an eagle spread its wings over a nest of twigs, a nest full of speckled eggs. A hallway led into a smaller room, a guest bedroom possibly or servant's quarters, with Tiffany floor lamps shedding a green and yellow light. It was still birds, but they were not so fierce.

She felt slightly relieved: she'd run the gauntlet.

In the small bedroom there was a pink bird that must be a flamingo, standing with one leg lifted gracefully on a mirrored pool. She leaned down to touch the reeds—reeds of glassy plastic, glorified Easter-basket stuffing. Ducks, geese, pheasants. She barely noticed the furnishings, so abundant was the stuffed game. The specimens were labeled now: a line of small plump birds, a mother followed by three tiny stuffed chicks, bore a shiny plaque beneath that read COMMON QUAIL, OLD WORLD. She leaned in close to it and wondered if the chicks were real. How could you shoot something so small and put it together again?

Past the bird rooms she came into a large study, ceiling-high bookshelves all around but no ladder in sight. It had the other hallmarks of an old-fashioned library—wainscoting, reading lights with beaded strings to pull, end tables that gleamed with a cherry warmth beneath their patina of dust. An antique brown globe on a stand, crossed sabers over the mantelpiece. She was displeased to see she was back among animals with sharp teeth and claws. Bears protruded from the walls between shelves, fangs bared, black and brown bears of varying sizes. One stood upright and ferocious in the corner, beside a coat stand. Its head was huge and marked on the plaque were the words KODIAK, ALASKA.

She knew it was irrational but still she felt nervous, alone in the house with the predators. Their glass eyes followed her.

But that would be easy enough to set right, she thought, looking for the nearest door—she would escape the eyes by stepping outside, get out of the dark wood and fustiness and old fur and take a free, full breath. She would have the stuffed animals cleared out as soon as she could, hire some movers to get rid of them. Not wishing to insult her uncle's memory, though, she couldn't throw them in the garbage, she'd have to donate them somewhere—a third-string natural history museum, maybe, or a moth-eaten roadside attraction. She would redecorate the place from top to bottom. It would be an ambitious project, a difficult task—a task so large in scope that it could occupy her for as long as she wished it to.

Finally she found a door that led outside through a small utility room, in which she blundered around until she found the lightbulb cord. Daylight shone at the end but there were obstacles crowding in: she made her way around the handles of vacuum cleaners and mops in buckets, toolboxes and stands for sewing machines, piles of yellow ripple-edged phone books on metal shelves, a roll of chicken wire that snagged on her skirt. At last she stood in a shaft of natural light from a frosted window. Beneath it was a rusty bolt, which she struggled with till it slid open, her fingertips sore. When she stepped outside there were cobwebs on her face. A dot-sized red spider skittered up her arm. She brushed it off and blew the strands from her eyes.

The backyard was nothing like the front. It was overgrown in places, drying in others but still gorgeous, a sumptuous dereliction. There were ponds, filmed over and stagnant, shrubs with flowers, shrubs browning at the base. There were mounds of reedy grass, birdhouses, delicate hummingbird feeders of blown glass. There were trees of all kinds, tall conifers towering, and paths wended back into the undergrowth, half covered by leaves and pine needles. She felt she could barely walk without ruining her shoes but went out anyway, pushed along over the muddy litter on the paths till she was coolly shaded.

One of the ponds, outlined in smooth, rounded river rocks, was partly covered in lily pads and a scum of green algae so light it was almost luminescent. She thought she saw something move beneath the dark surface and stopped, holding her breath. A slow bubble burst on the water.

There was a fragrance in the garden, not just the smell of decay but also the pines, or spruce, or whatever they were, in the sun, and flowers—jasmine possibly, she thought, sweet and rich. At her elbow were the leaves of a huge rhododendron. She found a fruitless avocado tree, which she recognized because she'd had one in her backyard as a child. There was an orange tree, a lemon. She wondered how far back the garden went, kept walking even when the paths seemed to trail off through the bushy undergrowth. It look several minutes to reach the very back: a wall taller than she was, a pebbled wall. At the wall she turned back and gazed at where she'd come from. Her path wound through trees, between bushes, beneath limbs. The house was only visible in pieces through the complexities of green, its creamy white ramparts. But it stretched far to the right and the left; it did not seem to end.

True, it was not the ocean. She had planned for the ocean,

when she considered a new home. The ocean was what she had foreseen. She had always been drawn to the sea, to the symbol of it more than what you could see—she thought of the untold depths, the deep blue mystery. But then, from the beach itself, the ocean could be flat and unknowable. The beach itself was mundane, compared to this—the beaches of L.A., at least, with the throwback hippies of Venice, the crowds of sweating tourists, bimbos rollerblading in headphones and bikinis.

Here it was lush, there was a hidden splendor. To the ones that had it, anyway: minutes ago she had been on the other side of the line, now she was here. A minute ago she might have hated who she was now. This sumptuous luxury.

The real selfishness, she thought, the only real selfishness was wealth like this. The commandeering of places, their fencing in, the building of palaces there—arches, gardens. No other selfishness mattered. All other selfishness was petty, as tiny as blown dust.

Her heart was beating fast, her cheeks were hot though she shivered when a breeze passed through the branches. She disbelieved it, then she couldn't help herself. She was filled with elation.

3

Susan invited Casey to the big house and Casey nodded and mumbled assent but didn't show up. Her grief seemed to be shifting to melancholy—lighter and less oppressive, though still she was prone to sudden retreat: she would be talking or doing routine tasks and then fall silent. Many days she continued much as before, at least on the surface.

Often when Susan got to her apartment T. was there, cleaning or fixing things or putting away groceries. He carried Hal's boxes in, arranged them neatly in a closet; he ferried Casey back and forth to his mother's place. Apparently Casey was curiously fond of Mrs. Stern, who remembered almost nothing from one day to the next. Susan felt a pang that her daughter chose to spend so much time with another mother, as though the two of them were in competition for her affections—she and a woman with no memory, a faded blond dowager from Connecticut who showed every sign of presenile dementia. Who, by the way, was blissfully competing with no one, while Susan had to work to pin down her daughter for dinner despite the fact that they were both bereft. Still it was good for Casey to spend her time with someone worse off than herself, Susan thought—she had to be grateful for any straws Casey could cling to. She tried to suppress her jealousy.

Before the closing with the buyers she and Casey and T. drove over to the old house. Opening the familiar front door, she thought how shabby this place was compared to the big house in Pasadena, this place where they'd spent all those years—a humble bungalow with no pretensions. With the furnishings gone it was a stack of boxes with hardwood floors and creamy walls, the wood pocked and scarred but still giving a tawny glow. T. pushed Casey's chair through the empty rooms as she looked around, Susan lagging behind.

Without their belongings it could be any house, any house where once a family had lived. Was there even a trace of them here? Only the appliances. Their appliances had been left behind. But it was hard to get teary about an appliance. Although she did remember shopping for them—the washing machine and dryer at Sears, the dishwasher later, when they had more money. For most of her life she'd washed dishes by hand. They'd bought the dishwasher in the evening of a day in which, bored and listless, she'd met a man named Najeem in a motel room that had indoor-outdoor carpeting (she remembered it still, a muddy brown flecked with yellow) and he turned out to be gay. She and Hal had been slaphappy that day, both of them, hysterical with laughter for their own unknown reasons. She would never be sure whether Hal had caught her hysteria or had his own wellspring. It could be ambient; hysteria caught like a yawn, that was clear, hysterics and yawns had their contagion in common.

Outside the mall, in the parking lot, they had run hard, chasing each other, and laughed even harder when she fell, surprising themselves. To this day she had a line of black dirt embedded in the skin of one knee.

This was where they'd been living earlier too, when the accident happened. Susan had got the call here, standing in the kitchen, and this was the space they'd adapted to accommodate the wheelchair, before Casey told them she wanted to move out. It had worn wooden ramps on the ground floor, to the elevated section that held Casey's bedroom.

Susan left her daughter and T. staring out the bare window at the next-door backyard, where a kid was creaking slowly back and forth on a yellow swing set. She made her way upstairs and stood silently in the empty master bedroom.

She and Hal had slept here together for years. Once, only once, had she let someone else in. Fantasy Baseball. The memory made her wince.

She stood still, wondering how sharply she would feel the rising tide of shame. She had never expected Hal to die young. She had assumed they would be old together, absentminded, dreamy and tottering. She had hardly ever thought of it, but when she did she saw them—a bit sadly, a bit nostalgic beforehand for the youth they had lost—nodding while quiet music played from dimly lit alcoves, drinking strong cocktails every night or watching the sunset, say, from the verandah of a restaurant—the games of children long forgotten by then. The selfishness of their youth left behind with their looks. That was how it would be, she used to think, when one of them finally left.

While he was alive she'd never felt squalid. Alive he had given a resilience to the fabric of things, his dry humor had warmed the rooms. But this was his death, its painful sanctity. Its coldness.

God damn. Death made everything serious.

This gray severity was the hard part—the punishment for her lifestyle, her callous practice of adultery, as a friend had put it once. Only three of her friends had known, and one had moved long since to New Zealand from where, every two or three years, she sent a postcard of craggy mountains and wild meadows, green ridges towering over a blue sea. The other two were more gone than that—one had succumbed to cancer in her forties, the last to manic depression and a group home in Northern California, not far from the ancient redwoods . . . faces blended and faded, their features more and more obscure.

That was the abstract cost of this, the cost beyond Hal's death: his memory was compromised. What should be a full and vivid remembrance of him was fractured by her separate life and blame—her separate life infringing on the life they had, the history he deserved to own.

The queen-size bed that had stood here might well have been the origin of his dying. She closed her eyes and saw the bed again, its sheets and blankets in disarray. She'd been careless here once, just once, with Fantasy Baseball. She had no way of knowing, of course, that Hal would have a minor car accident and appear at the house in the middle of the day, when she was still washing off in the shower. She had brazened it out, pretended there was nothing to acknowledge, and Hal had seemed to go along—but then soon after that he'd known, too soon for pure coincidence.

She should have erred on the safe side and never brought Baseball here. It had not been her practice to bring men home. Pure laziness: Baseball's apartment, where they usually went, was at Fairfax and Wilshire and she'd wanted to avoid the lunch-hour traffic. And she was not in the mood for the apartment's frat-boy furnishings, free weights on a vinyl bench, neon Budweiser sign and running shoes tumbled in a pile near the door with dirty socks crumpled into them.

That it was Baseball, with his stolid lack of foreplay and solid grasp of box scores, kept multiplying the offense, but the fact remained that she was sorry for symptoms, sorry for side effects most of all. Not for all of it, only what slid off the rails. It could not be her fault and all of it was her fault. She was a murderer and a victim, she felt the strain of trying to find her footing on uneven ground. Then also she was changeable, prepared to be someone else. She had fluidity.

She said goodbye to Hal again. She had left him once in the casket, once at the funeral and now in the bedroom. She would leave him again, she suspected, hundreds of times in near-invisible gestures, like the blur of a moving limb in a photograph.

Downstairs she passed Casey's doorway and saw T. stand up quickly from the level of the chair; he caught her eye and smiled. She wondered what was between those two these days. Before he went away there had been a close friendship that had ended; Casey had pushed him away, run from him even. Susan had suspected then that she had a crush on him. Casey liked to beat men to the punch, since the accident, reject them preemptively before she could be rejected. Understandable. Typically, though, she chose losers to take up with, insulating herself. That part wasn't so good.

But now—the look on his face as he rose—when it came to Casey Susan was unsure of her own instincts.

He had better not be leading her daughter on, she thought, with an edge of anger. T. dated women who resembled models— not that they actually were models, only that the prerequisites for seeing him seemed to be poise and classical looks. The girlfriend who had died, whom Susan had met only a handful of times, had been a slim, light-skinned black woman with a surprising movie-star charisma, who turned heads wherever she went but was also self-effacing and modest. The combination was rare. And then this rare, humble beauty had suddenly died: her heart had stopped with no warning and she was gone, as though to prove the unfeasibility of her goodness.

Casey was a rumpled child by comparison, a tomboy, a brat and a squeaky wheel. Not to mention the paraplegia, an attribute unlikely to be on his wish list.

She was defenseless, more so than ever. Susan would speak to him if she had to.

They dropped Casey at her apartment and headed to the office, where Susan would be introduced to the work of dismantling the business. T. had hired some kind of lawyer who specialized in charities. He was waiting for them.

"James," said T., and she and the lawyer shook hands. "He'll be helping with the transition."

"Call me Jim," he said easily, and held her fingers a little too long as his hand fell away. A good-looking man with a bit of a spare tire. She noticed the wedding ring.

Everything she owned was in the big house now, where she slept in an upstairs room. It featured the "horned beasts" of Africa; this theme was painted on a rippling scroll over the door. The horned animals were a water buffalo and a wildebeest, whose heads she'd taken off the brackets and piled beneath the sweeping curved staircase. Only the backdrop remained. The walls of the bedroom were painted diorama-style, long grasses growing up from the wooden trim along the floor and then, rising above them, the same flat-topped trees that were carved on the mansion's front door.

The heads themselves, alone in her room at night, had been too much company. But she liked the murals. In the distance, beyond the trees and the grasses, flat giraffes grazed and a herd of rhinos hunkered down, waiting patiently to be taken as trophies.

There were eight bedrooms on her floor, each with a geographic theme lettered above the door. One was titled THE RAINFOREST, with stuffed snakes and parrots and a sloth. Another was labeled THE ARCTIC, with caribou and a white Arctic fox. Icebergs were painted on the walls of the Arctic, expanses of blue water and a pale sunset. A third sign read THE HIMALAYAS, where there were snow-capped mountains, a stuffed white and black cat, an otter, and something labeled HIMALAYAN BLUE SHEEP, which to her looked neither blue nor sheeplike.

She'd chosen her own room, HORNED BEASTS, for its large bay windows that overlooked the back garden, the glittering oblongs of ponds. She could see the thin flagstone walkways weaving between the ponds, the feathery sweep of willows. In the mornings she liked to stretch in front of the window, leaving behind her dusty canopied bed whose linens smelled of mothballs. While she stretched out her limbs the sun rose and filtered through the dirty panes in strips. Her boxes lingered unpacked, save for the clothes and the toiletries: organization was a goal she kept ahead of her, fixed at a safe distance. In the meantime she liked her old life fine inside cardboard.

When the landscapers came the first morning to start work on reclaiming the garden she noticed one of the crew, Ramon: he had a pretty, unlined young face and ropy muscles and worked in a plaid shirt that hung open over a tank top and silver crucifix. She wondered if he was illegal. She would welcome that for she was illegal herself, far more criminal than Ramon would ever be.

•

Increasingly she wanted to know about the old man, as she was coming to think of her great-uncle. In the big house he was a ghost that walked alongside. But the ghost had the vague outline of a croquet mallet, the player piano. She wished it would take human form. She wanted to picture him. And she wanted to find out about his mania for collecting, if he had hunted or merely gone shopping. It seemed necessary to know.

She tried to ferret out his personal belongings but it was not even clear to her which bedroom had been his; the house was sprawling and uncentered. She found only piecemeal evidence that it had ever had a live-in tenant—a few old dress shirts marked ARROW and VAN HEUSEN hanging on the dirt-caked banister of the attic staircase, their faded pinstripes in mustard yellow and orange; a cast-iron bootjack in the shape of a Texas longhorn.

In daytime the house had the character of a dusty labyrinth whose caretakers had vanished, but by night the dust receded and she felt the solidity of the walls. At night the house was more like a honeycomb, a thick-built hive with hundreds of compartments. She could nest there cushioned and unseen.

After a few days of looking she found a desk in the library that might once have been a minor center of operations. It was less than it should be in that role; all it held was yellowing bills and checkbook registers, bundles of letters and postcards paperclipped together. But it was as close as she'd come, so that night she took the bundles to the kitchen and sat down at the table beneath a wall of fish.

The kitchen was mainly fish. She'd read in one of the old man's books that most fish trophies were replicas, so she thought these were probably also fakes. They shone with an unnatural flare and their colors had the high-contrast brightness of plastic. There were the usual suspects, a trout, a bass, a marlin, but there were also odd-looking specimens with peeling labels beneath them that read like poetry—a deep pink fish with large eyes labeled BLACKBELLY ROSEFISH, an evil-looking dark creature with white eyes labeled GOLDEN POMFRET, a tiger grouper and a bow-fin. She read beneath them with a bottle of wine at her elbow. The more she drank, the more dazzled she was whenever she looked up. The wallpaper was red and white and the fish on the walls were gray and blue and a lurid peach; their lines of contrast vibrated . . . in spidery writing on the back of a cruise-ship post-card from 1948 she read the words *Lil and I are having a swell time.* On a card from the Lincoln Memorial, *The hotest place Ive ever been.*

Now and then she had to get up, pacing with a letter in one hand and her wineglass in the other. The letters were impen-etrable somehow; they gave her almost no information about the old man. But one of them she wanted to keep for herself anyway. It was written on delicate yellowing stationery and was from a diplomat in Indochina, marked *Hanoi October 29 1945.* The dip-lomat described a cocktail party for Ho Chi Minh.

Ho is a seasoned old professional revolutionary, has done time for agitation in French, Chinese and even Hongkong jails. He is amazingly pleasant and gives the impression of being a Chinese scholar type . . .

Further down the letter writer described a person called the Emperor of Annam, who had also attended the party. *The Emperor is a very sophisticated gent, about 40 or 43, and looks much like what you'd expect of a modern Rajah. He is said to be inter-ested mainly in sports, chiefly hunting. There is wonderful shooting a couple of hundred miles from here.* A hint, she thought, a clue, a piece, but then it went nowhere, for there was no further men-tion of hunting. She forgot what she was looking for, in the wine and on her empty stomach, and only wished that she was in that time, long gone, when there were those habits of politeness and a person might reasonably write *much like what you'd expect of a modern Rajah.*

Then she was finished with the bundle of letters and there was nothing left but money. In a water-damaged register she found electricity and gas bills, even milk bills from the days when you could have it delivered, but most of the entries were illegible. There were a few invoices from travel agencies, which might have led somewhere if there had been enough of them, but in the end they yielded nothing of interest and she threw them away. The old man must have had photo albums, at least a box of curling old snapshots, she thought next, and started to search the library. But the task was too daunting.

Still she was stubborn and for a while at least she had nothing better to do, so she drained the wine bottle and combed the dusty shelves, pulling out one oversized book after another, flipping them open, then sliding them back into place. She lost track of time. There were volumes on coats of arms, on the children's crusades and the history of war, biographies of Napoleon and Douglas MacArthur. In a corner there was a small, primitive television and a pile of old movies: *Lion of the Desert, Little Big Man, The Bridge on the River Kwai.*

She would hire a cleaning woman, she decided, trudging upstairs at three in the morning with the dim old wall sconces lighting her way. People with big houses had cleaning women. Those people were not her, which she never forgot: rich people were not her. She looked at the sconces as she passed. Full of moths, hundreds of off-white moth bodies piled in the yellowing basins like pencil shavings. Were they a fire hazard? A cleaning woman could search the library. Or maybe a student could do it. With money, you could pay.

At the landing was an open window, its gauzy curtains blowing inward in the mild night breeze. Standing at windows had become a pastime. If she could, she would stand in the frame of an open window forever—the perfection of it. The peace. There you were, enclosed by the assurance of walls yet turned to the air. Stretching before you was the land, as though you were beginning it; the rest of being floated ahead, a movie in a darkened hall. Its possibilities touched the planes of your face, not too close, not too far, a scene of earth and sky that asked for nothing and forced nothing on you. There at the border and the rim, the real was also a mirage. The evening air cooled her cheeks and she felt exhilarated—her windfall house, a new life. The life of someone else.

Then the loneliness swelled, guilt pulsing at the base. She was a murderer.

She took a deep breath. Murderer, murderer.

She had to agree with herself. She had levied the accusation in the first place and now she had no choice but to acquiesce, accept graciously or she would never relax again, would always be defending herself against her own judgment. So yes: she was a murderer. Or worse, had done a negligent homicide. In an assassin at least there was purpose.

She felt her heart rate slow. Slow and steady. The fresh air cold on her skin. That was all right. She could be cold. She could be frigid. She held her arms out to receive the chill.

She was alone now. But on the other hand she was also a

queen, the private, unseen monarch of a kingdom of dust and faded velvet and the great horns of beasts. She dwelled in a palace. So she had nothing and everything at once, had been struck down and raised up.

In one respect it was not surprising, because the world's systems tended to elevate crime. Those systems knew about crime, those systems were forced to reward it. It would be wrong to say the world's systems liked or encouraged crime; that would be superstition, as the world had no opinions. The world neither liked nor disliked criminal acts; it was amoral, not immoral. It had no agency but it did have structure, and because of its structure it tended to reward criminal acts. As long as the criminal was not too overt and her movements agile, bad actions typically brought profit.

Inside there might be suffering, but externally, for all to see, profit and gain arrived. It would be incorrect to say society, for it was not society alone that had brought first Hal's death, then her windfall. Certainly society had created the big house. But other elements had also been required to bring her here—a molecular current was needed, a shifting too microscopic to attribute to people and their social compacts.

Broadly, the world could not say no to an act of selfishness. Selfishness burned at its core.

Above the core there was the good soil, the dirt of continents, the water of seas, the winds of the atmosphere. Moon and stars, firmament: the ocean and the sky. This second part of her life was two kinds of freedom and two kinds of blackness. The future yawned over her, the heavens were endless. They were an observatory. Was that what plenty gave you? Everything was offered, nothing was necessary. She was less bound, standing there at the window by night. She had sails, she had wings, she had the lift of low gravity.

She also had the shudder of regret, a sadness that clung forever. She was the sliver of rot in the wood.

Airborne, though, maybe she could stand it. Before her the indigo sky of predawn, the black lacework of sheltering trees. She and Hal had never been poor. They'd always had enough income to qualify as middle-class, at least until it came to Casey's medical bills. But this life was something else by an order of magnitude—a state of exuberance, a lazy abundance that bristled with energy.

One morning she stood at the bedroom window half-naked while Ramon was working alone in the backyard, and then, when he looked up, she smiled.

That was all you needed, typically. He was young, shy and deferential, and you had to be obvious with men: she had learned that early. To get what you wanted without undue worry, obvious was the key. Men would take anything that was offered, as a general rule. Most were so surprised they never contemplated refusal. That was the advantage of other women's submission.

In a society of aggressive or even merely confident women, she would be overlooked; but since most of them were passive, and most men were lazy, the field was wide open.

She led him into the Himalayas on impulse because the bed in there had new sheets—the only sheets in the house that didn't smell of mold. She had made the bed for herself before she chose horned beasts and not yet bothered to switch the linens, preferring to sleep in dust and oldness every night, half out of apathy. And he was clean, cleaner than average, she felt, and smelled slightly of aftershave or soap—eucalyptus, maybe—which she found she didn't mind. He gave an impression of instinctive knowledge: something about the fullness of skin, a generosity that made the context fade.

But then he stayed shy, downcast eyes and an expression of regret or modesty, hard to tell which. She guessed he was ashamed of them, that their behavior nagged at his Catholicism. Maybe the age difference made him awkward, maybe she reminded him of his mother. She would prefer not to. Younger men were a recent event for her, a passing accident. Usually it was competence that attracted her to men more than the way they looked, and older men were more likely to be competent, though they didn't have a monopoly on it. Baseball had been almost incompetent, which made him less than compelling in the end. Ramon was not; Ramon had competence enough to give solidity to his attractiveness. Also he did not have a girlfriend—she had asked—and so she was unsure where his regret came from, save maybe shame about pleasure.

She always tried to meet shame gracefully where she found it, felt sympathy for those who believed that pleasure deserved punishment (although she herself even suspected it sometimes, more superstitiously than anything). She felt the sadness of this inheritance, religious, social, even a casual hand-me-down, and tried small tender gestures to soften the exchange. Often she suspected these gestures were only perceptible to her, though—too subtle or subjective to convey.

They were surrounded by clarity in the Himalayas—the snow-topped mountains in two dimensions, the robin's-egg skies above. Around the king bed was a menagerie: the goat-like animal labeled BLUE SHEEP, the otter, the cat whose glass irises were a deep-spiraling well of gold. She turned her head to the window. Inside the square were power lines and palm trees and above these a yellow-gray haze of smog. The brief white frame divided those elements from the painted landscape of the peaks—one of which she was almost sure was Mount Everest, another K2, because she knew the shape of them from movies. She wondered if the old man had done this, lain on this very bed when he was young. The animals blindly seemed to watch; in former days, possibly they had watched him. The animals did not watch, of course—dead they were blind—but still they seemed to. You watched but did not seem to; they saw nothing while seeming to fixate on you . . .

She shivered. Do not look at the cat, do not think of old fur. Of skinning, of tanning, what happened to the real eyes. Someone had skinned these creatures once, someone had flayed their bodies raw. In Century City the lawyer sat behind his desk and hissed: *He died without issue.* She closed her eyes for a time, but to look at Ramon she had to risk the sheep in her peripheral vision. Its horns were symmetrical, rounded, rising from the head in graceful arches—but even this was a distraction, even this brief observation was not what she meant to be doing, seemed like a form of disrespect.

Then the condom came off and Ramon was embarrassed. She slid her hand around it and disposed of it onto the floor, rummaged in the nightstand drawer for a new one. She smiled at him while she reached for the packet, the smile always a key to continuity: she struggled to maintain the grace they'd had, smooth over his humiliation, struggled to do so without the appearance of struggling. Men could be sensitive to interruption.

She wondered what he made of the house, the moth-eaten mounts everywhere. The new condom went on and they were off and running . . . the old man's library contained books on taxidermy. Apparently aficionados called the animals *mounted*, not stuffed—both about sex, of course—the beasts, the prey, the caught, the shot. Ramon knew the place was new to her, that these were not her oddities but someone else's, inherited along with the house. That much she hoped, at least, from the fact that he was here working for her in the derelict garden, if not from passing remarks she'd made. If he'd listened.

Suddenly in her mind she was an old woman in a rambling house full of pelts. Nothing could be less appealing. And yet Ramon did not notice this sour flash of identity. He showed no outward sign. He did what he did. Here he was.

She pushed the pelts to the back of her mind, closed her eyes again and tried to feel her fingertips, her toes, the long glide of her legs over the backs of his. He said something under his breath, a compliment, she thought—it sounded like *You're beautiful*—and she appreciated the kindness but doubted that he meant it. It was not true; she knew she was not beautiful but attractive at best, the kind of woman few men noticed unless she wanted them to. She had a symmetrical face and a graceful, smooth body, once you got her clothes off—her body was still better than her face, even in middle age—but overall she had quiet looks.

She tried to forget the details of herself. She would be no one—Let me be no one at all or all of them. Let me be anyone. That was the privilege of the rich, wasn't it? They could feel like anyone, where the poor could only feel like themselves, trapped in themselves forever. The rich were infinitely free. Or the suddenly rich, at least. Those born that way were bound and tied, as much as anyone. But the manna from heaven . . . let us lift off the bed, let our skins absorb the streams of particles, of blood, water, the electricity, the storms—

She washed the smell of latex off her hands afterward and ran a shower for Ramon in the adjacent bathroom, whose tilework must have dated from the twenties: they were minute one-inch ivory tiles trimmed in black and a powdery pink. A large, rusting showerhead over a clawfoot tub.

She said to herself, almost aloud: Never again. Next time she slept with a stranger it would be in her own room, where all that watched them was the long, flat grass.

Ramon clearly felt pressed to get back to work, though the whole episode hadn't lasted more than twenty minutes and fit into his morning break. He stepped out of the shower and stood beside her, watching from the bathroom window as his supervisor arrived, pulling into the driveway beneath them in his white van with a logo of black leaves.

"You can say I made you do something for me," she said,

handing him a towel. "I mean, if you want to. You can say I made you carry something heavy."

•

It let her feel regal to stroll through the house out into the back gardens. Laughable—an emperor with no clothes—but still real. The rooms were cleaner now, the gardens tidied and replanted where they had died, trees and bushes pruned, ponds repaired and refilled, irrigation systems patched and put on an expensive timer. She picked out fish from a catalog. She spent her days clearing the house of what she knew she didn't need—at first only the small debris of the old man's life, gathered combing through drawers. There were scores of well-used packs of playing cards, held together with rubber bands and bearing an unmistakable old-card smell, the ancient dirt of fingers. There were board games, as though families had come through here frequently despite his having been a bachelor, despite his having died without issue.

She found Parcheesi, a game she remembered from summer nights in her grandmother's house. She found ashtrays by the score, glass with seams of bubbles along the edges or in the shape of French poodles, plastic printed with fading beer or tobacco logos, thick clay slabs with crude scallops and the denting prints of children's thumbs. She found a shelf full of faded badminton birdies and wooden tennis racquets, a worn football, croquet mallets. Somehow these conjured parties for her: elegant guests in evening dress with cigarettes in long holders, spilling out onto the patios and gardens in a gleaming night.

The furniture was dingy, and there was too much of it: every space was a hodgepodge of styles and colors. She had the ruined and homely pieces removed and watched with satisfaction as the rooms they left behind became airier. She loaded knickknacks into boxes and drove them to Goodwill; she scrounged through cabinets until they contained only items for which she could imagine some future use.

But when it came to the animals she was undecided. At first she had been determined to rid herself of their carcasses with all possible speed, but curiously the impulse was fading: the longer she lived with them the greater their hold. Some needed repair, were bald in patches with broken horns or ragged tails. At first, as she walked through the great room with its foxes and otters, this had made them ugly or pathetic; but more and more it made her feel protective.

Their arrangement added to her confusion. She understood the rooms on the second floor—their classification by geography, rough and general though it was. But the ground floor was a jumble. She did not know why the common raccoons of the great room kept company with the foxes, the possums, which were apparently marsupials, or the beavers, classified as semi-aquatic rodents. (She had to look this up.) The old man, she guessed, had not planned at all when he began to collect. At first the assemblages had been thrown together without forethought. A room of BEARS OF THE WORLD, he must have thought, hell yeah. A room of heads with racks. A room of brown mammals, why not.

As the collection grew he'd moved toward a better scheme— still rudimentary but at least organized—placing each mount in a more logical grouping. He'd been unable to help himself, and the more he acquired, the more he had to impose an order. She could see him, in her mind's eye, being forced toward it. Because without order there could be no true collecting. Without order there was only acquisition.

When she'd been living in the house for six weeks Casey finally paid her a visit.

By then Ramon had moved on to another job—he turned out to be neither an illegal nor a student but the youngest son of a claims adjuster, with ambitions in auto detailing—and she'd started sleeping with Jim the lawyer. Jim was an intelligent and slightly petty man on the surface, but beneath it he was tender. She thought he might be the kind of person who, in the right circumstances, could kill someone. She wondered if this would be a bond between them.

The combination of circumstances required for Jim the lawyer to kill, she suspected, was so specific that it would likely never occur. That made him a would-be murderer at best, unlike her, and a fairly safe bet. Not that he was vicious or cruel—on the contrary, he was mild and gentle. Still she thought he might have a blind spot of rage, some hair trigger that would unleash a buried anger. Many men did; it was hardly unique.

Jim impressed her because most of the adulterers she'd known liked to lie naked and panting beside her and offer up a disquisition on their marriage. It was a common impulse. She herself had learned early on not to talk about Hal, that discussing her husband with others was off limits, but some men treated illicit sex as an entry to marital therapy. And surprisingly by her third time with Jim he had still not brought up his wife, other than to acknowledge he had one. She liked this disinclination to confess.

She was standing over the bathroom sink lazily after he left, gazing at the lines on her face in the mirror, when she heard gravel scrape on the circular drive. Cinching the belt on her bathrobe, she felt around on the floor for her shoes with an outstretched toe, then craned her neck to see out the window. Beyond the branches of an oak—Ramon had told her what each of the trees was in the garden, both the front and the back, and she had faithfully written them down on the landscape map to commit them to memory—she could make out the hood of Casey's car.

When she invited Casey to come by anytime she'd been sure she'd have ample warning; her daughter didn't do drop-bys often. She'd assumed the drive to Pasadena was unfamiliar enough that Casey would have to call for directions. Still, now that Casey was here Susan was excited to show her the place, and as she reached for her jeans she wondered if her daughter had seen the lawyer's car leaving. It was a light-green BMW—unmistakable since Casey knew it from the office.

Also the two of them hadn't talked about Casey's livelihood since the airport but Susan knew they would have to discuss it sometime—it ached like a bad tooth at the back of her mouth. She would hate to lose her moral high ground, or the carefully guarded illusion of it. On the other hand, with T. around so often it was doubtful that Casey could be spending much of her time on the phone.

"You're kidding me," said Casey, when Susan opened the front door.

She was sitting out on the edge of the cobbled drive, a few feet from her car, with boughs of oak and laurel dipping over her head like a bower.

"What?" asked Susan.

"You're fucking kidding me," she said. "All this?"

"I told you," said Susan.

"You said a big house," said Casey. "You didn't say the Taj Mahal. This is ridiculous!"

"It's eccentric," said Susan.

Despite herself she felt puffed up by Casey's admiration, as though the house was her personal creation.

"Come on, honey. Come see the back. The grounds are almost twenty acres."

"No way," said Casey, and followed her onto the tiles of the patio and past the tennis court.

Lonely, sometimes, that there were two of them—moments like this, when they were single-file.

It also struck her that Casey should have a new car, that her car was cramped and dinged and there was plenty of money now.

"Do you want a car?" she asked impulsively, turning. "We can get you one. With some of the money from the old house. The sale. I mean look, there's some cash for once. There are taxes on this place, there are repairs I'm paying for, but other than that, with the proceeds from the house sale, maybe your father's life insurance, eventually, we're practically rich."

Casey stared at her, surprised, and then over her shoulder.

"Are those—parrots?"

Susan turned and looked and saw light-green wings flapping and blurring near the tops of the alders.

"They look like parrots," she said uncertainly.

"They are parrots," said Casey. "It's a whole flock of them. Look!"

A flash of red on their heads, yellow beaks, beady eyes. Susan wished one would alight nearby so she could see it closer up. Get a good look. But they blurred. Why did they have to fly the whole time?

"Parrots," she repeated.

They watched the parrots, which made a racket with their squawking. People spoke of the beauty of birdsong, but not when it came to parrots. They were the exception that proved the rule.

"They give me the weirdest feeling," said Casey dreamily. "It's like they remind me of something I never saw."

"My whole life I never knew we had wild parrots in L.A. County," said Susan.

"Did they escape from somewhere?"

"So many?"

"I'm pretty sure they're not supposed to be here," said Casey. "When I see nature shows, typically, they don't feature parrots in Southern California."

"This is the first time I've seen them," said Susan.

"Huh. I should ask T. He has this animal hobby," said Casey.

"I meant to ask you about that," said Susan. "The turnaround, the whole charity thing. So you don't think he's—unstable?"

"I don't know about stable. But he's less of an asshole now."

"High praise," said Susan.

The parrots flapped and squawked, raucous screeches fading. Presently there was silence and the high branches stopped trembling and were still.

"So now," said Casey. "About that car."

4

The koi was hanging beneath lily pads, long and bulbous and graceful—like a zeppelin, she thought. Orange and black fins flicked back and forth, barely moving. She knelt beside the pond and gazed.

A man's voice interrupted.

"I hear people pay two thousand bucks for those things."

She jumped to her feet, squinting and brushing dirt from her bare knees. It was her cousin Steven, the computer guy, dressed for leisure in khaki Bermuda shorts and a polo shirt; he wore highly reflective sunglasses in a giant wraparound visor, so the whole upper half of his face was missing in action. He was futuristic, a man who came with his own windshield.

She had to get the gate fixed, she realized. Then she could keep it locked.

"Yeah, there's breeders and shit, all these fancy Japanese, like, fish farms," said Steven, nodding sagely. "Big one outside Fresno, they sell the things to Chinese restaurants or whatever. For atmosphere. Not, like, for food. I know. I set up their network."

"Mine was twenty dollars at the pet store," said Susan.

"The things are what, obese goldfish?"

"Obese seems, I don't know, judgmental."

"OK then. Fucking fat."

"They're distant goldfish relatives, I think. A kind of carp."

"So they're like, goldfish on roids. Do they get roid rage?"

She found herself gazing at him.

"Hey!" he went on. "You should do mandatory drug testing."

"Ha," said Susan wanly. She looked down to the pool at her feet, the gold patches gleaming beneath the surface.

"Well, here we are, huh? Uncle Al left the whole dog-and-pony show to dear little Susan," said Steven, with a quick sting of anger that took her by surprise.

He looked around, head bobbing in what seemed to be an ongoing skeptical nod. At least, she assumed he was looking around: his head swiveled slowly as it bobbed and sunlight flashed on his metallic lenses.

"Not so little," she said, still taken aback and stalling. It had never occurred to her that he might feel entitled. Not once. She never had, herself.

She blundered on. "Middle-aged Susan, more like."

"Nah, really. You don't look a day over thirty."

"Aw. Can I get you a cup of coffee?"

"Gimme the private tour."

"Come on in."

Inside the music room, which opened to the pool and backyard and was full of sheep and goat mounts, he looked around and whistled. Except for a faded, wine-colored velour couch the room was almost empty, only a stand with some colorful guitars in a corner and a dusty double bass with no strings.

"Old guy was crazier than I thought," he said.

"I didn't know him well," said Susan.

"So why'd he pick you?"

"Honestly, I have no idea. Were you two still in touch?"

"We did a couple Turkey Day meals. That kind of shit. Mostly at our place, though, when we lived over in Reseda. He would come in from out of town with a pile of gifts for the kids. So they kinda liked him. Deb didn't. She thought he was an old lech."

"Oh yeah?"

"As far as invitations, he didn't return the favor. Last time I was in this place I was a kid myself."

"He had a player piano, remember? I haven't found it yet, though. Maybe he got rid of it. The kitchen's over here," she said.

"Building's massive. Jesus."

"It's large."

"Guy musta had a full-time taxidermist on the payroll."

"Was he a hunter? Do you know?"

"Well it's sure as shit not roadkill."

"Do you remember what he did? For a living?"

"It was like, commodities trading maybe? He was abroad a lot. He was traveling all the time."

"What can I get you? I have coffee, tea, sparkling water—"

"No beer?"

"Oh. At ten-thirty . . . ?"

"Gimme a Bud, if you got one."

She opened the refrigerator as he paced the room peering at the stuffed fish.

"Dos Equis OK?"

"Mexican pisswater? Enh, sure. I'm not picky."

She almost decided not to hand it over, then reached for the bottle opener.

"What is that, a marlin?"

"I'm still learning. Whatever the label says."

To occupy herself she reached into the freezer for the bag of coffee.

"So. What brings you by? Wanting to check out the place?"

"Yeah, you know. Though we probably won't make a claim."

"What claim?"

"Against the estate. You know."

She gaped at him. The sunglasses were propped up on his head now, but his eyes didn't tell her much either. He raised his beer bottle and drank.

A wave of illness moved through her.

"No—what?"

"Like I say, we probably won't. Tommy's giving me some pressure. He says it's the principle of the thing. But listen. I'm like, she's had a bad year already. That woman has nothing. Zip. Nada. She needed something like this. I go, She needs it more than we do, Tomboy."

She was unsteady.

"Well. Thanks for that, Steve."

"Yeah. Well. You know."

"It was pretty clear in the will, wasn't it? I mean what do I know."

"See, though," and he shook his head, taking a swig from the bottle, "the non compos thing. Not of sound mind."

"Was he under care or something? In an institution?"

"He lived here by himself."

"So what makes you think he was—?"

"Shit, woman. I mean the guy was a hermit. There's no one to say if he was crazy or not."

She might be having a panic attack. Her breath felt constricted. Spite, she thought. Spite and malice. She wouldn't be surprised if the old man had left her the house expressly to make sure it wasn't given to Steven. Possibly when he saw the guy, on holidays, the guy had irritated him. Possibly she was projecting, but possibly Steve's poor character had been the source of her own good luck.

She fumbled with the coffee grinder as her breathing evened out. It was an excuse to turn away; she'd already drunk her coffee quota. As she pressed down on the lid and the grinder spun and shrieked she raised her eyes to the wall above her, which featured a mako shark. She felt reassured by it. She was a murderer, after all. For once it was a comfort to think so. Being a murderer made her equal to Steven.

She lifted her hands from the grinder and waited till it wound down, then pulled off the top and tipped the grounds into a filter.

"Well, I'm glad you convinced Tommy I wasn't worth suing," she said humbly.

A murderer, like a shark, must have rows of hidden sharp teeth behind the ones at the front.

What he said was true, of course, though his whole bearing filled her with resentment. Resentment and unease. Of course she didn't deserve the house. No one deserved a house like this. She didn't deserve anything, she knew that. But he deserved even less, she suspected. All she could think of to do was flatter him. She would show him some gratitude, presume a kindness in him and will it into existence. Maybe he would follow a rare generous impulse and leave her alone.

"You liquidated this property, we're talking megamillions," he said.

A month ago, T. might have bought it himself. Made her his partner, bulldozed the big house and converted the lot to rows of houses like cupcakes on a tray.

"I would hate to sell it," she said softly. "They'd tear it down and build a subdivision."

"Ee-yup."

"But it's beautiful," she said, in a subdued tone. Needing somewhere else to look, she opened the refrigerator with a pre-occupied air.

"Spacious accommodations for a single lady," he badgered.

"I rattle around in here," she said, though this was not at all the way she felt. In truth she glided through chains of rooms streamlined, perfectly graceful in the long halls. Perfect not in and of herself, but in and of the house.

"Yeah, no kidding."

"I'm not sure what to do with the house yet. I admit. But I will do something."

"Do something?" said Steven, and drained his beer. "Like what?"

"You know there are parrots that live wild in the neighborhood?" she asked brightly. "Whole flocks of wild parrots!"

•

When she was ushering him toward the front door, two beers later, he stopped to pick through a box of odds and ends on a tabletop—she had it ready to go out to Goodwill—and lifted an old keychain. A dusty bronze ornament dangled.

"Oh yeah," he mused. "Shit yeah. You know about this?"

"About what?"

"Some club. It's the logo of that old club he was so into. You don't remember? Only thing I remember from when I was over here as a kid. Those fuckers were already ancient. They used to hang around the place with walkers and oxygen tanks."

She held it up to the light: gold and red, with a lion. There had once been words, but they were too worn to read.

"Drive safe," she said, as he got into his car. "And I really appreciate you respecting the spirit of the will. Going easy on me. It means a lot, Steve."

Maybe her self-effacing tone would ring in his ears when he thought about litigation. She crossed her fingers behind her back like a schoolgirl and hoped hard, into the bare air, that he would not return—that he and his son Tommy, of high principle, would leave well enough alone.

He backed up in a spurt of pebbles and rolled out the gate; she watched through the holes in the hedge as his car flashed away. She clutched the medallion.

•

Later she stood out on the poolside terrace drinking wine with Jim the lawyer and listening to the fountain at the end of the pool, where water flowed over jumping marble porpoises. He came over once or twice a week in the early evening, when his wife worked late or had made other plans. There were no children.

"Look at me. Already I'm jealously guarding my property," she said. "As though I earned it or something."

"You don't want your asshole cousin coming in and trashing the place," said Jim. "It's hardly irrational."

"Because it's *mine*," she said, shaking her head. "My personal Club Med."

"Club Med is pathetic," said Jim.

"You know what I mean."

"What I think is, you've had the rug pulled out from under you twice in your life. This house is the first good thing that's happened to you in a long time. Naturally you want to keep it. You're human."

"But you're not," she said, turning to press herself on him, holding her wineglass out to the side. "You're a lawyer."

"Your best bet is just to play defense. Wait and see. See if he bothers to make a claim."

She looked up at his face, its gray, heavy-lidded eyes. He never seemed to open them as far as he could. His lassitude was calming.

Reading in bed, she put down her book and reached for the old letter from Hanoi. She held the yellow paper carefully and reread the looping, faded script: *The Emperor is a very sophisticated gent, about 40 or 43, and looks much like what you'd expect of a modern Rajah.* It bore an embossment at the top, Charles Adams Sumter III. She flipped the papers over: his signature said *Chip.*

Chip had known the old man, she thought. The old man had known him. Long dead, no doubt.

A plane crossed the sky, blinking, and she lay back on the pillow. But then she woke up and it was early morning. She remembered the plane as though it should still be there; she had the sense that only a second had passed. It was so early the outside was still almost silent, and through her wide window she saw the yellow streaks of dawn. She reached out for her telephone. 411.

She said his name and the operator asked for an address.

"I don't have one," she said.

"Three listings in the metro area," said the operator briskly, and rattled them off as Susan reached for a pen.

At the first number a woman answered, groggy, and mumbled something in Spanish. She sounded young. Susan apologized for waking her but didn't regret it. The second number was out of service, and the third was an answering machine that seemed to belong to a young family.

She went downstairs to forage for breakfast but a stubbornness nudged at her so that midway through her bowl of cereal she got up and left the cornflakes soaking to call Information again. This time she asked for more listings, listings for the whole state. She had no evidence he was here, if he was even living, but it was her only lead. There were eight numbers in all, not too many, and she sat with her coffee at the kitchen table, the list in front of her, and dialed methodically. One man had an English accent, which gave her hope at first—maybe because it imbued him fleetingly with age or stature. But he hung up when she asked more. The next number gave her a voicemail with a generic message, so she left her own. The third rang for some time until she heard a distant voice at the other end: the name of a business, and she was disappointed. Then the words came again. *Sunset Villas.*

"Are you—I'm sorry. What are you?"

"We're a residential community. For seniors."

She stretched out the coils of the phone cord on a finger, then released.

"I'm looking for a Mr. Sumter. A Mr. Charles Sumter."

There was the buzz of static, then nothing. She'd been cut off. But no—a click and someone else picked up.

"Switchboard. Mr. Sumter is away from his room," said a second voice.

She asked if he went by Chip, but the woman didn't know. She asked how old he was, and the woman didn't know that either. It was an 805 area code, Santa Barbara.

•

The villas were condos that overlooked the sea, a blocky off-white complex built around a pool. It was a gray day, with a cold wind whipping down the coast, and the concrete paths that led between the buildings were mostly deserted. Here and there a palm tree with dry fronds scraped and flapped or a square bed of bright geraniums was laid flat by the wind. There were no signs on the paths so it was hard to know where the lobby might be. After a while she came up behind a woman with a walker, who was proceeding slowly enough to be caught easily. The woman pointed.

Stepping through the automatic doors into the reception area, with its turquoise carpet and framed posters of old musicals, she was surprised; it seemed low-rent for oceanside real estate. To her right was a wall that blared OKLAHOMA! and CATS, and to her left was a glass wall into a small cardio room, where elderly figures looked haggard but determined on StairMasters and treadmills. Their legs pumped doggedly beneath them and they were looking straight forward, looking right at her. She had to turn away quickly lest one of them suddenly collapse.

The woman at the desk gave her a photocopied floor plan of the kind they handed out at motels, with an apartment number circled, and then she was up a long ramp to the second floor, along a catwalk and at the room, ringing the doorbell. A nurse opened the door, a nurse in a baby-blue dress and sneakers, or maybe she was a cleaning person. Susan followed her down a white-walled hallway, their footfalls noiseless on the off-white carpet.

Chip sat on a floral couch in front of a large window. He was a dark form with the light behind him, but she could tell he was very old and thin, with white hair. He wore an argyle sweater. He must be in his nineties. Wind chimes hung behind him in multitudes: glass butterflies, aluminum pipes, hummingbirds dangling beneath bells.

But there couldn't be wind; it was a picture window and did not open.

He struggled to rise, but she shook her head.

"Oh no, please. Mr. Sumter," she said, and bent down to hold out her hand. His own was very soft. Behind him the fuzzy, blue-gray ocean was visible: he had been given a good room. Not all the residents could have so clear a view.

After she sat down across the wicker coffee table the cleaning woman brought them tea and poured the contents of two pink packets into his cup for him—or maybe not a cleaning woman, given the tea service. Her role remained unclear.

Susan told him who she was and asked if he had known her uncle, and when she said her great-uncle's name a smile broke on the old guy's face.

"Good old Bud," he said fondly, and picked up his cup of tea.

"So how did you know him?" she asked. She was prepared to explain herself but Chip did not need an explanation. He was happy to talk and spoke slowly and carefully: they had known each other through the State Department, where Chip had been in service. But her great-uncle had not been in the department because he'd failed some kind of Foreign Service test, though Chip did not use the word *fail*. So Albert had not been a diplomat but because of his line of work, which was import-export, he had been a fixture in various expat communities during a certain era.

In Bali, said Chip, and Peru, and Japan, and Indochina under the French.

"He moved in our circles, you see," said Chip warmly, and sipped his tea.

She remembered the phrase he had written. *Much like what you'd expect of a modern Rajah.*

"I found an old letter you wrote him," she said, and fumbled to pull it from her purse and pass it across.

"Ah," said Chip. He reached for his glasses, thick black-framed bifocals perched on an end table on top of a large-print book. He put them on and reached for the letter shakily.

"And I was wondering," she said, "if you knew where he got so many trophies. I mean all the—I'm his heir, and the house is full of these—"

"The club," said Chip. "Oh yes. Old Buddy ran the club."

"He did?"

"He loved the hunt," and Chip nodded. "He did. He loved the hunt. He liked the ponies, too."

Then he was saying something about a horse race and a particular horse—the Belmont Stakes, he said, when it was won by the son of Man O' War—did she know Man O' War? Did she know Secretariat? The hats worn by the women, in times long past, he mused. The lack of hats in horse-racing nowadays—sometimes he went to Santa Anita, he said, or Del Mar or Hollywood Park to wager on the horse races and he was dismayed by the casual dress. In former times the ladies had worn hats.

"What club?" she asked.

"He started the club in that house, you see," he said. "It moved, later—into the desert somewhere . . . published his own record books, even back then. The members' books . . . trophy records, you know."

"I haven't seen those," she said.

"All the big-game trophies. The trophies, owners' names, the year they were taken . . . skin length."

"There are so many," she said. "There are hundreds."

"Now, Teddy Roosevelt," said Chip dreamily, "took down twelve thousand on his African safari. Of course some of those specimens were insects. Not all big game, you see. Big game alone, I think there were only five hundred. Had your rhinos, your elephants . . . my father knew Roosevelt. Called him T.R."

"He knew him personally?"

The old man nodded absently.

"Buddy started the competitions. Started them and ran them, ran them for years. Who could have the most kills, you know. One of every kind of deer. Every bear. You won them all, you'd have to take maybe three hundred all by yourself . . . used to give them to the Smithsonian. Like T.R. Needed their help later to bring in the rare ones. After they passed the laws . . . back when I used to go over there, wasn't any of that. At the beginning, the soirees were nothing much. No girls, you see. The ladies weren't much interested in that. But later they came. Yes they did. The wives, the girlfriends. When he gave out the awards, and so forth. He would throw these . . ."

He started to cough and shook his head.

"Here you go," said the nurse, and handed him water and pills.

"I went for the parties, mostly," he said, after he'd swallowed the pills and taken a sip. "A bachelor back then, you see. I didn't go so often after I married."

"My uncle was always single. Wasn't he?"

"Never found the right special lady."

"If you don't mind my asking, do you have any old pictures? Pictures of him? My family, we weren't close. And I haven't been able to find anything in the house."

He got up with difficulty, leaning hard on her arm, and made his way slowly to a bookshelf. She gazed around the room: shelves with framed pictures on them, a philodendron, tourist posters of

Greece and Hong Kong, an old map. Finally he pulled out a thick
ochre-colored album but it seemed too heavy for him, balancing
on the edge of the shelf, half out and half in, as he stood help-
lessly with a feeble hand on the spine. She rose quickly before he
could drop it.

"Oh here, let me . . . thanks, thank you so much," she said,
and sat down with it.

"Might be one of Buddy near the beginning. Long time ago,
you know. My wife marked everything."

The photographs were elaborately annotated in a spidery,
awkward hand, words standing on the gluey ridges of the paper.
She sat with the scrapbook open on her knees as he puttered over
to a cabinet in the corner, which had an old turntable on top, likely
of seventies vintage: fake wood-grain on the sides of the platform.
It took him some time to remove a record from its sleeve, so long
that she considered offering to help but then reconsidered in case
it might give offense. Instead she paged through the heavy leaves
looking for her uncle's name. They were all black-and-white
at the beginning, then sepia-toned; there were color Polaroids
throughout the 1960s.

It seemed the wife had even gone back and archived Chip's
photos from before they met, since one caption, under a black-
and-white of Chip and a young blonde in evening dress, read *Chip
and his girlfriend Lettie "Lulabelle" Mae, May 1953.*

Finally she hit paydirt with a caption that read *Chip with,
l–r, Arnie Sayles, Lou Redmond, Frank Davis-Mendez and Albert
"Bud" Halveston. Spring Banquet, 1959.* It was a row of middle-
aged men in white dinner jackets, their arms around each other's
shoulders. Her uncle, at the end, was thin and angular with a

cigarette hanging out of his mouth and a wave of shining hair standing up over his forehead.

She closed her eyes and tried to remember him like that. She had been thirteen years old; she would have known him then.

Still nothing but the croquet and the player piano.

Chip's record was opera—a mournful aria. When he sat down again he was less lucid, rambling about the ancient festivities as she paged through his album. Once there had been famous people, he said. Bud was well known for lavish cocktail parties, catered dinners, fancy-dress balls . . . he remembered women with tall feather headdresses, feathers and sparkling beads, the fund-raising events for charity, the hunting expos and sportsmen's banquets. The Reagans were there once, and Henry Kissinger. Zsa Zsa Gabor one time when she was between husbands. Ice statues in the swimming pool.

"Charity," said Susan, clutching at straws. "So what were his charities?"

"Oh the club, freedom to hunt, like that," and he flapped a hand wearily. A moment ago he had been eager but suddenly he was tired. She wondered if she should call the nurse.

The opera played behind them, suddenly more subdued.

"I'm trying to figure out what he would have wanted," she went on. "What his wishes would have been, for the house and the collection. My instructions, more or less. I don't know who he *was*, is my problem."

"Of course his pet project was the legacy," said Chip, nodding.

"The legacy?"

He bent forward, coughing, and the nurse was back beside them with another glass of water.

"So what was the legacy?" asked Susan, when he had calmed down again.

"The legacy," he said.

She saw the letter, on the coffee table in front of him, was half soaked in water. It was no good anymore, she thought, and felt a curious sadness.

The old letter was gone.

"I'm sorry, the—?"

"That actress, what was her name, she had—oh, who was it—I heard that Buddy showed it to her . . ."

"Time for your doctor visit," interrupted the nurse. "We have a checkup downstairs." She was pushing a wheelchair.

"May I walk with you, then?" asked Susan.

The nurse held one of his elbows as he rose, steering him to the chair. His other hand pointed waveringly at the record player, so Susan went over and lifted the needle, trying for delicacy. In the silence after the *ffft* she could hear the whine of a car alarm cycling outside but the apartment itself seemed airless and sealed.

"You were saying," she urged gently, walking beside the nurse over the carpet. The wheelchair squeaked slightly under Chip's weight.

"Saying?" he asked.

"What was the legacy?"

"Wasn't allowed to go in. Not in the inner circle anymore. Bitsy was very softhearted, you see, she didn't like the hunting and so forth . . . that was where all his fortune went . . ."

"*Where*, though?"

No use.

The apartment door closed behind them and they were on the catwalk now, the car alarm shrieking louder and nearer. She had to squeeze in beside them due to the narrow passage. He looked up at her and smiled broadly and she thought, with a lift of hope, that he would say something oracular. He pointed past her and she turned and looked: a small plane passing over the ocean, pulling a yellow aerial banner. But there was nothing on it, or if there was the words were facing out to sea.

Later she half wished she'd asked for the picture of her uncle or even slipped it surreptitiously out of the scrapbook—what were the chances Chip would ever have noticed it missing? Instead of a constant reference point she had a new ghost image of her great-uncle Buddy that moved along beside her: a thin man in a white dinner jacket with Brylcreem stiffening his hair.

It was better than nothing.

To resolve the guilt she tried to be frank with herself. She was a murderer when she got up, a murderer when she walked, a murderer whenever she was moving. It was only during the quiet times that she tried not to think of the new title. With momentum behind her she could embrace her status: a murderer without a prison sentence, without a trial or a defense attorney, a secret and sure-footed murderer ranging beyond the confines of the penal colony. But when she was trying to get to sleep it was more difficult to reconcile. Doubts intruded. At first, before she knew she was a murderer, they had been doubts about her innocence. Now that those doubts were answered with the certainty of her guilt she thought she should be sure of everything. She should be past equivocation and bargains, now that she had embraced the murdering. Yet tensions still arose. It wasn't enough, in the dark, to know your own sin. It wasn't enough to admit it. There was still the silence that followed the admission.

When she felt restless in the night she got up from her bed, pulled on a fleece sweater and went down the hall, touching a switch to bring on the dim lights of the sconces. She went to the carnivore rooms usually; she found their open mouths in the dim light, their dark maws studded with the white teeth, and rubbed the points of canines with a finger. She slung her arms around the musty fur of their necks. There was something she should be learning from them, but she didn't know what. The hawk was no more to blame than the rabbit, right? She'd done her own killing in the passage of daily life, not because she wished to inflict pain. The cats and the wolves only did it for food: they looked cruel but they weren't, she told herself. By contrast she looked innocuous and that was equally deceptive. She'd been greedy, she'd been selfish: maybe greed was her sin, or the variant of it that was lust. She was irreligious but sin was a neat description: lust, gluttony, avarice and pride. In the end all of the sins seemed the same to her, softer and harder forms of the same murder.

Once she accepted her own judgment, there was also the question of whether more sinning would make for still more murder. If she kept being a slut, would someone die again? It was foolish to think so, but after all, she thought, she was a fool. If any sin was murder, she might have to start behaving.

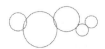

They did their best to ignore Christmas. Casey went to a movie in a mall somewhere, maybe the Westside Pavilion—with a guy, Susan assumed, though it was left unsaid. Jim the lawyer had gone to Tahoe to be with his wife's relatives and everyone else she knew was occupied celebrating, so Susan rented a couple of videos and picked up Indian food.

On New Year's she made a resolution to be different, though she was still unsure. She had murdered once, so she would always be guilty. But that didn't mean she had to be a serial killer.

She decided to tell Jim.

"So listen," she said, in bed.

"No."

"No what?"

"No, we're not breaking up."

She propped herself up on an elbow, curious.

He'd grown on her. At first she'd thought he was average, and then, slipping sideways somehow, the fact arrived that she almost loved him. At any rate she liked him far too much. She saw him only once every few days, but she'd come to depend on it—the pleasant welcome of his face. She wondered in passing if it was all about his skin and its sweet smell: his skin that reminded her of Hal's, smooth and flawless.

He lay on his back now, eyes closed. Curiously at ease. There was a crescent scar near one eyebrow, a shallow nick.

"And how is that your call, Jim?"

He shrugged lightly, his shoulders barely moving.

"We're not, is all."

Despite herself she was impressed.

"What if I said I don't like you?"

"But you do."

"What if I said it was—I mean, better late than never—the fact that you're married?"

"I'd say that fact was none of your business."

She turned and lay on her back beside him, gazing at the rings of light on the ceiling. One, two, three, the yellow circles intersecting with their invisible overlaps like a Venn diagram, the lamps on the nightstands, the floor lamp in the corner. They were on the ground floor for a change, in the small guest bedroom with the green Tiffany lamps. There were waterfowl around them. The waterfowl were an exception to her usual rule against sex with stuffed animals watching. The ducks, the geese, the pink flamingo on its single leg bothered no one. They had beady little eyes but clearly no interest in looking.

"Of course it's my business. Motherfucker."

"Come on, sweetie," said Jim, and touched her briefly on the side of her leg with fingertips, not moving his arm. She liked how he expended no energy unless forced to. Male lions were like that, according to her uncle's old encyclopedia. They slept all day in the sun and let the females do the hunting. "Let's not argue."

"I want to be better," she said after a while.

"You're good enough for me," said Jim, and turned his head slightly to rest his face against her shoulder.

"Obviously you set the bar low."

"Don't jump to conclusions," he said quietly.

"There's a third party," she said. "My new plan is not to be selfish."

"That part is my life. Let me worry."

A car passed somewhere outside, light glancing. Of course it was his life, but if she let herself off this easy her resolution was meaningless.

"I don't want those boundaries," she said abruptly, and sat up. Her robe was puddled on the floor beside the bed—she was still damp from the shower beforehand, she realized—and she leaned down to get it. "You don't want to tell me, fine. It's your business, I agree. But then I get to say if you stay or go."

She stood and threw the robe over her shoulders. She felt glad of its lightness, its shine in the lamplight. She could make a smooth exit.

But also her slippers were somewhere lost in the dark of the floor. In the big house she almost never went barefoot. Sharp things were lodged in the elaborate tilework of the hallways, old, permanent dirt blackened the soles of her feet even after the women came to clean. She widened her eyes, tried to look harder. There, on the mirror lake with the long yellow reeds like Easter-basket stuffing, a flip-flop lay between a duck's feet, the other tumbled beside it.

He mumbled something. She couldn't quite hear and turned back to him as she pulled the robe's belt tight.

"Sorry?"

"No love," he said.

"No love?"

"She doesn't love me."

His eyes were still closed. She saw his chest in the light, hairless and lightly muscled. She'd even come to like his stomach, even its small roll. In the quiet she thought of asking him if he was sure, if he was just saying that, if he was rationalizing. But something in the tone of his voice stopped her.

"No love at all. Not for years. Really, I promise you. She doesn't give a shit."

"Then why are you still together?"

"Susan," he said slowly, almost growling, and this pleased her. She remembered Fantasy Baseball and the way he'd said *Susie*, and how she had disliked him for it. She almost shivered. "Let's not."

She considered for a few moments and lay down.

•

In the morning she woke up and found he was still there, for once. He seemed unworried by the novelty of the infraction. He got up and shuffled around the kitchen in a T-shirt, boxers and his unlaced dress shoes without socks.

"Those shoes look ridiculous," she said fondly.

"Next time I'll bring the slippers and pipe," he said, but didn't glance up at her. He was breaking eggs for an omelet.

They shared it on a single plate, sitting on either side of a wrought-iron table at the end of the pool. Above them were the branches of a weeping willow. Then they smoked two of his cigarettes and drank their black coffee. Their faces were in the willow's shade, and she shivered and felt good.

He was consulting his watch—it was a weekday morning and he had to go to work—when T. came around the corner from the front of the house, followed by Casey.

Jim looked sidelong at Susan, squinting and crossing his legs. She had only the robe on, the robe and her flips, though her hair was brushed and she was clean. He was less so, half-dressed, his hair mussed, the boxers a dead giveaway. The situation was clear.

She watched Casey's face as it neared.

"How awkward," she said.

Best to be brutally frank. Her daughter was.

"Chill out," said Casey mildly.

"Sorry for the intrusion," put in T. "I wanted to see the place."

She looked from Casey's face to T.'s as they came toward her alongside the pool. They were relaxed.

"I made him drive over here, actually," said Casey. "So you should blame me."

Susan recognized her own position, hers and Jim the lawyer's, and at the same time she knew the position of Casey and T. It was the same, she was surprised to realize. She had thought so before, she recalled, but had never known.

She felt relief brimming in her. Relief.

"I called," said Casey, "but no one picked up."

She and Susan looked at each other, both of them in their chairs. Susan felt a beam between them, a generous current. Casey was happy, she realized, and this made her lighter in her bones, made her happier, she felt, than she had been for so long. Neither of them had been this happy before, at least not since the accident. Her daughter's happiness was her own. She had forgotten it for a while.

Even if Casey was hurt by this in the end, she had to think next—and rapidly she was squeezed at the heart, narrowly constricted and wrenched by fear, then just as rapidly loosened—still it was better this way. Open again, after these years.

As she gazed at her girl in the wheelchair a cloud moved and the sun fell on Casey's pale face, backlit her hair golden. In a trick of thought her daughter seemed young, eternal, all ages of herself that passed in wonder before her mother's eyes—when she played outside in the sun often, her hair turned lighter blond. Now once again it might look as it used to when she was a little girl, a little girl in a blue swimsuit on the beach with her parents. Susan was almost back there, years ago sitting on a dune, almost sitting on the sand with Hal beside her as Casey ran up to them from the water, stopped and shivered, hands clasped in front of her, grains of sand on her skin. Then she was off again, down to the waves, shivering and running as they watched her go, wet braids on her shoulders. How children shivered—with passion, without reserve. They shivered with their whole bodies.

She loved them for it, the freedom of that shiver.

The scene retreated. She wondered idly if Jim would get up in front of Casey and T. and walk around in his boxers, whether the button fly was undone and gaped open.

"If it's no trouble," said T., "Casey can show me around."

"It's no trouble," said Susan, and smiled at him.

She and Jim sat and watched them go around the house to the back, voices fading.

"If you want," said Jim, and cleared his throat, "I could come over for dinner."

She was confused for a second. A breeze lifted the branches

around them and she thought Hal was here—not gone, then gone, still gone, gone still. Old, dead leaves from last fall were also stirred, moving along the pool's deck. She felt so grateful: the turbulence of currents—the best of weather, the best of earth, a small whirlwind. Green branches wavered and jumped in the gusts over her shoulders and at her feet their leaf litter swirled and dove like swallows.

The air was warm. She was so lucky to exist.

And Hal, Hal would have done anything to see their baby happy like this again. He had, she thought, he *had* done anything—was he a saint after all? He had returned to earth. A sacrifice was made, the son came home, and now their daughter was happy.

She rose on a wave of love and grief—he had accomplished it, at the greatest possible cost. He had brought it all here, given it all to Casey.

Nonsense—sentimentality. Nothing but circumstance. Accident, manslaughter, or coincidence.

But for a fleeting second she thought she felt him in the marrow of her bones, the small hairs lifting on the backs of her arms before the tingle and the chill dissolved.

Molecules, molecules and atoms, sweet tiny points of being.

It was Jim across from her, inches beyond the table edge, and yet it could so easily not be.

5

First she thought she'd have the housewarming catered, for ease and novelty. She'd never thrown a catered party and this occasion was ceremonial: an end, a start again. But then she decided to invite Steven and his son, who wanted to contest the will. She didn't want to see them, of course; it was a purely diplomatic move, a hope that sociability would sway them. To that end she decided a caterer was out of the question: at the sight of such pretension, or at least such disposable income, the cousins might well descend upon her in fury.

So she called a cleaning crew to mop and vacuum and dust the mounts; she placed strategic vases of flowers. She enlisted Casey's help with the groceries and they bought prepared foods in plastic trays, frozen appetizers in cardboard boxes from Costco. In the unlikely event that Steven and Tommy mistook the hummus and dips for gourmet fare, she planned to leave the empty containers, with price tags showing, piled on the kitchen counter. The slovenliness of the gesture would irritate her, but she was nervous enough for petty schemes. Would it make a difference to them? No doubt it would not: but it made a difference to her. She couldn't help herself.

She invited a couple of women she liked from the old neighborhood and some teaching friends from way back. Casey invited friends of her own, some of whom were in chairs—the big house was finally equipped with ramps, rails and door retrofits—calculating that their presence might make the gathering more sympathetic. "That asshole Steven," she said, as she watched Susan take a tray of small crab cakes out of the oven, "if he sees how you're basically a halfway house for cripples here, how can he sue you then?"

"I think you overestimate Steven."

"Oh, and you know who else I invited?"

"Who? Oh no. Wait, don't tell me," said Susan. "Sal."

But she was secretly pleased. Sal was her favorite of Casey's ex-boyfriends because he was a spectacle; Sal could be counted on to misspeak and offend. There was the possibility he should be kept from the cousins, but on the other hand, not unlike them, he was a blunt instrument.

"Who else?"

"Nancy. Plus she's bringing Addison, but he's a walker. And then there's Rosie. You remember her, the one at UCLA? With the MS?"

Susan looked across the island. There were no shadows under her daughter's eyes anymore, no purple crescents. Her insomnia must be gone, she must be sleeping again . . . but the guests, she thought: the list was familiar. It was the guest list from Casey's last dinner party, from the night before Hal flew out of the country. The last night they ever saw him. The last night anyone did, or at least anyone she knew, anyone here. Except T., of course, who had walked with him in the tropics, talked to him, sat with him in a shallow rowboat.

She would ask T. She had to. This flashed across her mind now though it had never flashed before, there had been no previous flash. She had these blind spots, since the death, these failures to inquire. She would ask him how it had been.

He had seen Hal long after she last saw him, had known that other Hal, whom she had only talked to by telephone. That man altered unknowably by his destination, a high arc toward disappearance, long gone from them and frozen in time before dying—somehow committed to that death, alone in the tropics. She saw him looking out to sea. She put him there, on a beach she'd never seen. He stood there eternally, looking to the horizon, one hand raised to shield his eyes from brightness. Sun on his face, wind-scalloped waves.

The white, white, white, white sand.

"And some others," Casey was saying. "But those are the only gimps. Four of us, in total. What can I say, I had to call in some favors so we could make a strong showing. You know: I don't have an unlimited supply of wheelchair buddies. There's no spigot. There's just the ones from the support group, that's it."

"Who else?" asked Susan, but she was distracted and forgot to listen.

Now she had an idea of tropical islands and death. She was

in the grip of a memory, the gentle trade winds stirring the palm trees and then the stillness and the wavering heat. The stasis of an island in the middle of the sea. As a child she had gone to a cut-rate Caribbean resort on a family vacation; her parents ate jerked pork and drank frozen drinks, but all she did was snorkel all day long a few feet off the beach. She had a sunburn on her back in the shape of an X, her swimsuit straps. It was the island of St. Lucia.

She remembered the sound of thatch rustling on the palapas in the breeze that came off the water, that swept up her legs and arms and made her feel borne aloft. For years her most treasured memory had been of this feathery caress of the trade winds—a wistful memory that tried to capture the longing carried on that breeze. But now, she thought, the question was answered. Those pillowing winds whose touch had been a signal she would only receive long afterward, far in the future when the salt air of the ocean was gone. The smoothness of her skin gone too, the clearness of her eyes, the girlish hopes, who knew what they had been—to be unique, probably, beautiful or loved by masses of humanity. No doubt some kind of yearning; all young girls did was yearn.

That hush, that light stillness were ominous, had the quiet of an expectant pause. One day the tropics would bring her someone else's death. The lull, the sough, the doldrums—sailors had called them that, those equatorial calms that could be dangerous when stronger winds were needed to push their sailing ships—the trade winds blew like a soft dream of dying. Even the fragrant trees with their long names, their showy red blooms—*flamboyant*. That was the name of the tree that grew all over the Caribbean, planted on the resorts but native to somewhere else, a distant and vast continent, Australia or India, who could recall, and the locals said it like this, in their Jamaican patois: *flom-boy-on* . . . red flowers in the trees.

Possibly it was apprehension, fear of Steven and Tommy and their designs on her windfall, but she was in an unsteady place. From moment to moment her mood could change: a bitter taste rose in her throat and she felt herself falling into remorse. Morbidity shadowed her and she shrank from the knife—felt she was Hal, or imprisoned in Hal's body, and had a premonition of stabbing, a phantom pain in her side and wide-awake dreams of catching her stomach as it slipped out the slit. She leaned out, hopelessly reaching; beyond her fingertips were her falling intestines, slick and purple as tongues. She felt the knife cut every day—the anticipation of it, the wince. That was the part she'd been left with. Too often she winced at the thought of the knife.

That dinner with those people: she'd been in the dark then, blissful and unaware of her new status. She'd been completely in the dark when it came to that status—her status as a future murderer, a charter member of the Future Murderers of America. And then the next time she saw the dinner guests was at the funeral. The murder had been done.

She didn't remember talking to them then, though she might have, probably had—she'd been polite at least, she hoped. She recalled almost nothing outside the blur and only knew she had caught sight of them from the podium and been indifferent to their presence. But it was impossible to miss them entirely because they had stood out from the crowd, apart in their chairs at the ends of the pews. The support group had made a good showing—Sal, for instance, had barely known Hal and though clearly lacking in most social skills had come to the funeral to, as he put it, "like be there for Casey." On his muscled upper arms, often shown off by grubby tank tops, he had many tattoos including weeping roses, shamrocks and daggers; but at the funeral, though still garbed in the camouflage pants and combat boots that were his signature, he had worn long sleeves.

●

T. arrived at the big house early, with his mother in tow. Well-dressed and coiffed at the hands of a live-in maid who hailed from the former Communist bloc, she could pass at first for a business-woman or socialite—the latter of which she almost was, Susan thought, except that she had no friends.

"Susan, dear," she said, coming into the kitchen with T. behind her and holding out a frail hand. T. must have prompted her on the name.

"I'm so glad you could come, Angela," said Susan, and put her near-empty wineglass on the counter to clasp the thin hand in both of hers. The last time she'd seen Angela, Hal had been there too. They'd gone to her townhouse apartment to break the news that T. was gone, T. had been lost in the tropics and was unresponsive. She had served them Earl Grey and told them not to worry, vaguely protested that her son could take care of himself, and Susan had felt sorry for her.

But in the end she had been right in her confidence; Susan had been wrong. Come to think of it, if Susan had believed her—if Susan had not manifested a fussy, hen-like worry for her employer when even his *mother* remained unconcerned—Hal would never have flown down there. Hal would be alive now.

"I'm so very sorry for your loss," said Angela. Her soft lower lip trembled.

Susan felt a surge of fondness. The woman was a wounded doe—the straggler on the edge of the herd, the slow-moving one a wolf would select to bring down with sharp teeth. Though not a trophy hunter.

But before she had time to act on the passing fond impulse, Casey was there.

"Come with me," she commanded, reaching up to touch Angela's hand. "I'll show you things," and Angela smiled briefly at Susan and turned to follow.

The house was far too large for the small party so they had tried to set it up in the first-floor rooms that opened onto the pool—the music room, the dining room with its wolves and foxes, the long hall. At certain junctures, she realized, a tall man would have to bend down to avoid the antlers of moose or elk. The mounts were a hodgepodge in the corridors, hung without regard for the obstacles they might make. She opened the row of French doors between the terrace and the rooms, let their floor-length drapes flutter, and walked around surveying. The old hardwood gleamed, the faded rugs stretched at her feet . . . she checked the nearest ground-floor bathroom, which had been grimy when she moved in, the floor an ancient and torn-up linoleum in avocado green. Now the old flooring was replaced with tile and the walls had been painted.

The room's small window was open to the back of an oleander hedge, pink blossoms that could be lethal, someone had warned her when she was pregnant—vomiting, diarrhea, if a kid even *touches* an oleander he could sink into a coma, the woman had said. *And never come out.* You didn't hear that from a man, typically. As an expectant mother, or the mother of a young child, you heard many warnings from females but not so many from males. The females were protective, true, they spread their downy wings over the eggs to keep them safe and warm, but also they relished the gruesome. At least they relished the talk of it—tragedy, poisoning, accident, as long as it didn't happen to them or theirs, they talked it up as though it was delicious.

On a tall cabinet beneath the window there were candles and a bowl of pinecones and other domestic markings.

She was nervous.

In the dining room she moved bottles onto the counter of the bar—Jim would make drinks, since he was good at that—and set music to play from her cheap stereo.

He came in and touched the back of her neck.

She could get used to him, she thought; but then, no. He was married and he was not a replacement. Through the French doors the sun had sunk and the lower half of the sky was a pale orange.

"We shouldn't do that while the cousins are here," she said.

"Oh, you ashamed of me?"

"You know why."

Her friends would see she needed comfort, and if they didn't it would only be between her and them anyway. But the judgment of the cousins, so soon after Hal's death—the cousins would not spare her.

She heard brakes squeaking as a car pulled up and then Casey's voice as she went out the front door—it was not the cousins yet, only her daughter's friends. She realized she was far too nervous to hide it. She wouldn't be able to stand it if they took this place from her. She could hardly bear the tension of not knowing.

She said so. Jim poured her a fresh drink.

By the time her own guests got there—Dewanne and Lacy from the old street in Venice and a couple, Reg and Tony, from the last school she'd taught at—she was half-drunk and giddy. Time flowed faster, space was easier to move in . . . of course, she hoped she didn't sabotage herself with Steven. But he and the son still weren't there by nine-thirty and the other guests were scattered through the near-empty house, already drinking too much, already leaving empty cups on tables, smears of cheese and chip fragments on the floor. Around her she heard expressions of awe at the décor, at the plentiful zoology, awe sometimes tinged with horror.

She felt gratified anyway. She went to offer fresh drinks to Casey's friends, sitting in the cat room. Sal had two of them backed into a corner—not an easy feat in a wheelchair, but his chair was parked at an angle and blocked them effectively. It was Nancy and Addison, her nasal-voiced, stooping boyfriend. Susan had never understood what it was that Casey and Nancy had in common, beyond the chairs, she was thinking as she crossed over to them—Nancy had prominent hobbies, the obsessive reading of fantasy novels whose covers featured women with long swirling hair and elaborate chain mail and/or bladed weapons and the copious creation, via knitting, of bright-colored afghans, scarves and baby booties. Neither of which would ever be a pastime of Casey's.

Sal was thrusting his Walkman at her.

"It's Bridewarrior, man. Listen. This one song is so awesome. Wait, I gotta rewind it. The album's called *The Maiden Queens of Atlantis.*"

Susan remembered now: after Hal fell asleep on the bed in Casey's guestroom, at the last supper, Sal had orated to her for half an hour on the subject of rap music, rap magazines and the *East-West hip-hop rivalry*. There were New York rappers and there were rappers from L.A., like two big gangs that wanted to do rapid musical drive-by shootings. They chiefly battled it out by boasting of their prowess, however, and wearing big-bore gold-plated necklaces and rings, only rarely resorting to actual weapons. While Sal was into rap, Casey had said, the women he met were typically bitches and hos. This month he was into Celtic folk metal. Women were earth-mother goddesses and busty virgins wearing fur bikinis. Though in actuality as white as the driven snow, Sal had taken the name *Salvador* and liked to pretend he was Hispanic and/or black.

Curiously, some people appeared to believe it.

"Bridewarrior?" asked Addison. "What's that supposed to mean?"

"It's like this pagan deal. Ritual nudity?"

"OK, maybe later," said Nancy.

"We're just trying to talk here, Salvador," said Addison, patronizing.

"Can I get you something to drink?" Susan asked Nancy, who looked up gratefully.

"Sure, do you have cranberry juice?"

"Take a spritzer," said Addison.

Sal fumbled with the Walkman, pressing buttons.

"So this track's called 'Motherblood,'" he said. No one was paying attention. "Wait, wait. This other one rocks even harder. 'Black Carbuncle.'"

When she came back with the drinks they'd requested he was still declaiming.

"It's on *Cruel Scars of the Bone Beast*. Then there's 'Uterus of the Earthworm.'"

Susan leaned down with the drinks tray, feeling like a waitress.

"Earthworms don't have uteruses," said Addison.

T. had just come in and was standing beside Casey, smiling faintly at the conversation. He lifted his glass to drink.

"Not the point," said Sal. "It's a dark hellish vision."

"Well, but—" started Nancy.

"What she might mean," interrupted Addison, "is it's this, you know, kinda bad poetry."

"It's not fucking gay-ass poetry, man," said Sal. "It's *music*."

"But—"

"You just don't get it," said Sal, and shook his head in disgust.

"I had to dissect a worm once," said Nancy to Casey. "Back in Invertebrate Biology."

"Excellent," said Sal.

"Could you check on Angela?" asked Casey, as Susan began to move away. "She's lying down upstairs. In the room with the Arctic fox."

"Of course," said Susan.

She passed Reg and Tony on her way to the stairs, standing in front of an eagle diorama outside the birds-of-prey room.

"It's totally Natural History Museum," said Reg. "Circa 1950."

"I love it," said Tony.

"Me too," said Susan, and they gazed at the eagle. It had its wings back and talons out, coming in for a landing. Beneath it, on a gritty stretch of fake sand, a mouse cowered.

Walking up the stairs, she stopped and stood still on the landing, as usual. No airplanes, but there was a searchlight weaving back and forth across the sky. Always some light, in that black square—what you observed was forms of light—she tried to assess her drunkenness. She needed to drink more water, clearly. She breathed in, found a familiar body against her, and leaned back, contented.

"Ten minutes alone," said Jim into her ear. "I can get the job done in ten. Done and done well."

"I have to check on Angela."

She was drunk enough to have a pleasant feeling of chaos—a fluid chaos, not harmful but thrilling—she could welcome it, she could feel a kind of carefree anger against the cousins brewing in her and trying to supplant the fear of them. She walked with Jim along the darkened second-floor hallway and knocked on the door of the Arctic room, then, when there was no answer, pushed it open. Under the blaze of overhead light the white fox crept forever, but no older woman.

"She's nowhere," said Jim.

"She has this, you know, early-onset Alzheimer's, basically," she said in a low voice. "With some other things going on too. Mixed features, I think the shrinks call it. We need to find her."

They checked the other bedrooms, one by one—Rainforest, Himalayas, Indian Subcontinent. Then onto the barren wastes of Mongolia and The Soviet Union. She rarely came in here. Beyond an amateurishly painted Lenin, The Soviet Union had nothing but a massive, shaggy animal that looked like a bison, marked WILD TIBETAN YAK, and a sturdy horse marked EQUUS PRZEWALSKI.

"This guy shot *horses*?" asked Jim.

Finally they had checked every room save horned beasts. As

they approached she could hear the shower running from her own bathroom and in a flash she remembered: the woman had tried to kill herself in a bathtub once, after her husband left. The onset of her decline.

"Wait," she told Jim, and rushed forward to open the bathroom door. "Angela? Is that you?"

Only the small bulbs over the vanity were lit. When she flicked on the rest she saw Angela standing up in the bathtub—not naked, small mercies. She had a towel wrapped around her and her hair plastered down on her head and the shower water was spattering down behind her.

Susan was relieved.

"Are you OK?" she asked, and reached past Angela to turn off the faucets. Water fell on her hair and face as she stretched her arm out. She looked around hastily till she saw the hook that held her terrycloth robe. "Here. Put this on."

Angela looked at her blankly. Soaking wet, she was pitiable.

"Here, I'll—right arm—left arm—there you go," and she tied the belt around the slim waist and snaked the towel out from beneath. "Why don't you come with me."

Angela's clothes were nowhere to be seen so Susan led her toward the closet. Jim stood next to the open bedroom window smoking, holding his cigarette outside.

"Could you go find T.?" she asked him. "Or Casey. Either of them will do."

She wouldn't ask Angela what she had been doing in the shower—it seemed a rude intrusion. And when she asked about the clothes again the woman looked vacant, so she held up a dress of her own. "Do you think you could be comfortable in this one?"

Angela nodded but seemed distracted.

After some awkwardness she got the dress on, albeit with difficulty, as Angela stood limp and pliable in front of her. She was wondering if she had to find shoes for her too—whether they wore the same size—and then giving up and heading for the bathroom sink for a glass of water when T. came in.

He put an arm around his mother and steered her over to the bed to sit down.

"She suffers from trichophobia," he said. "Now and then. One of a number of complications."

"I'm sorry. I don't know what that is," said Susan.

"No one does. It's a fear of loose hairs."

Susan gazed at him dumbly, sitting on the edge of the bed with his mother, slowly patting her hand. After a few seconds she ducked through the bathroom door and filled a cup.

"It's intermittent," said T. "But when it—she tries to wash them off."

"Animal hairs, too? Because in that case—"

"I don't think so," and he shook his head. "It's long hair that's the trigger, mostly. This extreme disgust with long hairs. And it's if they're loose, only. Not if they're on your head."

There was fear of everything these days, she found herself thinking—as though it was magnanimous. A generosity of fear.

The fear of litigation. Was there a name for that?

She remembered an earlier impulse.

"Listen," she said abruptly. "I haven't asked you yet, but I do want to know. How was he?"

"How—?"

"In those—those days you were down there with Hal. How did he seem?"

T. gazed at her levelly, idly draped an arm around his mother's shoulders.

"He seemed all right," he said mildly.

"It's that—you're the only one I can ask."

T. nodded, his head barely moving, and gazed past her to the open window.

"He was worried about me," he said. "I was nothing to him, but he was still worried."

She waited. On the nightstand a clock was flashing 12:00.

"He was preoccupied, though," he went on. "He was down there looking for something."

"You," she said.

"Yes, but—yes and no, I got the feeling."

She preferred not to look at him straight on, so she switched her gaze to his mother instead, who was studying her own bare feet. The toes were polished light pink.

"I should say, I do know why he went down there," T. said gently, after a minute. "But in the end it wasn't that. I mean yes, he was recovering. He slept a lot. A bit of binge drinking. And in his spare time he was looking for me. But also, he was—I remember thinking he was like a child."

"A child?" she asked. It surprised her.

"There was something childlike about him. Like someone who's never left home. That's what it was: someone who's lived in one place all his life. And then suddenly travels to a new country."

On the wall beside them the African plain was palely visible. She reached out her right hand to sweep her fingers over the painted fringe of tall grass that grew up from the floor.

Of course, you couldn't feel the grass.

Still the smoothness of the wall was somehow disappointing.

"But he *had* traveled before," she said softly. "I mean we traveled together. Mostly before the accident. We did road trips. And we went to Europe, once. He was impressed by Europe."

"I didn't really know him," said T. "As you said. That was just how he struck me."

They sat there quietly for a while in the dim light of the bedside lamp, until T. turned and looked at the wall painting, one of the big spreading trees. Possibly an acacia, Susan thought idly. They looked different over there.

"Hunting, you know, it wiped out some of them," said T., scanning the animal figures in the background. "It's not a leading cause of extinction around here anymore. But Africa, yeah. Monkeys killed for the bush meat market, for instance. Elephants for ivory, rhinos for powdered horn. You know: some Chinese people, a folk-wisdom group that isn't actually particularly educated in Chinese medicine, think it's an aphrodisiac. Globally, mostly the driver is habitat loss. But soon the leading cause is going to be climate change. Or too much carbon, anyway."

"What?" asked Susan. "You're kidding."

He shook his head.

"Is it time to go home?" asked his mother, raising her head.

"I think so," said T., and helped steady her as she got up. "Sorry," he said to Susan. "We were hopeful she would last a little longer this evening."

"Please, no," said Susan, and turned to Angela. "It's fine. I'm just glad you're all right."

They left the room, T. and Angela walking slowly into the wide hall with Susan behind them. She flicked on the line of sconces as they passed; it was too dark for strangers, who knew what they might bump into—dim shapes of horn and hair, the lips of elk. Then she noticed the sconces still had their basins half full of light-brown moth bodies.

We're brittle and fading, she thought. Fading like moths, gray-blond mothers. With each day the population aged. Maybe not in the so-called third world, where there were plagues of babies, but here, where there were plagues of the elderly. Before long there would be scores of old ones for each of the young, their lives prolonged but rarely cherished—certainly not by the old themselves, who hung on by threads of pharmacology in stages of slow death. Not by their children either, the children moved away pursuing an idea of self, an idea of fulfillment as once, not all that long ago, nomads had followed the seasons. They lived their adult lives in distant cities now.

Soon all the young would be absent, lifted into the momentum of their speedy existences in which the past was only a minor point of information—the parents who had raised and loved them, even adored them with all their hearts, only the vaguest imprint.

Ahead of her Angela picked her way with care down the wide stairs, as though her bones were hollow. Yes, it was coming, the generations of the ancient would be left to their own end. The grandmothers would feed the great-grandmothers in their final falls, the ones in their seventies would tuck in the sleepers who were in their eighties, nineties, hundreds—

Hal, she thought, had been on the cusp of a whole new life.

Regret needled her, and something like envy.

"Oh," said Angela, as they led her past the eagle. "A beautiful birdie."

In the foyer the two of them watched as T. leaned down to

Casey to say good night—Angela smiling vaguely, Susan feeling a quick, guilty flush of pride in her daughter. Together they were beautiful, it couldn't be denied. Then T. took his mother's arm again and Susan followed them outside and helped Angela into the passenger seat of his car. The high-end black Mercedes was an affectation he still hadn't dropped, it turned out.

There was continuity there, at least. She felt reassured by the black Mercedes.

As she went indoors again she waved at Casey, who had moved outside and was sitting by the pool, talking to Jim and others in the dappled turquoise refractions. The lights in the library were on so she ducked in and saw piles of books all crooked on the floor, then Nancy and Addison, the quiet college girl whose name Susan forgot, and Sal. It smelled liked marijuana.

"Oh shit," said Sal under his breath, when he saw her coming. He had the joint in his hand and seemed to be casting around for an ashtray.

"It's fine," she said. "I've actually seen pot before." There was an ashtray on a sideboard, she recalled, and headed over to pick it up.

"Thanks, man," said Sal.

"So we've been looking at these antique anatomy books," said Nancy. "Animal anatomy. Some are from the 1920s. There are diagrams of earthworms."

"Informative," said Susan, and set the ashtray on an end table.

"It says here worms are gay," said Sal. "Listen. 'Two earthworms mate by attaching at their clitella and exchanging sperm.' They sperm on each other."

"It's not uncommon, in nature," said Nancy.

"The worms aren't gay," said the girl from UCLA, with some difficulty. It was the first time Susan had heard her speak—her voice was affected by the multiple sclerosis. "They are hermaphrodites."

"You want?" asked Sal, and held out the joint toward Susan.

"Maybe I will," she said. She drew on it and held in the smoke as she passed it to Addison. "Thanks," she said after she let it out. "Been a while."

It would allay her nervousness, she thought. If it didn't put her to sleep instantly.

Sal took the joint back and slipped on his headphones.

"Susan?"

She turned to see Steven and Tommy at the library door just as Sal began to recite the lyrics. "All virginal maidens / Satan will ulcerate . . ."

"Oh hey! Steve, Tommy. I'm so glad you made it!"

"Whoa," said Tommy. "I'm getting a contact high."

"Susie. I had no idea," said Steve, as though he'd stepped into a bordello.

"What can I say," said Susan, cheerfully. "It's California."

"But Mother Earth, she heals them," croaked Sal, head rocking, "By sending them to Hell . . ."

She would report to Casey: the possible benefits of wheelchairs were outweighed by the costs.

"Let me get you some drinks," she persevered, and went toward the cousins, leaving Sal and the others behind.

"This place is like that Haunted House ride at Disneyland," said Tommy. "Do you have one of those elevators where the pictures on the walls stretch out?"

She realized suddenly that she must not have seen him in years. He had thick eyebrows that met in the middle and cheekbones with a spray of acne. A show of affection was clearly called for, so she held out her arms and smiled.

"Tommy," she said, and embraced him, remembering as she drew close and smelled his strong deodorant that he was the one his father was proud of. Unlike the unfortunate art student, or whatever the other kid was. "The prodigal engineer."

He let himself be embraced but barely participated. She pulled back and noticed he was unsmiling.

The father, at least, could be plied with spirits.

"Would you like a cocktail? A beer? Please, follow me."

She kept up a patter as they headed down the hallway toward the room with the bar.

"What kind of engineering program are you in? Civil?"

"Chemical," he said. "Going into cement."

"Oh," she said, nodding, but despite casting around desperately could find nothing to say about this. Doubtless there were many people qualified to speak on the cement subject, but she was not among them. "Oh, I thought you were still a student."

"Graduating in May. Early recruitment. Already got my first job lined up."

"Congratulations!"

"Focus on GGBS."

"GGBS?"

"Ground granulated blast-furnace slag."

"Right outta college," said Steven. "Six figures."

"Wow," she said.

At the end of the hall, in the darkness under a rhino head, Reg and Tony were kissing.

"Are those two *guys?*" asked Steven. "Making out?"

"It's two *old* guys," said Tommy. *"Whoa."*

She checked her impulse to comment and went through the dining room door ahead of them.

"So what can I get you, Tommy?"

"I need a strong one after that," he said. "Gimme a vodka. *Man.* You got any Absolut Citron?"

"I don't think so," she said. "We do have some mixers."

"I'll take a Bud," said the father.

From behind the bar she could see Casey and Jim and some of her former neighbors outside. She missed them.

"Let's get some fresh air, shall we?" she said, once both of them had their drinks in hand, and led them through the French doors.

"Hah-ey," said Dewanne, smiling widely as they approached. She was a thrice-divorced Southern belle and more times than that cosmetically enhanced; she'd lived two houses down. She was also an avid catalog shopper, in a constant state of indignation at the perceived abuses of mail-order apparel companies. The indignation was a hobby. When they both had teenagers in high school—she was a housewife and Susan was substitute teaching—she would come over to the house in the late afternoon, a glass of white wine with ice cubes in her hand, and call 800 numbers to harangue operators about merchandise quality.

Susan had always liked her.

"Hi, Dewanne," she said, and reached out to grab her hand.

"So who have we here? Introduce me to your cute friends, Susan."

"My cousin Steven," she said. "His son, Tommy."

"Hey, Tommy," said Casey. "Last time I saw you we hadn't even hit puberty."

"Hey, Casey," said Tommy stiffly, but made no move in her direction.

"You were into *Star Trek*," said Casey.

"I don't remember that."

"Denial is common. But I remember all too well. You always tried to give me a Vulcan nerve pinch."

Tommy lifted his vodka and drank, projecting an aura of distrust.

"That was his geek period," said Steven, and elbowed his son in the ribs.

"All in the distant past now," said Casey, and grinned.

"He's got a job in Portland cement!" said Susan.

"Ground granulated blast-furnace slag," corrected Tommy.

"So, Tommy," said Casey brightly. "Let's catch up then, shall we? Come tell me all about that slag."

She inclined her head toward a nearby table, and Tommy shuffled off after her with some reluctance.

"Hey, name's Jim," said Jim, and held out his hand to Steven.

"Sorry, how rude of me," said Susan, and finished the round of introductions.

When Susan paid attention next Steven was saying to Dewanne, "So what are you, one of her teacher friends?"

"Just a neighbor," said Dewanne. "From the old neighborhood. And what do you do, honey?"

"I run my own business. In programming."

"Oh *my*," said Dewanne.

She would leave the two of them alone, thought Susan, and Dewanne might win him over. Dewanne graciously liked everyone, even sleazebags.

But really, for the cousins, forget the guest list and the food selection; she should have cut straight to the chase and ordered up some working girls.

"You ready for a refill?" asked Jim.

"I'll come with you."

Better this way—better to leave her relatives with people who could stand them.

She and Jim slipped away for ten minutes, snuck into the room with the ducks and locked the door behind them. But then, in the yellow-green glow from the stained-glass lamps, in the drowsy aftermath of the pot, she drifted. She woke up later in the quiet and realized it, alarmed. She had fallen asleep. She sat up with a jolt. Damn it, she'd missed her own party.

The house was still beyond the door, the clock on the wall read 2:48. She had not meant to vanish. How inconsiderate, how wrong. Also, she'd screwed up the cousin thing. She felt panicky.

She got up and pulled her clothes on in a rush, the dress, the heels. The music was turned off, she thought, or she'd be hearing it. Her guests must all have left, gone to their homes. Some must have asked where she was, some must have felt ignored or irritated—but anyway she had to know, if there were any still here she had to go out there, play the hostess, take care of them.

She left Jim sleeping on his side, mouth agape on the pillow, opened the door and stepped out into the silent hall. A few lights were still on, here and there, but overall it was dim and on the edges of her vision she had an impression of orange and black shades in the rooms, great caves looming off to the sides, beer bottles on the tables, wineglasses on the windowsills. Ashtrays, empty food bowls on surfaces—how many guests had there been, after all? Thirty, she thought, thirty guests at the most, but now it looked like more, it looked like forty or fifty.

She passed the ballroom and saw the doors. They all stood open still and the drapes rushed out in rills when the breeze came up. It was a chill breeze now, in the small hours. She would close the doors, she thought, and went into the room. In the dimness she stepped across a trail of crackers, crumbling to powder underfoot, and walked toward the pool, visible through the line of doors with its wavering aqua light. She started to shut the doors and then thought she saw something outside, a movement in the back garden beyond the corner of the pool enclosure. For no good reason she thought of burglars, then chided herself for paranoia.

But someone was still here, she thought. Someone remained.

She went through the doors, planning what to say if it was Steve or Tommy—how to appear gracious and pretend she hadn't retreated into a back room to get laid and then, stoned as a twelve-year-old on his first high, abandoned them. As though, somehow, she was controlled and prim. This was how she wished to appear in their eyes: someone who was responsible, grateful, and unduly burdened. Someone straight as a pin and fully deserving of their charity.

Give it up, she told herself, moving onto the patio.

Alternatively she could confess her guilt, make a clean breast of her character flaws and throw herself on their mercy. She went around the pool and opened the gate on the far side, heard it creak behind her and stepped out onto the path that led between the koi ponds and the willows. There were footlights along the pathways and she was glad of them. She stopped on the flagstones and listened. She thought she heard a whisper; she didn't want to interrupt anything. But then—she stopped again, holding her breath—maybe it wasn't intimate, maybe it was just talk.

Further along the path the bushes were closer beside her, there was less room to move, and the sound of her heels on the uneven stones seemed louder. She peered through the dark. There was a bench in the trees, back there, with footlights around it—a small paved area, one of the round wrought-iron tables, and she went toward it cautiously. There were shapes under the trees, near the bench—a wheelchair, facing her, more or less, and sitting in it a girl with long hair, her face down. For a second she thought it was Casey, before she knew it wasn't.

It must be the college girl, she thought—still shocked, in the background of her recognition, that her own daughter was *not* a college girl, apparently would never be. It wasn't Nancy, because Nancy's hair was shorter. It had to be the younger girl, the one who had multiple sclerosis.

She was about to say something to her, was wracking her brain for the name, but then she blinked, her eyes nearly aching from the strain. She could make out another figure, on its knees, its head in the young woman's lap. A man, must be. Because of the footlights she could see lower but not higher up—see the man's bent legs, the vertical planes of the soles of his shoes, even their patterning, with the orange light from the sodium lamp shining onto the grooved rubber surface. She moved around to try to make him out, so the wheelchair was more in profile. But his head was down and she could not see his face. Indistinct sounds of choking. Was it sex? No: the man was crying, or sniveling at least, and the girl was speaking in low, consoling tones. They were drunk, or at least the man was drunk—the man was well on his way to wasted. The girl might not be drunk at all, as Susan recalled, she probably didn't drink—her way of speaking had stutters and pauses, had slushy consonants—it was common with her disease, Casey had said. But the man slurred when he spoke, slurred and mumbled, and with him it was all drunkenness.

On a spying impulse she crept closer, screened from them by trees.

"It'll be OK," said the girl, and stroked the man's head, comforting. Who was he? Not enough light. She couldn't tell.

"One night you pet one," he slurred, "and the next night you come in and you have to kill it."

"You could change jobs," said the girl, in her soft, halting way. "If it's too hard."

"There's no one else to take it," said the man, and raised his head. He was sobering up now, or had stopped sniveling, anyway. There was a branch in front of him and she couldn't see his features. "Someone has to do it."

"I'm sure they do . . ."

"There's weeks when, though, I feel it's all on me, like the whole thing is on *me*. You know?"

Susan hit her anklebone on something hard, winced and looked down. It was a round river rock at the edge of a pool— mounds of rocks, dry reeds white in the nighttime, the black water. The still, black pools: she felt such an affinity for them. Who knew what he was talking about, some kind of mass euthanasia of unwanted pets? And yet the information was being dispensed as though he was a hero: he was a noble caretaker, he was a suffering martyr in his euthanizing. Repulsive.

Beneath her the pool was peaceful, black and smooth. So tranquil was the pool: look at the pools, pretend the pool alone was real, its dark relief, simplicity. She would creep backward, if she could do it silently and without tripping—back away from the conversation. After all, if these two were still here, there could be other guests lingering. She might still be able to redeem herself, as a hostess. She should sweep the rooms and make sure. She started her retreat.

Quiet.

"You're so pretty," said the man more loudly, in a different tone. His words still ran together, but now he was projecting.

"Shh," said the girl.

"Come on. Lemme—"

"No."

"Your eyes are nice."

"We'll get you some water," said the girl.

He was trying to force himself on her, pushing his face up to hers. Jesus, she thought, a guy who used dead dogs as foreplay.

It was a new one on her.

There was the sound of it, the flesh sound of arms or chests, of soft fronts blundering.

"Stand up," said the girl firmly. "It's alcohol. That's all."

A long moment and then the man stood up droopily.

"We'll go inside," said the girl. "We'll get you some water."

She reached for her handrims and Susan stepped back into a

nook, back behind a bush—the rhododendron, thick and waxy. In a minute they went past her, the girl ahead in the chair, the man slowly following. She recognized him from behind: Addison.

Where was Nancy? Asleep, maybe. Sleeping girlfriend in a wheelchair, dying dogs. That was the strategy. He was golden.

When they had disappeared she stepped up to the pool again and stared down into it.

•

There were others, she discovered, but they were fast asleep. Casey was lying on one length of the L-shaped couch in the cat room, a blanket pulled over her up to the chin, and Nancy was asleep on the other length. Sal was there too, asleep nearby but still in his chair—snoring, his head back to expose the jut of his Adam's apple. An annoying tinny beat issued forth from his Walkman earphones. She didn't see Addison or the girl.

She walked across to Sal and stood there looming over him for a second, deliberating. After a moment she reached for the dull silver cassette player lying on his lap. She lifted it delicately, turned it sideways to study the row of buttons, and gently pushed the one marked STOP.

Sal's head jerked up. He blinked at her blearily.

"Sorry," she said. "I thought you were . . ."

"I gotta have the music," he said.

"When you're—?"

"To sleep, man."

"Oh?"

"Can't sleep without music," and he took the Walkman back and placed it on his thigh again.

"I apologize, then," she said.

He grunted, pressed PLAY and crossed his arms, leaning back.

Down on the couch, Casey moved her head restlessly.

"Good night," whispered Susan in Sal's direction. She was turning to leave when she saw the two from the garden approaching—the girl ahead, Addison stumbling behind.

"He needs to crash," whispered the girl, and then: "I would—go home, but all of them . . ."

"You came together," whispered Susan.

The girl nodded. "In a van."

"It's always hardest for the sober ones," said Susan, as though she knew.

Behind the girl—possibly headed for the corner recliner—Addison tripped abruptly and fell sideways onto the platform that held the rearing lion. He turned and grabbed at it as he fell and the hind paws came up off the platform, ripping off their bolts, so that he and the lion fell together, in a clinch.

"Oh my God," said the girl.

"Oh no," said Susan.

Sal's head jerked up again.

"What the fuck," he said.

Addison lay on the shag rug loosely holding the beast, whose front paws stretched above his head.

"Passed out," said the girl, after a second.

"I think you're right," said Susan.

"No shit," said Sal, and shook his head.

"I'm sorry about the lion," said the girl.

"Me too," said Susan, and gazed down at the lion's ripped feet. She bent to look closer: the four gray pads of the toes, a yellow-white fur around them, another soft pad further back. It was torn open now with a bolt sticking out to reveal part of the white-plastic mold inside. Their pose, she thought, was like two animals on a shield or flag in one of the old man's heraldry books. Some flags pictured lions and unicorns facing each other, standing on their hind legs, or griffins and dragons. Two animals poised to pummel each other. Lying inert, Addison pummeled a lion.

"Why don't you come with me," she said to the girl. Sal was already nodding off. "There's another room on this floor you can sleep in. More comfortable than here."

They left Addison where he had fallen, tangled with the great cat, a high-pitched beat leaking out of Sal's headphones.

"They're going to claim he had delusions," said Casey in the morning.

She was in the bathroom with Susan, who stood up from the sink, her face dripping, and reached for the hand towel, her eyes squeezed shut.

"What?"

"Yeah. They've got a lawyer. They're going to say the will isn't valid."

"You're kidding."

"But Jim says that they're full of it."

"Jim knows?"

"Yeah, he was standing there when they told me."

Susan dried her face and walked out, looking for him. He was in bed still. She pulled the curtains open and flooded them both with whiteness, bleaching the flamingo.

"You didn't think I'd want to know?"

He groaned and rolled onto his back, feet splayed under the sheet, arms wide.

"Listen. I don't think you really need to worry."

"Don't need to worry? They're trying to take this all away from me!"

"The standard for legal capacity is low," he said, and raised himself onto his elbows, rubbing his eyes wearily.

"I don't know what you're saying, Jim. What are you telling me?"

"They'd have to prove that he was delusional under 6100, and there's no evidence of that. Or under Section 811, they'd have to have evidence he couldn't reason logically. Or recognize familiar objects or people. Or have any memory. They're not objecting to the trust. The trust is irrelevant to them. And that's a benefit to you, because with trusts the legal capacity standard is higher. There's no presumption of undue influence here, either. So chances are slim they'll prevail."

"Slim?"

"Very slim, Susan."

She was silent for a second, biding her time. Then she realized the legalese was oddly erotic. His competence. His knowledge of the probate code. She wanted to get back into bed.

The door was open, though, and outside in the corridor was

Casey, sitting impatiently in her chair beneath a woody canopy of fallow-deer antlers.

"You're not just saying that?" she asked him finally.

"I'm telling you. It's a long shot at best. It's frivolous, in my view."

"Do I have to—then should I do anything?"

"Try to relax."

Now that the cousins' decision was made, she saw, it was possible. The lawsuit was actually a relief; she could behave exactly as she wished. No more need to try to impress them, no need to fail so miserably.

She was smiling at the lawyer from the white-lit dust. Motes were adrift in the beam, and floated horizontally.

6

If you lived in a very beautiful house your life became the house, and like the house the life could acquire a quality of completion. It was something about order, she thought, order and its sufficiency. Before now, she had never seen how the mood of her life was defined by the spaces where she existed. Other people knew this—on one end of the spectrum architects and interior designers, on the other the guys who lived in appliance boxes in alleys—but it had never been so obvious to her.

When she left the house, three days a week on Mondays through Wednesdays, to drive to the office and do T.'s paperwork, she walked out the side door onto the driveway in a familiar path straight across the gravel. She parked the car in the same position every afternoon and so the path to it was always the same in the morning—behind her, as she emerged from the house, thick

English ivy and Virginia creeper climbing the mansion wall, lilac bushes on either side of what had once been a service entrance.

To her left as she went out the door was the pool enclosure: the sounds of the fountain, a bird dipping over the water, a flicker at the edge of her eye. To her right was the driveway as it stretched out toward the wide front gate, the straight line of it with a branch curving off to the right, as you moved to the street, to round the front of the house in a semicircle. From where she stood it was mostly a line between grassy expanses, a simple gravel line in the grass. Beyond it rose the hedge that screened her from her neighbors; this was the closest point of contact with the other properties—the towering oleander that guarded them, rising easily eighteen feet, already thick with gaudy pink and red blooms.

Once she pulled through the gate—which was fixed now and glided open before her—and the lush gardens and shady trees were behind her, the gray buzz of the city replaced the oasis. There was the confusion of crowding, sometimes of ugliness: the concrete of overpasses and buildings, air thick with pollution, black and yellow digital signs with words unfurling constantly, velocity and noise, the haphazardness of garbage, the pall of commerce and everyday filth. There was bumper-to-bumper traffic on the freeway, exhaust fumes, the possibility of bad drivers, hostile passersby, sudden accidents, contagious illness, but more overwhelming still than these variables was the slightness and insecurity of her position in space—she could be anywhere, once she was out of the house.

She understood agoraphobics. As soon as she left the perfection of home her location, if not exactly arbitrary, was constantly and sometimes impulsively changing. Her being was subject to the many conditions of wherever she was, the trivial details of her momentary needs; outside the house the sequence of events was chaotic, could not express a clean design. This situation, she realized, was tolerated by most of the five billion people on earth. But more and more she had no idea how they did it—this normal state of mutability and flux, which she had always presumed and often preferred, was not only displeasing but almost unacceptable.

In her old life she'd gone out looking to make things happen because home was a resting place between these happenings; now home was more like a temple, inviting a routine of poise and deliberation. She could move peacefully between the walls as though she walked a neat path in history, as though her time and place were not the product of chance at all but of an ancient arrangement. She lived in the soft footprint of a ceremony. And the longer she lived there, the rarer were the thoughts of the knife. The winces as she expected the blade, awaiting the invisible cut, receded noticeably whereas out in the city she was anyone again. Anyone, to whom anything could happen; anyone, which she had once embraced.

Not anymore.

•

With students from the Art Center—art students whose names she'd found on a bulletin board—she began reorganizing the mounts. Before she had them rehung and restaged she had to encode a new system, and for that she went to a reference librarian who helped her order museum floor plans. She studied the organizing schemes.

There was geography, there was taxonomy, and there was the collection itself, the variety of animals she had and the spaces she needed to house them. She made her own plan according to those needs.

The main part of the ground floor would be given over to North American mammals, each order with its own section. The deer, the bison, the sheep and goats and pronghorns would occupy the *great room*, as she thought of it now, where previously foxes and wild dogs had slunk along the sideboards. The library would hold the big carnivores—the bears and the cats, the wolves and foxes—while the smaller meat-eaters, the weasels and raccoons, would spill over into a drawing room off the front hall. Rodents would live in the music room, rabbits and hares in the ballroom. Bats fit into an alcove once meant for a telephone and a lone armadillo fit into a display case in the hall, where once a forest of antlers had interrupted the air. She made a reptile room out of the old breakfast nook to house tortoises, alligators and snakes; birds of prey now had the rec room to themselves—the rec room where the lion had stood before it was rudely felled by Addison. Owls perched there, hawks, falcons, eagles and a lone vulture.

She knew the second floor should follow the same principle, but she loved the dioramas. Also the foreign collections were small, with the exception of Africa—Africa, land of safaris, was a horn of plenty, and when the African cats migrated from the ground floor, the gazelles and the zebras along with them, it was clear that the horned beasts room could never fit them all. So she took herself out of it and reinstalled the buffalo and the wildebeest. Two of the art students were mural painters so the wide

hallway, too, turned into Africa: out the walls of her former bedroom flowed the grasses and the great lonely flat-topped savannah
trees, curling to the right and left as they emerged from the doorway. Long yellow grasses grew up from the hallway floor as they
grew in horned beasts, and then, along the hall, ceded the way
to wetter and greener terrain as the plain became a jungle. And
on the Rainforest walls the art hangers put up a small colobus
monkey, an antelope, a spiny lizard, and a gray parrot.

The birds seemed to demonstrate a lack of interest in her
personal business, so she put her bed in Birds of the World, which
once had been Russia. She had the squat, dun-colored horse and
shaggy yak moved, and in the former Soviet Union students
painted over Lenin and sketched the lines of treetops in a light
sky, arching branches and tree hollows. She watched as the lines
were filled in and dimensions came out. On a wooden platform
a whooper swan raised its wings; against the wall that faced her
bed stood a peacock with its shimmering tail open.

But in the other bedrooms the collections stayed where they
were, in their quaint geographic compartments. She told herself
that even the Natural History Museum in New York, even the
British Museum in London, whose floor plans she had photocopied, displayed a less than symmetrical arrangement.

When the project was finished the house had a globe-like
aspect in its sectioning off, its variety of scenes, its separation by
palette. It was multicolored like a globe, and also like a globe it
represented reality only partly, with the failure of all maps but
also the same neatness, the same quiet satisfaction. The Himalayas and the Arctic were cold rooms, light-blue and gray-white;

the tropics were emerald green, with the bright splashes of toucans and macaws, the savannahs yellow and gold, and in two of the rooms there were sunsets, pink and mauve.

She had loved austere institutions, as a child—old churches, universities, art galleries, museums. She'd cherished the high ceilings, the deep walls, the wide doorways. Now she thought she had also liked what she hadn't recognized back then: an air of permanence and contentment, the happy captivity of precious things.

Jim the lawyer had an attitude of indulgence when it came to her interest in preservation. It was the kind of indulgence you would rarely find in a spouse, she thought—the benevolence of a third party with little stake in the matter, someone whose agreement was not required and therefore not contentious.

It wasn't only the taxidermy; there were trees in the garden that were historic, which the state declared it was illegal to cut down. She learned the names of all these trees and tried to find out about them, and then the trees gave her an idea for the house, for how to keep it the way it was. It had never been put up for historic status but it could be, it might well qualify if she pursued that course . . . and she decided she would, in case the cousins won their suit, in case the place passed out of her hands. She'd try for state landmark status, Criterion 3: *Embodies the distinctive characteristics of a type, period, region or method of construction or represents the work of a master.* She'd need to hire an architect to evaluate the place—she thought it would qualify as an example of California Mediterranean, like Pasadena City Hall—but first she needed the records.

So on a Thursday morning she drove down to the permit center to pull the old building plans. She filled in forms, waited in lines, paid fees for duplication and processing, and at the end of a dreary morning was handed some rolled-up plans. On her way across the parking lot she unrolled one of them: an architect's drawings of additions to the main building made in 1928—outbuildings, a shed near the pool. There was a greenhouse, she saw, which sadly had since vanished. Sitting in her car with the curls of paper spilling off her lap, she found, to her annoyance, that there were no plans of the original construction in all of it. There was a drawing of a garage renovation done in 1950, a 1954 repair of the dome, and an old schematic she didn't pretend to understand. But there was no drawing of the building in its entirety.

There was the name of an architecture firm on the 1928 drawings, though, a firm that had been absorbed by another one and moved from Pasadena to Westwood. She made an appointment to consult with an architect there.

Coming into the office one morning—the new, small office in Culver City to which T. had downsized—she found a message on the answering machine.

They'd gone away for a while, said T.'s calm voice. While they were gone, it would mean a lot if she could look in on Angela every so often.

"You've got to be kidding," she said aloud in the empty, airless room. It was still full of unopened white boxes of files, stacked into crooked towers that stood around awkwardly. The venetian blinds were angled open slightly so that, standing beside the desk, her finger on the rewind button, she registered the dark masses of cars flicking past.

She wished Casey had told her.

The message didn't say where they'd gone or when they planned to come back. T. had left a few jotted instructions about the business on a legal pad, but that was it.

"I can't believe this," she muttered.

The only people she saw for the rest of the day were a FedEx man, a guy selling copiers, and, when she went out to move her car around midday, a woman walking a dog.

•

Still, a few days later she did as they'd asked. She set it up so that Jim could come with her—made a late reservation for dinner on Abbot Kinney and scheduled the visit to Angela between that reservation and an early date at a bar. The trip would seem less dutiful then; they could stroll over from the bar half-drunk, in the moist sea air of early evening, and be garrulous the way drinks let you be. Angela wouldn't mind. She wouldn't know the difference.

She met them at the door in what appeared to be a kimono, orange and satiny with stylized white birds. They stepped over the threshold shaking hands and smiling. Behind the counter that divided the kitchen from the living room, setting crackers onto a tray, Susan saw the live-in helper, formerly of Bosnia-Herzegovina, whose name she always forgot.

"Vera," said the woman, without being asked.

"Of course, of course," said Susan to Vera, apologetic. "Hello. Susan. And this is Jim. He also works with T."

"A criminal, like my son," said Angela smoothly. She turned to a small wine rack with flourishes of grape leaves and began looking at bottles distractedly.

"I'm sorry?" said Jim.

"It's one of those days," said Vera, rolling her eyes.

Her English had improved, thought Susan, since she first started with Angela.

"Yes, my son is a criminal," said Angela, with a measure of pride. "A criminal mastermind. Would you like white? Or red?"

"Oh, whatever you're having," said Susan quickly, and stole a sidelong glance at Jim. He was gazing at Angela and grinning faintly.

"Look," said Angela, smiling delightedly, and lifted one of the bottles by the neck. "A Zinfandel. A Zinfandel is cheap and stinks like shit."

"Oh!" said Susan. "Yes?"

"I never heard that said," said Jim.

A look of sadness crossed Angela's face and she shrugged regretfully. "I love it very much," she said.

She turned her back, wine in hand. They followed her into the kitchen, where Vera handed them a tray with olives and pickles on it. Jim took a pickle.

"Often they blame it on the parents," went on Angela, as she rummaged in a drawer. They stood back, spearing olives and biding their time. "The worst criminals are often caused by neglect. There was a television show . . ."

"Oh, but not in T.'s case," said Susan.

"I'm sure, not with him," agreed Jim.

"Really?" asked Angela. "But you're a criminal too, aren't you?"

"Some would say," agreed Jim gravely, and inclined his head.

"I've heard of those," mused Angela. "A criminal lawyer."

They stood beside each other and watched as she struggled to open the bottle—"May I?" asked Jim—but Vera was already taking over.

"You would know better than I would," said Angela, and turned from Vera to take a dish towel out of a drawer. It was cheerfully patterned with strawberries; she swabbed it up and down her arms as though cleaning or drying them. "So you tell me. Did they neglect you too? Was that why you did it?"

"I wouldn't say they did," said Jim. "No, I really can't complain. My parents were pretty nice to me."

"The Zinfandel," said Angela, and proffered two glasses.

They sipped expectantly, waiting for the next remark. But instead she ceased to perform, and for the next half hour was gracious and comprehensible. She made tactful and sympathetic remarks about Hal's death; she knew what T. was working on, discussed the mission statement for his new foundation; she understood that Jim was a lawyer for nonprofits and remembered that he had met T. at an alumni party for their college fraternity.

Frat boys, both of them, realized Susan with vague astonishment. In her youth she would never have gone near one.

They walked away slowly, afterward, in a mild daze.

"I like her," said Jim.

•

The architect came to the house a week later, a tall, thin man with glasses and a prominent nose—more or less an architect cliché, as far as Susan could tell. Together they toured the grounds. He studied the building from various angles and then accepted a cup of coffee and went inside with her to examine the interior features. He said he was hopeful the house would be granted state historic status and she felt a surge of confidence: now, even if Steven and Tommy somehow won their suit, she had an ace in the hole. Not that she had the money to pay them off without selling the house anyway, in the event that the decision went against her, but she would cross that bridge . . . she would rather lose all the money she had than sacrifice the house.

When she walked him out to his car he popped the trunk and brought out a long yellowing roll. "The 1924 drawings," he said. "You can keep them. We've made a copy to put back in the archives. Technically we don't need to keep even the copies this long, but since the file's been reactivated . . ."

"Thank you," she said, rolling the thin rubber bands up and down on the tube.

He got in his car, and she stepped back as he started it up. Then he put it into reverse and rolled the window down. "Hey, if I come out again you'll have to show me the basement," he said. "On the plan it has a surprisingly large footprint."

"What basement?" she asked, but he had already backed up out of earshot with a light wave.

At the kitchen table, beneath a blackbelly rosefish, she spread out the drawings. There were several pages and she wasn't good at correlating the lines on them to the real house, but soon she had glasses weighting the corners and could study the one marked BASEMENT & SUBCELLAR. She wondered if it had been filled in since—was that even possible? She'd never noticed a door to the basement, yet there it was on the plans. As far as she could tell it had been as large as the ground floor, had extended over the same area—maybe nine thousand square feet. The subcellar was smaller and seemed to have been designed for wine storage: there were built-in racks on the plan, if she was reading it right.

She called the architect, who had a phone in his car.

"Could it have been, I don't know, filled in or something? I've never seen a basement here. I mean, I've lived in the house since December."

"Tell you what," he said. "My lunch meeting just canceled. Let's look for it."

He was back in half an hour.

"So you've never seen a door?" he said.

"Never," she said firmly, and shook her head. "They're not where the plan says they should be. See? Here?"

"The plans indicate there—there—two doors, two staircases," and he tapped the flattened paper. "Let's go look."

He lifted the glasses off the drawings and took the plans with him. She followed him out of the kitchen, along the main hall to the raptor room with the sunken floor.

He looked around for a second and then consulted the drawing.

"Huh," he said, and turned around a few times.

"What?"

"I don't think this room was ever built as the plan stipulated. Either that, or it was gutted and rebuilt from the ground up. See? This should be a supporting wall. Nothing. Instead the support's over there," and he pointed.

"So what does that mean?"

"First we check where the other staircase was supposed to be," he said, shaking his head, and this time she followed him to the music room.

"No," he said, and shook his head again. "Hmm. Surprising."

"Will it affect the application?" she asked abruptly, quickly worried that her curiosity had jeopardized the house's future.

"Oh no. Shouldn't be relevant," he said vaguely, looking around and then back at the drawing.

"Oh good. Good."

"OK. We'll have to walk it. We can start from the east end," he said finally.

"Wait. Are you hungry? I know you're missing your lunch hour right now. Would you like me to make us some sandwiches first?"

"Thanks. Appreciate it."

In a few minutes they were standing with their sandwiches in the parlor off the cavernous front hall—the drawing room, full of raccoons and ringtails and coati, weasels and otters and minks.

"Procyonids and mustelids," she told the architect, as he nodded and masticated his ham and cheese, casting his eyes to the molding and ceiling beams.

She liked knowing the nomenclature, even took pride in it. They were beautiful words, the terms from Greek and Latin: careful words to be kept and valued, along with the collection.

"All this furniture has been here? Since you took possession?"

"This room is unchanged, pretty much, except for the taxidermy. That's all been moved around. But I don't think it blocks anything."

He walked along the one interior wall, rapping with one hand, sandwich in the other.

"Moving along," he said, when the last bite of sandwich was gone.

He checked the hallway next, the wall behind the grand staircase; he went back and forth between rooms, measuring closet spaces and the depths of walls with his eyes. She was impressed by this, how he could know measurements without using a measuring tape. He knew the volume of hidden spaces without seeing both sides of them at the same time. But in room after room he shook his head, and finally—by this time she was impatient and the balls of her feet were hot and sore from standing—they had made it to the west end of the house without new information.

There had been some shelves and cabinets and wardrobes they'd need to get out of the way, he said, if she wanted him to be sure—some walls he couldn't get to without the furniture being moved, pieces that were too heavy for just the two of them to shift. He wrote down the list of rooms and the walls he needed to check if she wanted a definitive answer.

"I can send over a couple of burly guys who work for one of our contractors, if you don't mind paying his fees," he offered at the front door, consulting a sleek wristwatch. "Some cement guys or roofers or something."

"Yes, please send them," she said. "Or give me the number. Whatever's quick."

"The secretary will call it in to you."

It hadn't occurred to her to sleep with him, she thought, despite his competence and a passing attraction. She wondered at this, and when he was gone she put her feet up on the couch in the library and gazed into the face of a black bear.

"Vera's gone," said Angela.

Susan had picked up the phone at two in the morning, with Jim asleep beside her.

"What?"

"She's gone. She had to go away."

She sat up, discomfort growing.

"You mean—she's coming right back, though?"

"She had to go because someone was sick. But now I'm all alone."

She could hear thinness in the voice, a lost quality.

"She—Vera left in the middle of the night?"

"She left in the afternoon."

"And she didn't call for a substitute?"

"No substitute has come."

"No one's with you? No one?"

"I'm all alone."

"I'm in Pasadena, you know. There's really no one there with you?"

Silence.

"Angela. Why don't you give me the agency's number and go back to bed, and then I'll call them for you first thing in the morning?"

". . . I'm all alone," said Angela again.

Susan sighed, sat for a minute in inertia and resentment, and then got out of bed.

"What?" asked Jim, as she flicked on the closet light and stood blinking at the clothes hanging.

"I have to go make sure she's OK," she said.

"She? Who? Casey?"

"Angela. Her attendant apparently left her. Unless she's making it up, for some reason."

"You're kidding."

"Have to drive over there," she said.

"There? Where?"

"Santa Monica."

"It's the middle of the night. Why you?"

"There's no one else."

"But why . . ."

"There's no one else," she repeated, and reached into the hanging clothes to grasp the folds of anything.

•

The drive was faster than usual since the freeways were empty, but it still took almost forty minutes. When she got to the townhouse the lights were all out. After several minutes of her knocking and waiting, increasingly impatient, Angela appeared at the door in a lacy dressing gown and old-school hair curlers.

"Did you go back to *sleep?*" asked Susan. "After you called me?"

Angela shook her head firmly. But there was a waffle pattern printed on the side of her face.

Irritated that she'd driven across the whole city for what seemed to be nothing, Susan slipped past her and flicked on the overhead. Apparently Angela was fine with shuffling around in pitch black.

"OK, listen," she said. "I told your son I would check in on you while he and Casey were gone. So I'll sleep here tonight, until I can call Vera's agency in the morning. I'll just sleep on the couch, right here. And you need to go back to sleep too."

"I'm sorry. T. will be back soon," said Angela, lucid for a moment.

"Well, good," said Susan. "I'm glad. And I have to say, I'm surprised at Vera. Even if she had to leave on an emergency, she still should have made sure you had someone."

She plumped a pillow on the edge of the couch and slipped off her shoes.

"Back from the honeymoon," said Angela, and nodded.

Susan stared at her.

"Pardon me?"

"Back from the honeymoon."

"Vera went away on her *honeymoon?*" asked Susan, and studied Angela's face, her pale blue eyes and carefully plucked brows. Maybe Vera did the plucking for her. Personally she wouldn't trust Angela with a sharp pair of tweezers in the eyeball vicinity.

"Not Vera, T.," said Angela.

Not lucid anymore.

She had to be inventing it—very likely she was. Still, Susan remembered what Angela had said about T., when he was missing in the jungle and she herself was convinced he was dead. Possibly the woman had some kind of savant deal going on.

"Let's get you back to bed," said Susan gently, and took her arm. "Here. I'll walk with you to the room. Were you going around in the dark before I got here?"

After she'd left Angela in her room she tossed on the couch for a while beset by images of Casey with vanilla cake smeared around her mouth, Susan not there at all, Susan all alone and separate and completely forgotten. Casey in the middle of sunlight, sunlight and other people who knew her—flowers and dresses, pomp and circumstance, ceremony and dancing, white frills and hideous ruffles.

●

In the morning she waited till Vera's replacement arrived, a pretty young Latina who walked expertly on black stiletto heels. Susan opened the door for her and right away Angela eyed her tight clothes with suspicion.

"My name is Merced," said the woman, and smiled. "You must be Angela?"

"Mrs. Stern," said Angela coldly.

"Of course: Mrs. Stern," said Merced, not missing a beat.

Angela ignored the outstretched hand but Merced took that in stride too and patted her arm kindly.

"Don't worry, Mrs. Stern," she said. "We'll do fine. I'll take good care of you until Vera comes home again."

She put down her purse on the counter.

"So what happened?" asked Susan, as Angela wandered out of the room.

"It was an unfortunate situation," said Merced. "The receptionist was a temp, because the regular girl just went on maternity leave, and then this temp, who I guess, it turns out, is bipolar?—she just all of a sudden walked out on the job. So no one got Vera's message. And then . . ."

"Something could have happened to her," said Susan.

"They're extremely concerned about the error," said Merced, and nodded earnestly. "Are you the family?"

Susan was explaining when Angela came back in and began to rearrange items nervously on end tables and shelves.

"Excuse me, Susan? May I speak to you privately?" she asked after a minute.

Susan followed her into her bedroom, where she shut the door behind them.

"I don't *know* that woman," said Angela. "She's a *stranger.*"

"It won't be for long," said Susan. "Probably just a few days."

"I don't know her at all. And she doesn't know me."

Angela had flipped open a jewelry box on her dresser and waggled her fingers in its miniature compartments until she found a sparkly rhinestone brooch in the shape of a bow.

"It'll be fine. She's a professional. Just like Vera. When Vera first came you didn't know her either, but still you got along fine. Remember? This one's good too. She knows what she's doing."

"But she doesn't know anything about me," said Angela.

"Is there anything you'd like me to discuss with her, before I go?" asked Susan.

Angela had opened the pin on the back of the brooch and was picking at her cuticles with the sharp point, agitated. They were already torn into ragged hangnails and soon they would be bleeding.

"I tell you what," said Susan, reaching out and taking her hand to stop her. She pried the fingers gently off the brooch pin as she spoke. "You try to get along here for the day with just the two of you. All right? Because I have an appointment. I have some men coming to the house to move some heavy furniture for me. So I have to get back to Pasadena now. But if you still don't feel comfortable with Merced by dinnertime you can call me. And I'll come back again. Does that sound fair?"

Angela said nothing.

"I want you to relax," said Susan. "She'll take good care of you. She really will."

"She's low-class," said Angela, and put out her bottom lip in a sulk. "She looks like a prostitute."

Infantile, scattered, then distant and poised—but after all it must be par for the course. If Hal had lived, if both of them had lived together into their dotage they might have been like this. They might have ended as ancient children, half-gone, fumbling, and rarely if ever themselves.

"It's the style," said Susan. "She's young. They all dress like that these days."

As though she and Angela were already the same—old biddies far past sex and fashion.

"Prostitute shoes," said Angela.

"Look, I like her," said Susan, thinking that maybe a more personal testimony would help. "She's nice. Give her a chance. I think she'll grow on you."

After a few more minutes of wheedling she was able to steer Angela back into the kitchen and persuade her to accept a glass of iced tea. Quiet in the background, she slipped out the door while the other two were talking—fled down the walk gratefully in her slept-in clothes, her teeth gritty and unbrushed.

●

Construction workers came and moved the large pieces of furniture from the walls marked by the architect. When they had gone, dark, massive old wardrobes stood anchorless in the center of rooms.

It bothered her. The investigation had to be finished quickly or she would grow restless at the disorder. But when she called his office the architect was busy with *real work*, he said testily. He pawned her off on a junior associate who could come by in his stead.

The associate was a young recent graduate named Leigh, her hair pulled back in a tight platinum-blond ponytail, wearing the same trendy horn-rimmed glasses favored by her colleague. Susan admired her self-possession and wondered if all architects had this—a punctilious, almost rigorous and pared-down sense of style, clothing with clean lines and expensive labels. Leigh showed no interest in the mounts, only the house itself—as though the animals were not there, as though she saw right through them.

Susan could tell she was less expert than the older guy but

she seemed to know enough for the purpose. She rapped on walls and moved a small yellow stud finder over their surfaces, Susan watching as its green light flashed on and off again.

"Nothing there," she said in the first room.

"Nope, nothing," she said in the second.

"My guess would be crawl space," she said in the third. "Not enough room for stairs."

"Sorry, no," she said in the last room.

Susan was disappointed.

Only then, resigned to a nonevent and walking the architect girl to the door, did she remember the slab.

"Wait," she said excitedly, and stopped. "There's this one place in the yard—it's not that near the house, actually, it's in the backyard, way back there in the fir grove—but when I first moved in, we were doing some garden work and we found it. It's just a piece of concrete sunk into the ground. You don't really notice it, normally. He said there might have been a root cellar under there once, something like that. I mean, it's just a slab. Cement or whatever. With grass growing over the edges. But can you quickly take a look?"

Leigh followed Susan out the service entrance and around to the back, where they picked their way down the flagstone paths toward the copse at the rear of the property. The further they went the more discouraged she felt: it was too far from the house. It was unlikely to be connected.

A few steps into the fir trees they ducked under some boughs, crunched over a sparse litter of cones and then stood over the slab: overgrown, concrete, about three feet square.

Almost nothing.

"Enh," said the architect girl, and shrugged. She poked at the slab with the smooth toe of her pump. "It doesn't look like much to me."

•

The intercom buzzed a little past midnight. She looked out the window of her new bedroom—it faced the crescent drive instead of the backyard—and saw a taxi waiting at the front gate.

She was hoping it was Casey, and she took the wide stairs quickly, lightly, two at a time. But when she pressed the button to talk to the driver he said, "I got a Angela here. Angela Stern."

She almost said *Oh no* right then. But instead she sighed, buzzed open the gate and went out front to meet them.

"Does she know where you are?" she asked Angela, as soon as she stepped from the taxi.

It could mean Merced's job, she was thinking.

"She fell asleep," Angela said.

"We have to call. She'll be worried sick by now."

Angela walked slowly, peering down through the dark at her footing as the taxi's headlights swept back. She was wearing a long winter coat, a coat she'd never have a use for in L.A., over a sheer lacy nightgown.

"So what went wrong?" asked Susan, a hand on her arm to steer. As they drew near the house again the motion sensors were triggered and the outside lights flicked on.

"It wasn't safe. It was *unsafe*," said Angela, and shook her head. "Unsafe."

"What if she stepped on you," said Angela. "Those shoes— those shoes would be like daggers. They could stab me."

"Uh-huh," said Susan.

It took her a moment to register the words. And then she found Angela was standing there stricken. Her face looked white.

"I'm so *sorry*," she said, exactly as a person might who wasn't insane at all. "I shouldn't have said that."

"Don't worry. It's all right," said Susan.

Inside she sat Angela down in the kitchen, gave her a glass of water and called the apartment, where Merced picked up the phone right away.

"She'll stay with me," Susan told her, resigned. "She'll stay till Vera gets back. So have them call me as soon as that happens. Would you?"

She looked over at Angela, who was sitting very straight on her kitchen chair under a fish and holding her water glass carefully, with two hands. She put her to bed in North American Birds.

When the children returned, Angela was still there. They showed up at the big house one evening around dusk, while Susan and Jim and Angela were eating Thai on the patio beside the pool—though Angela was not eating. After the food arrived she'd decided she distrusted food of any "ethnicity" and had requested instead a Tom Collins.

Casey was brown from the sun and T. wore faded jeans. The three-legged dog loped along beside them.

"Oh, dears, dears!" called Angela joyfully. "How was the Mexican wedding?"

Susan rose as they approached the table, rose and put down her napkin.

"Good," said T., and rested a hand lightly on Casey's shoulder. "It was good."

1

She wanted to show she was happy about the wedding news. And for the most part she was, or she would be when she assimilated the information—she felt a kind of rising anticipation on Casey's behalf—but there was also petty confusion. Her pride was injured as much as her feelings. She would have been grateful for anything—the most nominal warning, the most casual tip of a hat.

"I didn't tell you because I didn't know," said Casey.

They'd gone to get a bottle of white wine from the kitchen. Susan didn't keep champagne in the house, so it would have to serve.

"But Angela did," she said, rummaging in a drawer for a corkscrew and trying to contain the seed of resentment. No whining; keep it pure and simple, be remembered well.

"Oh yeah?" asked Casey. Give her credit: it sounded like real surprise.

"She told me you were on your honeymoon," said Susan.

"Huh. Not exactly," said Casey. "In the first place, I only went along for the ride. At the last minute. I wasn't planning to. It was Baja—the Sea of Cortez. A whale stranding."

"A *whale* stranding?" asked Susan, looking up from the wine.

"A mass stranding. There were over twenty of them. Beaked whales, which is a kind that dives deep, I guess? They look like dolphins to me, they have those kind of long noses. Anyway the biologists inspected some of the dead ones and said they had these hemorrhages around the ears. They think navy sonar caused them. You know, the navy does this sonar in the ocean? It's for detecting diesel submarines, or something. So anyway the whale guys think the sound waves hurt whale brains. They get confused or they're in pain and it disorients them and then they beach themselves. They lie there baking in the sun and dying. It's one of the worst things I've seen. You wouldn't believe the smell."

"So what did you do?" asked Susan.

"We helped get some of them back in the water. Yeah, yeah, I know what you're thinking. Answer: I sat on my crippled ass behind a folding table and handed out bottled water to the volunteers. Tame shit like that."

"But it's good," said Susan softly. "I'm glad you did."

"T.'s idea, he got on some kind of emergency phone tree for marine mammal rescue. He's on a bunch of lists now. Your basic Good Samaritan shit. Some of it's just giving out money. Like with the foundation. He just paid a bunch of poachers in Africa to stop shooting rhinos. They sell the horns to make into, like, fake Chinese aphrodisiacs. Now they're getting a salary for guarding the rhinos instead of killing them. Who knew?"

"That sounds like a great idea," said Susan drily.

"But with the whales I kinda got into it," said Casey. "It was a life-or-death thing. It had—I don't know. It wasn't nothing."

"You take the wine, OK? I'll take the glasses," said Susan, and handed down the bottle. She put five goblets on a tray and they started out of the kitchen, toward the patio. "So where did, you know, the getting-married part come in?"

"Spur-of-the-moment," said Casey behind her. "That was his idea too."

"You going to have a reception? At least a big party?"

"Fuck if I know," said Casey happily. "Haven't thought about it. He's moving in, though. He likes my place better than his."

"I like it better too."

"He does things," said Casey. "You know. I miss how walking on sand used to feel. I was telling him that, after the whale thing was over. We were on our way out of town, we'd driven down to the shore to look at it one more time. So he picked me up and carried me down to the waterline and put me down and he got down there with me. And then we kind of crab-walked. We walked on our elbows. There were waves, you know, and I can't go fast on my elbows, I'm not built in the shoulders like Sal or someone. Anyway, I'm not going to say it was some romantic shit, because actually it ended up sucking. I mean after three minutes I was soaking and shivering, I had these scratches on my knees from dragging them, because there were pebbles in the sand too, shit, there were probably syringes, what the hell would I know. And then the finer sand, for like *days* after that, was killing me. It got way down in my goddamn ears and I couldn't get it out of there. I was afraid it would do some damage, if you want to know the truth. To the ear drums or whatever. Then I'd be crippled *and* deaf. So finally I had to go to a Mexican doctor, on our way back up here, in some shitty border town crossing into Arizona where the doctors make most of their salaries selling Ritalin prescriptions to American *turistas*. For snorting, not for the hyperactive kids. I had to go to one of those guys and get my ear canals irrigated. It was actually disgusting."

They passed through the French doors, saw the other three talking and laughing at the poolside table.

"The guy tried to sell me a scrip for Ritalin just as an extra bonus. After he squirted six gallons of warm water into my ears."

"Sounds like T. showed you a really good time," said Susan.

"His heart was in the right place, though," said Casey.

As they drew near the table Jim glanced up, smiling. T. was smoothing a lock of his mother's hair behind her ear.

Family, thought Susan. She was surprised.

"Don't look now," said Jim, a couple of days later. They were on the tennis court, whose clay surface was far too cracked for serious players. Luckily they were not serious. They had two old wooden racquets from a closet in the rec room and a bag of dull gray balls with hardly any bounce.

"Don't look where now," said Susan, walking up to the net.

"Outside the gate there's a guy with a camera, taking snapshots of us," said Jim, and bent down to pocket a ball.

She turned to look.

"Well shit. What did I just say," said Jim, shaking his head. But he didn't seem upset.

"Who is it? The cousins?"

Jim shook his head. "Doubt it. They have no incentive to document us."

"But then—who would?"

"I think maybe my wife," said Jim. "Apologies."

Susan had been reaching down for her water bottle, at the end of the net, but stopped and glanced up.

"Your wife?"

"Someone who's working for her, anyway. They're gathering ammunition."

"Ammunition?"

"For the divorce."

She lifted the bottle to her lips and gazed at him steadily as she drank.

"I had no idea," she said, after she wiped drops off her lips.

"It doesn't matter," he said.

"Can't she—you mean for alimony, or something?"

"Ha. No. There was a prenup. She's wealthy, her family made me sign it. Evidence of infidelity means I won't get anything."

"Oh," said Susan. They stood opposite each other, wooden

racquets in hand, with only the net between them. The top of the net was cracked, like the court, its white hem barely holding together across the top of the sagging green mesh.

"Sorry for the invasion of privacy," he said, and gazed down at his shoes. They were Converse; Hal had owned a pair.

"I don't care," she said. "But are you—I mean we could call the cops or something, couldn't we? That's actually my property there, where he's standing. I think he might be trespassing."

Jim shook his head and shrugged. "I always knew it would happen. She's been waiting me out. Waiting for me to do this. For years. So now she's free to get rid of me. Even before, any settlement would have been minuscule. Fine with me. But she likes to win completely. She didn't want me to see a penny."

"So why did you—I mean, why did you stay? If you weren't in it for the money . . ."

"Why do you think," said Jim. "Let's hit the ball, OK?"

He backed up.

"You love her," said Susan, nearly under her breath. "You love her even though she doesn't love you."

He stood and tossed a ball, waiting for her to move into position.

"I can't help it," he said finally, as she walked to the service line.

The ball came early, while she was still turning toward him to receive. It bounced and hit the fence.

Vera was not coming back; a sick relative needed her in New Jersey. Angela was upset by the news and sequestered herself in her bedroom.

"She won't eat anything but candy," reported Casey over the telephone. "She refuses to have anyone else come and stay. Except for T. or me, but we can't go there every night. She drinks water from her bathroom tap, out of the toothbrush cup. She eats these little bags of red licorice. She had them left over from giving out to the kids at Halloween and she took them in there with her and now she won't eat anything else. If you try to give her real food she lets it sit there and rot."

"Maybe," ventured Susan, "maybe it's time to consider—?"

"Not happening. We're not putting her in an institution. First of all, she would hate it. And T. doesn't like the idea much either."

"I don't know what to tell you," said Susan. "Taking care of her is kind of a full-time occupation."

She was looking out the window at the backyard, where the guys who serviced the koi ponds were dipping tubes into the water to test it.

"Yeah. Yeah," said Casey distractedly. "No. It is. Plus T. wants to go to Borneo."

"Borneo?"

"Saving-the-rainforest deal."

"Huh. He's hell-bent for leather on the nature stuff, isn't he."

"What can I say. He's always been a workaholic."

After they hung up Susan wandered out the back door, over to where a technician stood beside a pond with a small bridge arching above it. He was young, freckled and sported a crew cut. Once she might have seen him as a prospect.

"You don't happen to know anyone who could tear up a piece of concrete for me, do you?" she asked. "Who has a jackhammer or something?"

"I could find out for you," he said. "Sure. How big of a job is it?"

"It's pretty small," she said.

"So what's in it for me?"

She looked at him for a few seconds. He looked at her and smiled slowly.

"You want a finder's fee?" she asked finally.

It wasn't what he meant, clearly.

"Nah," he said. "I was just kidding. I'll get you a number."

But he seemed disappointed, as though he'd expected otherwise. She must be giving off a trace amount of desire, though she was not, in fact, currently a slut.

•

The taxidermists were busy. It surprised her: there seemed to be a booming business in animal stuffing in Southern California. West Virginia or Texas she might have expected, but not here. Her repair jobs were often accepted but then put on lengthy waiting lists; sometimes the taxidermists turned her down outright. One came to the house to look at the collection and tell her what maintenance it needed, but he was a hobbyist, not a professional. Lacking experience, she decided to entrust her charges only to the practitioners whose livelihoods depended on their skills.

On her computer, which was finally unpacked after the move, she kept an electronic log of the mounts she sent out, when and where, with estimated completion dates. *Meerkat,* read the spreadsheet. *African Taxidermy, (818) 752-9254. Out 2/5/95. ETA 4/15/95. Oryx head, Dan's Taxidermy & Tanning, (510) 490-9012. Out 2/7/95. ETA 6/1/95.* Once, making an entry, she thought of something the aging diplomat had said—something about a record, a log book the old man had kept, a list of which skins were taken, when, where, the hunters' names. It occurred to her that the names in such a logbook could be helpful—one of the hunters, if any were still alive, might know what the legacy was that Chip had mentioned, might be more lucid than he'd been. It was possible the old man had wanted some of the better-quality mounts to be sent to a museum or something, and the possibility nagged at her so she called Chip's resting home to ask him about it.

"Mr. Sumter's room, please," she told the receptionist.

"Oh. I'm sorry," said the woman, after a pause.

She should have called sooner, should have been more grateful. A small thank-you note after she left.

She poured herself a cup of tea and cut a slice of lemon. The single apartment with its beige carpet, glass wind chimes catching a cold light. Even a butterfly could be ugly in the form of a wind chime . . . the chimes would have been his wife's, likely. Two posters of foreign cities—what had they been? It was already faded. Maybe Venice or Rome. Hanging from the ceiling, a spider plant with brown tips. An opera playing. It was the one with a clown on the front, she had noticed as she left: the opera about clowns. You didn't have to know anything about opera to recognize it. There was a famous scene from that opera in a gangster movie: the tough Italian mobster was deeply moved by the plight of a clown who was crying inside. Robert De Niro as Al Capone, one moment weeping at the tragic beauty, the next bashing heads in. He stove in a man's cranium with a baseball bat in that particular movie, if she remembered right—a baseball bat at the dinner table. Not much subtlety there.

A caterwauling song by the heartbroken clown hero. It rose to a crescendo: *Ree-dee, pah-lee-ah-cho* . . . It was a caricature of opera, which was already a caricature of tragedy. Men's tragic qualities were closely connected to their cluelessness; the tragic men suffered from a lack of self-awareness. Once you painted their faces in tawdry clown makeup and forced them to sing in high registers, at that particular point, frankly, the tragedy turned into chewing gum on your shoe.

She tried to recall the details of what Chip had said. He had called it a trophy book, she thought—maybe a trophy log or a trophy record, words to that effect. But in the library she would never find such a record book, even if it was stowed somewhere, because as usual she felt overwhelmed as soon as she went in. The books weren't catalogued and there had to be thousands. She would need to hire someone if she wanted to get them in order—either that or go through them herself and in the process get rid of those she didn't have a use for: the many shelves on heraldry, for instance. Maybe she could get a library science student to help her. She already had landscapers, art students, architects, taxidermists; she had a small army. Her friends these days were paid for their service.

Except Jim.

"So," he said, the next time he was over. He had the Sunday paper and was reading the real estate classifieds. Rentals section.

"The divorce will come through sometime this spring. Not long. There aren't any disputes."

"You're moving out soon, right?" she asked.

"Next few weeks."

"So what are you thinking?"

"Still looking," he said, and shrugged. "Silver Lake, maybe. Echo Park. Los Feliz. Say, little Craftsman bungalow."

"You gonna do the whole running-every-day thing? Getting fit after the breakup? Diet? Sit-ups? Lifting weights and trying to feel young again?"

"Uh-huh," he said, and turned the newspaper page.

"Maybe I should go jogging with you. We could buy matching tracksuits. A his-and-hers type thing."

She couldn't help but think of the many rooms of her house, without inhabitants. But there was still Hal to consider.

*

The jackhammer man showed up only after she'd left several phone messages for him saying to come anytime, she was usually home, etc. She'd finally given up because he never answered the calls himself, and when he did call back he left messages that told her nothing. Then he was at the front door, a yellow unit of some kind pulled up behind his truck and parked in her driveway. She led him into the back and down the stone path into the trees and showed him the small slab.

"You want me to haul out the pieces?" he asked, cigarette dangling as he took a packet of earplugs out of a pocket.

"That'd be great," she said. "Yes."

"Not sure I can stretch the cord all the way to the compressor from here, where my truck is parked now. May have to drive onto your grass a bit."

"OK. Try not to run over the flowers, though."

"OK then."

She left him unspooling an orange cord, thick as her wrist. A few minutes later one of her broken mounts was delivered and she forgot about the jackhammer as she stood in the entry hall and opened its crate with a crowbar. She wasn't handy with tools, had only bought a kit when she realized they always sent the animals back to her in a mass of Styrofoam peanuts, packed deep inside wooden boxes that were solidly built and sturdily nailed. Leaning back and straining, she popped a nail out too suddenly and it hit her on the cheek and stung; then she snagged her shirt on a splintery board-end, tore a rent in the fabric and swore.

It was one of her favorites among the crocodilians: a small alligator in a swamp setting, dark-brown acrylic mud wrinkling around its clawed feet, a dozen white eggs in a twiggy nest behind it. Its green eyes, gone cloudy over the years as though with cataracts, had been replaced with clear new ones. The squat feet had polished-looking claws instead of the ragged toe ends that had preceded them; discolored patches on the leathery hide had been touched up. She was pleased. The whole assemblage was remarkably light—she could carry it herself.

So she lifted it, though its bulk was awkward, and walked slowly toward the reptile room, where she put it down on the table while she unlatched its glass case and raised the lid. As she did so she thought of archosaurs, the dinosaur lineage of which only birds and crocodilia remained . . . that was the problem with organization: it was never perfect. Sometimes she wished she could have laid out the house in evolutionary terms—put the birds and crocodilians together, for instance. But then there would be the strangeness of genetics to contend with, the oddness of the fact that some animals who seemed to be nearly the same had borne almost no relation to each other over the course of history, according to the scientists, and that, conversely, some animals who looked like they had zero business together were actually close relatives.

Only as she left the reptile room did she register the far-off drone of the jackhammer, still drilling. She wondered if the slab covered an old, capped well—they must have had wells here once, she thought. Pasadena had more of its own water than Los Angeles proper, she'd once been told. Maybe she could have her own well again, in that case, ask them to drill deeper, deeper, down to where cool water flowed beneath the soil, to where it trickled through the rock, the caverns of the earth. Maybe she could make the whole house into a living kingdom then—its flora and fauna, both dead and alive, its circulatory system of ponds and rivers . . . vegetables growing, the fruit of the trees to eat . . . but no. That was a pipe dream. It was a terrarium, the house. It should not attempt to simulate nature.

There were zookeepers, in the order of things, and curators. Previously she had been neither, but now she fell into the curator category. She was not going to keep a menagerie here, she was not going to farm and live off the land, clearly. Living, even the koi were too much work for her alone. But the dead animals were enough. In any case the dead were almost as beautiful as the living, sometimes more so. They had far fewer needs.

No: this was a museum of killed animals, pure and simple. An amateur museum, yes. It was not professional. But no less beautiful for all that—maybe more beautiful, even. She welcomed the flocks of suburban parrots as they alit in the trees and she wanted to keep the koi, could even foresee adding to them—bringing in native frogs or toads, maybe, or the cocoons of butterflies, as long as they weren't a kind that would defoliate her trees. These were mere accents, of course: the center of the house was the skins hung on their plastic bones. The center of it was the crouching, leaping, preening, the frozen poses, the watchful blind eyes; it was a house of ghost prey, ghost predators, innocent killers trapped by the less innocent.

"Mother," said Casey.

She jumped. She'd had no idea she wasn't alone—had been staring at nothing. Staring at a door lintel.

But there was Casey, in the hall. Clearly had just entered.

"Jesus! You scared the hell out of me," said Susan.

"Sorry," said Casey. "You know—I have that clicker in my car now. For the gate. I didn't think you'd mind."

"No, no," said Susan. "Course, make yourself at home. You want something to drink?"

"What is that, construction?" asked Casey, and cocked her head at the jabbering noise of the drill.

"Some cement in the backyard I'm having ripped up," said Susan.

"Ground granulated blast-furnace slag?"

They smiled at each other. Susan knelt and put her hand on Casey's arm.

"How's married life treating you, honey?"

"I really like it."

"Good. Good," said Susan. "I'm really happy, then."

She thought she might choke up at Casey's unaccustomed sweetness.

"Angela came out of her room," said Casey.

"I'm glad to hear it," said Susan.

"But here's the thing," said Casey.

Susan's knees were hurting so she stood up again.

"Yeah?" she asked. "Follow me to the kitchen, I'm thirsty."

"Wait," said Casey. "Seriously."

Susan waited, listening.

"We're going away."

"The rainforest thing?" asked Susan.

"Malaysia. Malaysian Borneo."

"Oh," said Susan.

"And it would be a lifesaver if you could take her again. Her and the dog. Both of them."

"Her and the dog," repeated Susan.

"And T. says we could pay for someone else to live with you here and help her. A new Vera. So you wouldn't have to do much in the way of like, care or whatever. Just let her *stay* here, just give her one of the bedrooms. Because we've got her to come out of her own room finally but she's still shaky. And there's nowhere else she'll willingly go."

Casey leaned forward suddenly and clasped both of her hands.

"Please," she said. "Please?"

Susan was gazing at her, confused and slightly panicked, when there was a knock behind them and the jackhammer guy clomped in from the back, covered in dust and leaving white bootprints all over the ancient rug.

"You got a manhole in your backyard," he said.

"A manhole?"

"Problem is, the cement was poured right onto the plug, you know, the metal lid on the hole. I got most of it off but you still got that metal plug there, and the thing's not moving. Possibly rusted over, maybe locked from the inside, hell if I know. If you want to open the lid you're gonna need to bring in something like a backhoe and dig up the whole deal. Or blow it up. Hell. The drill won't do any more for you than it's already done."

"Oh. Well. Thanks, though," said Susan, disappointed.

"Is it like a city manhole?" asked Casey. "It should have that stuff written right on it, right? Like initials or something? Seems to me the city would need to deal with it, not us. What if there's some high-voltage line or shit like that under there? Or toxic raw sewage?"

"No letters I could see," said the jackhammer guy.

"I'll call the city anyway," said Susan. "OK. So. Thank you."

"I still gotta load up the truck. I'll come back in when I'm done. Be a hundred fifty," said the guy. "Cash or check."

When he was gone they were back in their awkward pause—Casey's request hanging between them. Susan flashed back to their last such pause, or the last one she had noticed, in the minutes before they found out Hal was dead. They had been standing in the airport beside the baggage-claim thing, the particular luggage conveyor belt always shaped, come to think of it, like a bell curve. There'd been a poster of a high-rise on the wall, in Rio de Janeiro or Buenos Aires or some other far-south city where there were beaches littered with half-naked women in thong bikinis and the apartment buildings were white. Now when she thought of the phone sex, of Casey and phone sex and her maternal anxiety, she would always think of tall white buildings. There was nothing she could do about it; the association was simply lodged in her mind. Neurons firing the same way repeatedly, carving out a deep rut—it was what happened, they said, with clinical depression. *In a rut* could be literal, could happen to neural pathways in your brain.

It struck her that she felt free to ask, finally.

"You're not doing that phone-sex job still, are you? Now that you're, you know, married and all that?"

"Nah," said Casey. "It was a momentary thing. Fun while it lasted."

"So I know this sounds like a mother and all that. But what can I say, I am one. Have you been thinking about what you want to do career-wise? I don't see you living off T.'s money. I don't see you just, you know, indefinitely flying around the world with him, handing out Evian at whale strandings."

"No," said Casey. "No. Not indefinitely."

"So?"

"Well, shit. I'd like to have an answer for you. I'd like to for myself. But the truth is, I don't know yet. So I'm going to give it some time. I'm going to have this honeymoon period. I'll go anywhere. I'll do anything. I'm free-floating. Say for a year. And then I'll decide."

"I see," said Susan, nodding.

"What the hell is that," said Casey, and gestured. "An armadillo or something?"

"A nine-banded armadillo," said Susan, surprised. "Of course. What did you think?"

"It's weird-looking," said Casey. "It's basically a freak."

"I really wouldn't say that," said Susan.

She felt annoyed.

"It's like a giant pill bug with a rat head and a long, ratty tail," went on Casey. "You know, those bugs that roll up into a ball? Or doodlebugs, some of the kids used to call them. It's like one of those, but bigger and uglier."

"If you're trying to get me to do you a favor, you shouldn't insult the collection," said Susan testily.

"Wow," said Casey. "You really like the thing."

"It's not a question of liking," said Susan, but she felt increasingly agitated. "And it's not a thing. Or it wasn't. Anyway. I'm going to the kitchen. You can come with me or not."

Casey followed, past a lone sea turtle in a case with a some fake kelp and a couple of lobsters.

"I dig the tortoise, though," she said, in a clear attempt to curry favor.

"It's not a tortoise at all. It's a green sea turtle," said Susan.

"I was just trying to get your goat," said Casey. "I do that to T. too. I know what a sea turtle is. I watch the nature shows."

"Uh-huh," said Susan.

"But he doesn't love all animals. He's mostly interested in the ones that are about to go extinct," went on Casey.

"Nice," said Susan.

"The more common they are, the less interested he is."

They were in the kitchen now, Susan opening the freezer to get a can of lemonade concentrate.

"I didn't mean to piss you off," said Casey.

"I know, because you're trying to get something out of me," said Susan. "So that would be a tactical error."

"Listen. For whatever reason, she's comfortable with you," said Casey. "She feels safe when you're around. And face it, I mean, the cousins are assholes, no question. But it's true this place is enormous. You probably wouldn't have to even see her that much at all, if you didn't want to."

Susan turned and leaned back against the counter, the thin coat of frost on the cardboard tube melting swiftly against her fingertips.

"So because I'm single and live in a big house, all of a sudden I'm in loco parentis to your senile mother-in-law. You think I have no life of my own, right? I'm some kind of convenient middle-aged caregiver?"

"Not caregiver," said Casey. "That's why we'd hire someone. More of a hostess. A rich relative offering room and board."

"Huh," said Susan. She peeled the white ring from around the lid of the tube and dropped it into the sink.

"It makes sense," said Casey. "You have to admit."

"For you it does, sure," said Susan. "Yes. It works out perfectly for you. Then there's me. If Angela decides she doesn't like the woman you hire, she's my responsibility. And I'm basically up a creek. Like with that nice girl Merced. Angela ran away from her because she didn't like her footwear. Did I tell you that already? She accused her of wearing shoes a hooker would wear. And then she showed up here in the middle of the night in a taxi that cost me like two hundred dollars. She left her wallet at home. Of course. I mean Jesus. I'm fond of T. and all, but I'm not the one who married him."

"She won't show up in the middle of the night, though, because she'll already be here."

Susan turned. She was holding up the tube, letting clumps of concentrate drop into the pitcher.

"I think you're missing my point there, Case."

Casey just gazed up at her, large-eyed.

"Fucking fine, then," said Susan finally. "God *damn* it."

Casey crowed with delight and threw her arms around Susan's waist.

•

After Casey left she went out to the backyard and through the trees. The jackhammer guy had left a gray moon of dust on the trampled grass around the manhole cover. She knelt beside the lid, traces of cement still adhering to the grooves, and studied it: no words, only a diamond pattern that reminded her obscurely of pineapples and beehives. Couldn't she just lift it up? But there was no handhold, no opening.

"Backhoe," she said to herself.

Certainly it was a fool's errand. Still, she would make some calls to the city.

Jim rented a U-Haul and drove his few possessions from the house he had shared with his wife in Palos Verdes, which Susan had never seen, to a small dove-gray bungalow in Silver Lake.

She went over the morning he moved in, carrying tall cups of coffee for both of them, and stood on the covered front porch with its square stucco columns. She liked the view out the uncovered wing of the porch, down to the bottom of the hill where the narrow street of cottage-like houses, about as quaint as you got in L.A., gave way to a dirty wide street of businesses and fast traffic. Rows of palms like truffula trees, with blowzy tops and spindly, bending trunks, stood out against the sky.

She liked the house, which was a finer, older version of the one she and Hal had lived in back in Santa Monica. It had more style but some of the same elements: the burnished-looking hardwood floors, the well-carved mantel over the fireplace, dark beams on the ceilings that crossed each other to make rectangle patterns against the white. She was impressed by the spareness of the rooms that contained Jim's pared-down life, the neat stacks of folded shirts, the three small cases of law books.

•

That afternoon the new caregiver took up residence in the big house to prepare for Angela's arrival the next day—a stout woman in her early sixties with dyed black hair and lipstick the color of traffic cones. It strayed over the edges of her lips.

Casey had decided to hire an older woman, essentially an imitation of Vera since her mother-in-law's brief track record with young women was poor. In fact she had chosen another Eastern European lady, this one hailing not from the former Yugoslavia but from some obscure yet quite large district of the Russian Federation, one that sounded like a mouthful of half-chewed nuts. Her name was Oksana and she brought with her a tall bamboo cage, two zebra finches inside.

Angela would sleep in the bird room, which Susan regretted since it would no longer be free for Jim and her. But it was the only room on the ground floor that was set up with a bed and its own bath; Casey had said that Angela got up at night, not sleepwalking but wandering around bleary and half-asleep without the capacity to notice her surroundings. She thought the second floor would be dangerous. Oksana needed a location nearby but the best Susan could do was the drawing room full of raccoons and minks, a few doors down.

T. brought in a daybed, which they set behind a pair of the old man's decorative screens, scenes of mallards swimming on glassy lakes with bulrushes in the foreground. Oksana hung up her cage, set up a small portable television with T.'s help, and unpacked her suitcase into the room's narrow closet.

"We don't know how long we'll be," he explained to Susan, as she surveyed the mounts.

She had to fix them in her memory. She wouldn't be able to go into the room whenever she wanted to now and she resented it, though admittedly Oksana asked for almost nothing. The Russian even lacked her own bathroom; she'd have to walk down the hall to use the toilet or take a shower. The house was large but it wasn't set up for assisted living.

Item 1: A coatimundi from Arizona needed repair; insects must have gotten to it recently because parts of the face looked mangy. Could be the larvae of carpet or fur beetles . . . and there was mold on it, she guessed, either mold or mildew; ask the repair people, install a dehumidifier if need be. Item 2: One of the minks was incorrect, she had learned from a reference book in the library. The teeth were not its own. Possibly they had belonged to a housecat. Replace. Also the eyes were bulging. The wadding inside had likely expanded: another humidity problem.

"So I've paid Oksana's wages in advance," he was saying. "Angela has an ample allowance. Let Oksana handle her food, her bills, all that, the same way Vera did. Here's hoping she's capable. I'll take a look at the debits and credits when I get back, but you shouldn't have to be involved at all. That sound OK to you?"

"Fine, sure," she murmured. She wondered if Oksana would be disturbed by the flash of canines at night, if, say, a car passed outside and illuminated the crouching raccoon. It held a half-bitten slice of lurid fuchsia watermelon, made of vinyl chloride.

Then again, she'd noticed, some people didn't notice the faces; to some, like the young architect girl, the taxidermy was nothing more than a design element, albeit a misguided one.

"Where we're going," he said, "there won't always be reliable telecommunication. Casey doesn't want you to be worried."

"I promise," she said after a minute. "This time I won't send anyone to track you down."

•

Jim was spending more nights in the big house now. While he did not seem overjoyed by the arrival of Angela and Oksana, he was not displeased either; he liked the arbitrariness of their encounters, Susan thought. He was amused by the sight of Angela wandering into the kitchen at some odd hour of late night or early morning, her hair twisted up into a peach-hued turban, matching kaftan floating out behind her as she walked and a muddy facial mask with holes around her eyes and mouth. He smiled at Susan when Angela summoned him into the bathroom to remove a stray hair from the sink. He enjoyed her sporadic remarks about the hazards of all-American dining chains like Denny's, to which she objected strenuously. It had to do with the portion size and the dominance of fried foods, apparently. Also the fact that the menus contained large photographs of each selection and were covered with plastic.

He found her humorous, Susan thought, despite the fact that her comedic value stemmed from mental decline. He was not worried about the moral dimensions of his entertainment.

Oksana also amused him. She represented an enigma.

"What's with the lipstick all over the place," he said after dinner one night, when the old women had gone to bed.

He and Susan were drinking wine in the backyard, watching helicopters cross the sky and listening to a chorus of far-off sirens. Jim liked the sound.

"Does she do it on purpose? It makes her look even crazier than the other one."

"I think it was the fashion once," said Susan. "To kind of draw on the contours of your upper lip. To make it look like you had, you know, these Cupid's-bow lips."

"Cupid's bow?"

"With two, kind of, bumps on top? Like Lucille Ball or someone."

"She wants to look like Lucille Ball? She looks like a bag lady. Seriously. With the dyed black hair that gets gray at the roots and the day-glo lips. We have a bag lady living with us. Are you sure she's a nurse?"

"She's not exactly a nurse. I don't really know what she is."

She dropped one of her shoes on the ground and trailed her bare toes in the pond water. She wondered if the fish would come nibble at them.

"Nothing wrong with a bag lady. It's not a criticism, per se," said Jim. "I'm just saying."

"Yeah, don't ask me," said Susan vaguely. She was feeling the water, soft and cool as her foot swept through it. "All I care about is that Angela likes her."

"So far," said Jim. "Don't get too comfortable."

•

The dog came last. Casey and T. dropped her off the day before they left. They were booked on a series of flights to get to Borneo—through Hong Kong, Taipei, and Jakarta.

"I still don't get what you're going across the globe to do," said Susan to Casey, standing talking to her through the window of the parked car while T. took the dog inside.

"His deal is, poor people that need to make a living, and then these dying-off animals," said Casey. "He wants to make it so people don't have a good reason to do things that kill the wild-life. So what there is, over there, is some kind of jungle forestry project. Community harvest of non-timber products is what they call it. It sounds so wonky, right? He's trying to help these local guys set it up so the people can live off this one forest without cutting it or burning it down. There's animals living there that need the forest. This Sumatran rhino that's practically gone. Also orangutans and pygmy elephants. He loves those little fuckers."

"So what are *you* going to do?"

"We've got this cabin lined up," said Casey. "It's primitive. No indoor toilets. But you can send faxes from this town that isn't so far away, you just give them to the driver who comes out with food deliveries. Two times a week, they said. And sometimes we'll go into town for errands and I can call you then. So my job? I'm going to handle the paperwork, to start with."

"Huh. No toilets?" said Susan.

"Other priorities."

"But what if . . ."

"What if what," said Casey.

"Health concerns," said Susan. "The lack of pavement."

"Oh please," said Casey.

Susan saw her wheels caught in rainforest mud, her chair sinking into quicksand. It seemed wrong.

"All settled in," said T., opening his car door and sliding behind the wheel. "She's in my mother's room right now."

"T. How's Casey going to get around, in Borneo?" asked Susan. "I'm serious. She has to have her independence. What about emergencies? Seriously. The *jungle*?"

"Listen," said T. "We don't want you to worry. We bought her an all-terrain wheelchair. A power chair with these big wheels. She's been practicing on it at the beach. But more to the point, the facility where we're staying is part of a research-station complex. It has gravel paths between the buildings. A couple are even paved. It's not all dirt."

"It just doesn't seem like an appropriate setting," said Susan after a few seconds, anxious.

"Fuck appropriate," said Casey.

"I don't—"

"And fuck setting," said Casey. "I'm not a lawn ornament."

"Susan, you have my word," said T. "If mobility is a problem, we'll leave."

"Don't get all paternalistic just because we're married," said Casey. "If I want to leave I'll say so. I have the power of speech."

"Not what we meant," said Susan.

"Yeah, yeah. I know. But I think you both get me."

"OK," said Susan. "OK. I just worry."

"You don't have to," said Casey.

Susan stared down for a while and finally leaned in to kiss her on the cheek.

"Do my best, then," she said.

She watched as the black Mercedes reversed, Casey waving out the open window, and pulled away.

8

"It's not one of theirs," said Jim, when he got off the phone with the city of Pasadena.

There were old women milling around them in the kitchen, wearing pastel colors and cheerfully garish prints. One blouse had numerous teddy bears, with pink and blue bows around their necks.

Angela had invited some friends over, unbeknownst to Susan, who had believed she had none. Without prior warning the house had filled with elderly ladies from a church book club.

Angela wore a delicate crucifix and went to mass now and then, when she suddenly felt the need, but her beliefs were opaque to Susan. The other churchgoers she knew were all old and most were also female; only the old attended church these days, she'd told Susan solemnly, unless you counted the poverty-stricken, ethnic, or Deep South states where, if you believed the statistics, millions were joyously awaiting the Rapture. But these were not Catholics. Angela's church was part white and part Mexican, she said, and the whites were all old because young whites did not believe in God. Thus the book group was elderly white ladies devoted to reading Christian novels and discussing them.

There were, said Angela, some old white men in the congregation too, but if they read at all they tended to avoid fiction, which they believed was frivolous. And anyway the novels favored by the book club often had a romantic bent, even though they contained references to Jesus, Mary, Joseph, the apostles, the saints, and other popular and interesting characters in the Bible. Some were historical, telling the stories of these biblical figures, while others were just about regular people now, Angela said—regular people who were godly. Usually they were also Catholic, but not always.

Angela had recently attended a meeting of the group on impulse, her first time. She quickly volunteered Susan's house for the next meeting, then forgot she'd done so until the ladies arrived. They'd brought food with them—macaroni casseroles, triangular white-bread sandwiches, powdered diet drinks and frozen layer cakes. Curiously they had also brought stacks and stacks of paper napkins, napkins by the hundreds.

"They don't know anything about it," went on Jim, over the white, wavy head of a half-deaf woman sipping lemonade from a paper cup. "The guy said he never heard of that—a manhole in someone's backyard that wasn't authorized by the city. I got the feeling he didn't actually believe me."

"I should probably just leave it alone, shouldn't I," said Susan.

"It could be part of some ancient sewage system the city doesn't use anymore."

Jim shrugged. The white-haired lady hovered between them, not moving or seeming to register their presence; she drank her lemonade with sucking sounds and stared with watery blue eyes into the great beyond.

"I don't know," he said after a minute. "You wanted to do something with that part of the yard, was that it?"

"I want to make sure there isn't a basement," said Susan.

"A basement? It's a manhole. It's hundreds of yards from the house."

"I know."

"Listen," he said, and looked down again at the white wave hovering beneath his chin. "I really need to get going to the office. It's halfway through the day already."

"So go, so go," she said, and smiled at him as the lady drinking lemonade kept standing there, clueless.

He loved his wife, she thought as he left the kitchen, or rather his ex-wife, now; he loved her and he always would. In this house there was unrequited love and there was love of the dead. She and Jim cherished these two streams of affection, at once different and the same: they lived inside two loves that went out and did not come back to them.

●

Casey had decided to send faxes instead of letters. Airmail from Borneo took too long, she wrote, while faxes were instant.

She had them sent to the machine in T.'s office, and Susan would come in on good mornings to find their curled pages waiting for her, thin and slick, some of them always fallen or fan-blown to the floor. The pages had no numbers, typically, only long disorderly paragraphs of Casey's barely legible scrawl interspersed with *!!!* and *???* so often she had to piece them together painstakingly, the last word of one to the first word of the next, before she could begin to read.

At first the places and even the facts seemed purely fictitious.

> *From here in Long Banga to the clear-cuts in Gulung Mulu . . .*
>
> *On the way we stopped in what claims to be "Berkeley's sister city": Uma Bawang.*
>
> *Among the Penan of Upper Baram, murder, rape, and robbery are unknown. Selfishness is considered a crime.*

After a few letters she stopped grinning reflexively every time she encountered a foreign word. It wasn't funny, of course. Indeed the current events Casey described were alarming: episodes of police brutality, conflicts between the natives and the logging companies, the wholesale liquidation of primary forests, the erosion of mountaintops and massacre of wildlife. But there was also the day-to-day, and Casey included rough, childish sketches of the local fauna, as though they might be added, by proxy, to Susan's collection.

She started with a mount that hung in a tourist lodge near the research station, a civet cat, and then moved on to living subjects. There was a male proboscis monkey with a huge dangling nose like an ancient drunkard, beneath which she had written *The big nose is thought to be attractive to females*; there was a pangolin, a distant anteater relative, with the legend *Talk about freaks*. The monkey had its dangling, pear-shaped nose, then also a large potbelly and beneath that a small red penis sticking out. Susan knew the color because Casey had drawn an arrow toward the offending organ and written *red*.

Next there were drawings of people, women with earlobes stretched all the way down to their chests, heavy earrings pulling down the impossibly long holes—six inches, seven or eight. *Orang Ulu*, wrote Casey. An ancient man with boar's teeth piercing the tops of his ears: *Village elder, Bungan festival in Punan Sama*.

Casey rarely wrote about herself or her feelings except to mention a casual fact briefly: *Our shower is a bag of water with holes in it*. Or *I do miss the junk food*. And *Sucks to do laundry once a month*. Still her daughter was close there, in the unkempt script and the abrupt turns of thoughts—in some ways closer than when she was home.

Susan hoarded the faxed letters. She read them to remind herself of the realness and texture of Casey whenever she felt afraid. One foreign place was not the same as all others; Casey would not fall under a knife. She kept the pages stapled, smoothed flat, although they wanted to curl, and pressed between two big dictionaries she carried up to her bedroom from the library.

But they did not last. She was distressed to notice how quickly the ink faded.

One afternoon she got home after a half-day at the office to find Angela leading some church ladies through the second-floor rooms, pointing out both the taxidermy and the house's architectural features.

"The building has been nominated for historic status," she said proudly, as Susan hovered in the hallway.

There was a message from the estate lawyer in Century City, whom Jim had pushed to give her case more attention: a date had been set for the adjudication of the cousins' will contest. She felt her stomach sink when she heard this—did that mean the case had not been dismissed, or something, as they had hoped it would? Or could it still be dismissed?

Jim would explain when he got in, she told herself, and went outside to where the church ladies were picking their way through the back garden, gazing down into the fishponds and nodding. Angela had her arm around one of them—the white-haired one from the kitchen, hobbling unsteadily.

Worried about the will, hoping for some distraction, Susan hurried toward them, on a path to overtake. As she came up behind the last in the group—an imperious fat lady in red and gold and another, in gray, who looked timid and thin by contrast—the white-hair with Angela stumbled and emitted a gasp of fright.

"You're all right, Ellie dear," said Angela, whose arm had stopped her from falling. "You'll be fine."

"Tripped me," said the lady.

"Let's see," said Susan.

In the pebbly soil between the flagstones of the path, at the white-haired lady's feet, was a thin piece of black tubing.

"Part of the irrigation system," said Susan.

"It's unsafe," said Angela.

Susan gazed at her.

"It waters my garden," she said after a pause, irritably.

"This way, honey," murmured Angela, but she gave Susan a punitive look.

•

When Jim came over after work three of the ladies were still present, in Oksana's room off the entrance hall. It was almost six-thirty in the evening and they had never left; they sat there in armchairs and, as far as Susan could tell, said hardly anything. There was the oldest—the white-haired lady—and the slight one in gray and the large one bedecked in the colors of the Chinese emperors. They each had a copy of a Christian novel nearby; this one featured a handsome angel who flew down to earth to help a single mother with a crippled child, then fell in love with her. A couple of them even had drinks beside them. The conversation appeared to be moving with exceeding slowness.

When Susan and Jim came to stand in the doorway Angela was telling the plot of the novel. The other ladies ignored them.

"The angel starts out too proud, you see," said Angela, and turned to Susan. "You see, the angels that come down to help people are often the proud ones. God gives them penance. Having to come down from heaven is a punishment for them."

In a corner, Oksana painted her fingernails fire-engine red and watched her small television. On the news, someone was dead.

"I mean it, they're not moving," whispered Susan to Jim, as they veered away from Oksana's door and down the hall to the bar area where they liked to drink their dinnertime cocktails. "They've been here since like ten a.m. It's like they've been installed. Like furniture."

"But you can't sit on them," said Jim.

She poured him some scotch.

"The lawyer left a message for me," she told him. "He said they set a court date. Is that bad?"

"It's neutral. Look, wills get contested all the time. But will contests are hardly ever won by the people who bring the objection. Keep that in mind."

"I was hoping maybe it wouldn't even make it to court, though," she said.

"I'll go with you. Don't think about it."

•

As the evening wore on she and Jim grew fixated on the question of when the old ladies would leave. When ten, then eleven o'clock rolled around both of them were making trips down the hall so that they could walk past Oksana's open door and see whether the ladies were still there. Then Jim would return or Susan would return to him, shaking their heads in disbelief. Susan was aware of acting vulture-like. The truth was it shouldn't matter to her— the ladies were quiet and infringed upon no one but Oksana—but she was intrigued by the unlikeliness of the ladies' presence, of their remaining in the room as though they were frozen there, as though they were inevitable.

Finally it was eleven and Susan hovered in Oksana's doorway like a parent executing a curfew.

"Let me run something up the flag," she said. "Maybe Jim or

I could drive you ladies home tonight? Because night driving can be dangerous—"

"Oh no, dear," said Angela. "No no *no*. We're having a slumber party!"

The faces turned to her then, all three of the visitors staring. Oksana continued to ignore them and ignored Susan too, eyes fixed on a late-night talk show on the television. Susan noticed she had put on a nightgown.

"A slumber . . ."

"Oh yes. We're sleeping in my room."

Was Angela lucid?

"Oh," said Susan uncertainly. "Ladies? Is that . . ."

They seemed to be nodding, though it was almost imperceptible in the dimness of the room. It struck her as absurd—either a comedy of errors or a group mania of some kind. They had to be in their late seventies and eighties; they must need comfortable beds, she thought, need their routine, their home environments; they must all have some complaint, minor or not, arthritis, bursitis, porous and brittle bones. There was no way they could intend to sleep in Angela's bed, no way they could have made that plan on their own. Had Angela misled them about the facilities? Had they been fed? Was she even taking care of them?

"If you're staying, please use the bedrooms on the second floor," Susan said finally. "OK? There are plenty of beds up there. Most have their own bathrooms, though some share. Jim will be happy to help you up the stairs, if any of you needs a hand. Because frankly I can't imagine you'll all be comfortable in Angela's room. There's only the one bed in there! You realize that, don't you?"

"Upstairs will be quite suitable," said Angela, with a certain smugness.

"But then the staircase is hazardous too, or at least it could be," objected Susan, recalling the white-haired lady—Ellen, she guessed—tripping on the small piece of black tubing.

"Young lady," said the portly dowager in red, turning in her armchair with sudden severity, "you know, we may be getting on, but we're certainly not deceased yet."

"Oh no, I didn't—" started Susan, but Jim interrupted from behind her.

"Oksana," said Jim, "why don't you come and get me when these ladies want to go upstairs. Or, of course, when you'd like to go to bed yourself. I'll be glad to accompany them." He looked at the imperious one. "No offense intended, madam. I'm a lawyer by trade. I'm thinking purely of our liability here as homeowners. Or call it responsibility. A broken hip could be costly."

With the ladies staring at him Susan withdrew and he followed.

"I can't believe you said that," she whispered.

"Angela's taking advantage of you," he said. "She should have asked first. It's bullshit."

"I mean, she does have dementia," said Susan.

"She's also manipulative."

•

It was almost midnight when Oksana came to get them, with tired eyes and traces of cold cream on her cheeks. Jim went to escort the women upstairs while Susan got towels out of the linen closet and sorted them into groups, a bath towel, hand towel and washcloth for each lady, and then carried them up the narrow back stairs formerly used by servants.

She went to the rooms and laid the towels out—a small pile each on the twin beds of the Arctic and another on the queen bed in the Himalayas—before meeting the guests in the upstairs hallway, where they stood with Jim under the dome. After they had shown them to the rooms, walking back to their own, she stopped Jim with a hand on his arm.

"I murdered Hal," she said. "I killed him. You should know that about me."

In the morning she went into the bright kitchen happy because Jim had been kind to her, Jim understood that she had killed and though maybe *forgive* wasn't the word, he saw and didn't give up on her. She came down in a good mood and found them seated around the table, four ladies in nightdresses with gleaming fish overhead, eating toast with marmalade and listening to some kind of quaint homily about daily life: National Public Radio. Angela had made breakfast for them, even brewed them a carafe of her weak, stale coffee from a can, which she preferred to Susan's gourmet beans.

Angela was animated, rising to get them fresh toast as it popped up in the toaster, and Susan saw she had been changed by their presence: the older ones made her energetic, gave her a central role, bustling around. But surely she couldn't sustain it, Susan thought, she'd have to absent herself again or even perform a broadly insane act, such as stripping naked or locking herself in a room. Then the ladies would quietly take their leave.

Jim had gone off to the office so it was only Susan and the ladies; her kitchen felt crowded. She spooned up some yogurt, drank a half-cup of the weak coffee and then went outside and crossed quickly to the shed in the backyard, where she chose a shovel from the dirt-encrusted fleet of them propped up against a shelf. Backhoe, she thought, wasn't that overkill anyway? She could find out what was beneath the manhole without the help of large earth-moving machines. Of course she could.

On the shelf beside the shovels she found an old, dusty gray pair of gloves, shook them in case there were spiders or splinters in the finger holes and then pulled them on. Last time she'd tried to wield a shovel she'd rubbed blisters on her palms and torn them open. A kind of water had flowed out when they ripped: was that pus? But it had been light—transparent, inoffensive.

We know so little of our molecules, she thought, the molecules we are . . . so little about them. A proof they're in control: they guide our hands, they make us grow, they form our children inside our bodies—miracles come from them, all that has ever been, all that will be. Meanwhile our conscious selves perform their rudimentary acts, those simple sums. What shall I be, whom shall I love: those are the easy parts, behaviors that we call ourselves, they're only icing, floral borders, all that we think we are is trivial while what we really are is not even known to us. If there is a machine, a ghost in the machine—they always said the machine was the body, didn't they? Philosophers?—but no! The body's both of them, machine *and* ghost. The body's not only the vessel but also its spirit, the body is visible but its animators impossible to see. Materialism, she thought, sure—she might be a proponent. But she didn't like the flatness of answers, the stolid and dull arithmetic of being, not at all! Rather the glory of the unseen. She believed in the ineffable, great mystery, great creation, only that it was lodged in molecules, in molecules, beyond the human ability to see.

The final authority of the microscopic.

She carried the shovel into the back, through the trees, stuck its blade into the ground a few inches from the manhole and then stood on it with one foot. She hopped awkwardly to sink it further, then dismounted, scooped and flung. And again. It was hard, boring work and soon she was dizzy and distracted. As the minutes passed she felt blisters starting on her hands again despite the gloves, felt dirt down the backs of her sneakers and in between her toes, and just as she was thinking how tedious it was the spade hit underground metal.

"Well of course," said someone, and she looked up to see the elderly dominatrix, now clad not in the red and gold ensemble of yesteryear or her ruffled nightgown from the breakfast hour but in a voluminous dress of deep and vibrant purple. Around her neck hung a crescent-moon pendant in silver, vaguely redolent of Wicca or perhaps the New Age.

Were there obese Wiccans?

"Of course what?" asked Susan, out of breath.

"You've hit the shaft."

"I didn't know there'd be one," said Susan. She stood resting, catching her breath. What a stupid idea, digging. Of course some Wiccans were obese. Sure—even morbidly so. No different from other Americans, most likely. One of Casey's best friends in high school had been Wiccan. She worshiped the moon goddess, the feminine principle, and told Casey not to use tampons. She advised Casey only to use sea sponges when she had her period. The use of tampons was a denial of the sacred nature of womanhood. The tampons were the patriarchy. Sponges by contrast came from the ocean, which some viewed as feminine. And also by contrast with the tampons, manufactured by companies that men owned and designed to men's specifications, the sponges were not shaped like penises or missiles.

But with sponges you had to wash the blood off in the sink.

Susan had run interference. She spoke of practical benefits. After the accident Casey lost touch with the Wiccan friend, who went to college and presently joined the Young Republicans.

Susan squinted at the purple-clad woman and tried to imagine her dancing at midnight before an altar to the horned god.

"You think it goes deep?" she asked.

"Too deep to tackle with that thing. Don't make me laugh. It's probably solid iron. You could be talking twenty feet deep."

"I'm sorry," said Susan. They'd never been properly introduced. "I'm not sure I even know your name! I'm Susan, Susan Lindley."

She stepped forward and stuck out a gloved hand, which the large woman took and pressed lightly. She wasn't without grace, Susan thought. Around her own mother's age, if her mother were still alive—older than Angela by almost a generation but clearly far more coherent.

"Portia," she said.

"Porsche?"

"No, not the sportscar," said the woman haughtily. "The moon of Uranus, for instance, discovered by *Voyager 2*. I myself predate the *Voyager*s by several decades, needless to say. I was, like the moon, named after the heroine of *The Merchant of Venice*, if you knew your Shakespeare. All of the Uranus moons are named after characters in Shakespeare. And Pope, of course."

"I don't know my Shakespeare *or* my planetary trivia," said Susan. "How many Uranus moons *are* there?"

"Perhaps you recognize this line: 'The quality of mercy is not strain'd. It droppeth as the gentle rain from heaven, upon the place beneath.' Sound familiar?"

"It does. The gentle rain part. Definitely."

"That line's Portia's."

"I'm glad to meet you, Portia."

"About the moon," went on Portia, lifting the too-large necklace off her chest, "little is known."

"I see."

"And to answer your question: there are twenty-seven."

"Many moons."

They were gazing at each other. Susan realized she tended to like the woman, found a kind of reassurance in the woman's pompous presence.

"Any*hoo*," said Portia. "What you need here is simple: a backhoe."

"I'm not sure I know where to get one," said Susan. "I did find a guy with a jackhammer. But a backhoe, that's a whole other level."

Hal had ridiculed people who used that turn of phrase. *A whole other level. A whole 'nother level.* Both, according to Hal, were not only annoying but also ignorant. His least favorite common phrase had been *Can I help who's next?* But Susan had stubbornly used the language he looked down upon. She saw his point, certainly, but she couldn't get behind the snobbery.

Like Hal, this woman seemed the type to value correct speech.

"Child's play," said the woman. "Leave it to the Yellow Pages and to me. If money is no object?"

"Well, it *is* an *object*," said Susan, as they started back to the house. She carried the shovel parallel to the ground, trailing clods of earth as they went.

The day of the court date Casey called. It was hard to hear her—a delay in the connection so that their voices often crossed. Susan talked over Casey without meaning to and only heard half of what she was saying.

She was hazy on time zones, but it was so many hours different there that it was almost the same time—was it across the international dateline? She did not know. She strained to hear over a kind of swishing windy sound—the sound of space, she wanted to believe, the sound of the stratosphere, of falling interstellar dust . . . though it was probably none of these, it was probably the sound of wires and circuits, metal and fiberglass. Casey was talking about bamboo—something about the properties of bamboo. Bamboo was good, was the gist of what she was saying. She mentioned the Dayak, who were apparently a tribal people. It rhymed with *kayak*.

Susan pictured them in loincloths, although she had no evidence for this. They would look better in loincloths than she did, that much was certain. Smiling, wearing loincloths, the whole ear thing, and now also carrying bamboo. Possibly in spear form, sharpened at one end, or then, in a more modern context, as strips of light-colored flooring. Bamboo floor coverings were increasingly popular.

Searching for something to prove her own attentiveness, though she could still only half hear, she asked after the other tribal people Casey had written about.

"But how are your friends, the Penan and the Punan Bah?" she asked loudly, enunciating as best she could, though as usual the names made her want to laugh wildly. No offense to the Penan or Punan Bah, she thought, none meant at all, it was the phonetics.

". . . *are* the Dayak, Mother," came Casey's voice.

•

Jim was supposed to meet her outside the court building so she was driving there in her own car. She was nervous, dressed neatly in conservative clothes with pearl earrings and flat, unglamorous heels, and she listened to the radio as she drove—she had always been irritated by NPR, all her adult life, and yet all her adult life she had listened to it faithfully.

One exit's worth of freeway driving was all it would be: first surface streets, then a mile on the freeway, then surface streets again. And yet as soon as she merged onto the 110—on NPR a well-known interviewer, Terry Gross, was earnestly complimenting a rap musician on his genius—she knew she would never make it. The traffic was stopped, bumper-to-bumper, as far as she could see, though in the opposite direction it was moving freely. Technically it was spring, but the smog was more like summer smog, heat rippling in the dirty air, and a torpor had descended over the long lines of cars. Up ahead people had gotten out of their vehicles and were walking back and forth, some standing aside by themselves and smoking cigarettes, others in groups, talking and gesticulating. It had to be an accident.

She wished she had a cigarette, but then she never bought them herself, only bummed them off Jim. She thought of getting out of her car, like the others, and asking one of the other smokers for one, but then that seemed too disgusting. Anyway she had never liked to get out of her car on the freeway, even when the traffic was bumper-to-bumper and at a dead halt. The concrete had a gray desolation and the air was unbreathable, and she knew a cigarette would seem even viler as soon as she stepped from the car. She waited fifteen minutes with the windows up, cooled by the air-conditioning, glancing frequently at the digital clock on her dashboard, jiggling her foot and occasionally swearing as the minutes ticked away and the hour of the hearing approached. When it was six minutes before the hour she became irritated with Terry Gross, whose earnest tone, it seemed to her, had grown more and more sycophantic. More and more, the intimacy of this trademark Terry Gross tone, as she spoke to the rap star and flattered him several additional times with her eager references to his *brilliance* and *creativity*, seemed to suggest that she, Terry Gross, was a longtime proponent and appreciator of rap music and even quite possibly a credentialed expert on the rap-music subject.

The longer Susan listened, becoming increasingly frustrated and impatient, the more it seemed that the impression being conveyed was that she, the white, middle-aged female Terry Gross—unlike she, the white, middle-aged female Susan—was a proud, savvy collective owner of what she lavishly called the *rap-music phenomenon.* Susan felt resentful of this pandering self-inclusion, of this proprietary, rap-music-savvy, rap-music-loving Terry Gross.

At four minutes till her court date she switched off the radio in a fit of pique and rolled down the windows all the way. Let the heat flow in, she thought, let it boil. The fumes from the idling cars almost choked her but stubbornly she refused to roll up her windows again. Not yet, she thought, not yet. In her annoyance and frustration, her incipient rage, she associated the rolled-up windows and air-conditioning directly with Terry Gross: if she closed the windows again and switched the AC back on it would be necessary to turn the radio back on too, and it would have to be NPR because the commercial stations were all men or products screaming at you, which was even more hateful in this situation of car entrapment than the quiet, earnest, middle-class, educated, and maddeningly empathetic tone of Terry Gross, and so the rolled-up windows meant letting Terry Gross and her sycophantic rap-music interview win.

Three minutes. Two minutes. One. Still no movement. She

wished she had a car phone, like T. or probably the rap guy. He certainly had a car phone; most likely he was using said car phone to converse with Terry Gross. Then it was fifteen minutes past, then eighteen, and the tension drained out of her because she had to give up. She had missed it. There was no reason for her to be sitting here anymore, no reason save the obvious fact that she was trapped.

A bearded man in a baseball cap walked by her car and she rolled the window down briefly to ask him if he knew anything. He told her there was a multicar pileup where the 110 merged with the 5. Cars had crashed and people were hurt, he said. "So count your blessings, lady."

She watched him in the rearview mirror as he continued down the line of cars, slouching, moving so slowly it seemed he felt no urgency at all. He walked like a defeated or dazed person, yet he had spoken sharply. Maybe he had seen something, maybe he was grieving.

When Casey had her accident there were courageous bystanders who went in to help the trapped and wounded victims. One or two of them talked to Hal and Susan later, in the hospital—told how the accident had changed their lives, too, though they had not been physically injured. Some of them never recovered fully, but wrote to Casey and told her how they had cried themselves to sleep at night for months after they came upon the scene.

And they had not been hurt at all.

After the man disappeared from her rearview mirror she surrendered to Terry Gross, surrendered completely. She closed her eyes and listened to the empathetic Terry Gross tone and to the rap-loving earnestness as it flowed over her. *I love rap music too,* she thought, making a generous gesture. She would reach out to Terry Gross, the rap guy and their mutual passion, thus elevating her own mood. I also find it creative and brilliant, she said in her mind to Terry Gross and the rap guy. It is brilliantly creative, it is creatively brilliant. Not only that, but *all* of it is brilliant, not just the white-friendly, woman-friendly versions favored by college students but also the gangsta version, the version with bitches, hos and gats, the completely misogynistic, racist, homophobic and violent, even nihilistically brutal version.

I love it, love it, love it. Mmm-hmm. I love it and I love all self-expressions, ironic and otherwise, all of them under the sun. I love pornography, gangsta rap, war video games, all fantasies of violence. These fantasies preoccupy the insane men and keep them from their actual work of angrily murdering. Let us not condemn these proliferating, vibrant simulations, these models of brutality. No, let us praise them as though they were condoms. Maybe that explained Terry Gross and her rap appreciation. Maybe the gangsta rap was viewed, by Terry Gross, less as an incitement to gangsta-type acting out than as an artistic, prophylactic screen against it. Maybe the rap Terry Gross and the Planned Parenthood Terry Gross were actually one and the same.

I am a nice person, Susan thought steadily. No one will take my house from me. She was a murderer, sure, like the angry men who did not listen to enough rap music—perhaps this was her own problem also, perhaps she needed a larger dose of rap—but not of the angry variety; she was a polite murderer, the white kind, white-skinned and white-collar. Although, come to think of it, she *had* liked an Ice Cube song Sal forced them all to listen to after the dinner at Casey's apartment, the night before Hal flew off. Hal had been sleeping then, passed out, and Sal played for them an album titled *Death Certificate*.

In fact the song had been hilarious. Her favorite part was a line concerning oral sex, where the slutty daughter ate nuts voraciously, not unlike, said Ice Cube, hummingbirds. It could be ascribed to poetic license, she thought, but let's face it: Ice Cube lacked a solid education on the subject of bird diets. He was funny anyway, whether because of the curious nut-eating hummingbirds, undiscovered in the annals of nature, or despite them. It was hard to say. The natural history of hummingbirds was not the point. The point was that they rhymed with *cummingbird*.

Too late. The probate court judge would either rule without her or not; it was out of her hands now. It always had been, of course. But still she should have left the house earlier, prepared for something like this . . . up ahead they might be carting a dead person away. Oh, poor, dead people. No more rap music for you. No more of Terry Gross either.

Hal had liked Terry Gross, but had not liked, as far as she knew, rap music, except for the kind sometimes referred to as *old-school*, from the seventies or maybe the early eighties, say "White Lines" or "The Message" by Grandmaster Flash. He had liked those very much when they first came out and he and Susan were younger, but the nineties brand of rap he'd had less patience with. He might have been surprised at this new Terry Gross version, this new rap-music-loving Terry Gross.

No ambulances had passed her on the shoulder, she realized—where were they all, the sirens and the lights? Maybe they'd passed this way before she came onto the entrance ramp herself . . . the man had seemed sure of what he said, sure it was a pileup. She opened the door and got out, stood beside her car and squinted ahead, searching for even the faintest sign of movement. But there was a gradual curve in the road and she couldn't see past it.

You didn't know what was happening out of view; you never did. You lived your life in a small part of the world, with only the faintest inkling of what was everywhere else.

9

To celebrate she thought she would sleep in. She would lie in bed and yawn and not get up for a long time. She had won, she had won, she had won.

When Jim called and told her she was gleeful; then she felt sheepish and somehow frustrated in the effusive moment of rejoicing by herself. Tonight they'd go out, eat at a restaurant for once—maybe have sushi or Korean barbecue, something they didn't get at home. And then they could stay up late and drive up into the Hollywood Hills and look down at the great sea of lights. She'd always liked it up there, the strange, huge agave plants with their ten-foot-high stalks that grew along the ridgelines and far beneath the millions of stars that signaled homes, rolling in waves all the way out to the Pacific.

Later, when they got home in the small hours, they could

sleep as long as they wanted to, sleep till the sun rose high enough to fall across her face and she woke up and cast off the too-heavy covers. Then she would feel the light and warmth and think of the long gardens of the mad, dead kings of France.

It was a thought of luxury but the luxury wasn't what made her happy. The luxury was an afterthought—embarrassing, ridiculous, and also now familiar. No, it was the safety of what could never be replaced, the house and the collection. It was the fact that the law said, now—on behalf of the house and the animals and the gardens and even on her behalf—the law expressly stated: No one could plunder them.

Then the doorbell rang and as she hurried down the wide hall to answer it she passed the church ladies, who were sitting in the rec room and playing cards—gin rummy was the usual. The oldest lady, the white-haired trembler named Ellen Humboldt, seemed always to be here these days. She stayed over three nights a week, whenever her son went out of town for work and couldn't be on call—stayed in Susan's house as an alternative to a rest home, apparently. The son was a commercial pilot. Angela seemed to have formed an instant attachment to Ellen, and Ellen to her. They walked everywhere together with a painstaking slowness, calling each other "Ellie" and "Angie" and holding each other fast by the arm.

"Susan!" called Angela from the card table. "We need to talk about elevators."

She shook her head in disbelief; yet she was almost giddy enough to say yes. Hell, they should just put beds in the music room or something, make more bedrooms on the ground floor for the benefit of the old people. She'd seen four of them at the rummy table, Angela, Ellen, Portia—as always, regal and in command—and the slight woman in gray like a shade, trying not to be noticed. Susan was always forgetting the gray woman's name but never forgot the name of her little dog: Macho. The elderly terrier came with her every time and so it was in the house at least three days a week, a curly black thing with bad breath and red bows on its head. It attended the Christian book club meetings, held on Thursdays, and liked to lie in the inside scoop of the three-legged dog's body—the three-legged dog, which was far younger than the old, small one, curled around it protectively.

There were two sweaty-looking men outside the front door, and behind them, through the closed gate, a yellow machine. The pedestrian gate had been left open, she saw.

"Here about the digging," said one of them. "Backhoe. A Mrs. Friedrich."

"Friedrich?" she asked, blankly.

"Portia Friedrich," said Portia, at her elbow. "I am she. The challenge will be getting it in without tearing up the vegetation. I ordered the smallest unit possible, of course, but still: that's going to be difficult."

Susan hung back as one of the men drove his backhoe in the gate, up the driveway, and through the garden, weaving slowly between trees and fishponds. Portia walked backward in front of him directing his steering; she wore a flowing robe with wide-open sleeves that made her look like a pudgy Merlin. When Susan tried to step in she was waved back impatiently, till finally the backhoe stopped, wedged between a rhododendron bush and a weeping willow.

"Great," said Susan, shaking her head. "Great."

"This was the only way," said Portia sharply. "Over there you hit the pond with the little cherrywood Japanese bridge. There's a steep grade on the other side, and the third option is over your lovely bed of angel's-trumpet. I'm sure you don't want that."

"My what?"

"Angel's-trumpet. The white flowers?"

Susan looked at them—large, drooping conical blooms, languid on their thick tussock of leaves.

"All things considered, I suggest you sacrifice this."

They watched the backhoe rip out half the sprawling rhododendron, dragging a tangle of severed branches behind it. By the time it had reached the area of the manhole it had left a swath of destruction in its wake—torn-up limbs and grasses, red-brown earth exposed beneath the stripped-up turf. She felt a stab of guilt and worry for the plants, for the disturbed symmetry.

All for a poorly placed manhole, which, for all she knew, covered nothing but an ancient septic tank—she was deluding herself. The aging women, their absent-mindedness and dementia: by osmosis she was becoming more and more like them. Or maybe, in her own aging, here at the tail end of her forties, she had drawn these women to her. But more likely they had drawn her to them via some kind of post-menopausal force. When young women lived together, after all, or even stayed for a time in the same area, their periods grew to coincide—the pull of pheromones, legend had it. Possibly this was like that, minus fertility. The other end of the life cycle: contagious senility. Because she was less rational with each day that passed, less grounded. Wasn't she? More closely tied to the place, but less closely tied to herself . . . she felt a quick, deep regret.

Once she had been pragmatic: once, when she was a younger person, she'd passed for normal on a daily basis. She'd been a teacher after all, first grade, second grade. She had personally been a trusted guide for children, had led them up to the new and tried to help them decipher it. She had felt the newness herself now and then—felt for an instant, as she showed them a simple picture of an apple, that she herself had never seen an apple before—never in two dimensions, never so flat. And so perfect.

In that instant she had a glimpse over the wall of a garden.

And society had let her do this, had even thanked her for it. Society had deemed her fully responsible, a shepherd of the dear flock. There had been small teaching awards; there had been offers of dull administrative positions as a reward for her years of service. The children had often loved her, the parents had smiled and thanked her profusely and the mothers brought her generic female gifts, soap or scented candles. Now—much of the time alone, far, far away from those glowing children—she roamed a big, dim mansion whose walls were lined with dead animals, herself growing old, surrounded by dust and fur, by remnants of fierceness, remnants of wildness, remnants of what had once been the world.

The old women weren't dying quite yet but they were feeble and growing paler all the time, pale speech, pale minds, pale hair, pale skin. As the youth fell away they also shed the pigment, they shed every last vestige of youthful color . . . maybe that was why old women often wore clothes in garish hues. She forgot what the theories were about aging—cells failing to divide, cells dividing too fast. But however the molecules were getting it done, the women themselves were fading, lost to entropy and washing out.

They went gray, grayer, white, toward the day in the future when they attained translucence. And so the reds, the violets, the pinks and emerald greens they wore were a desperate grab at pigment again, a simulation of life.

She was filled with longing. She knew what it was. She recognized it instantly. She wanted the small children back.

Yes, it was sentimental—it was pathetic, this yearning. But they were good; they were, almost always, so good. She missed their perfect skin—their beauty, the swiftly given trust. She wanted to see them again. She wanted them all around her. How had she ever let them go? Children! Come back. Come back now, dears, you dear beings. When I left, you know, I was only joking—a foolish joke, wasn't it. I wouldn't leave you. I'm here again.

When had this happened? Not with Hal's death. Not with his death—long before that. It happened with the accident. She had turned from the children because of a terrible certainty, a certainty of what was coming.

"Are you all right, Susan?"

She realized the backhoe driver was staring. He wore a tie-dyed T-shirt with large underarm stains.

"Why don't we let the gentleman begin his excavation," went on Portia. "I'd like to go inside for a few minutes and check up on the ladies." She tapped Susan's arm and they turned back toward the pool and the tennis court. Tie-dye, Susan thought, was limited in its appeal to those who were dropping acid. No one in a sober frame of mind could possibly find it pleasing to the eye—though possibly the old women admired it for its garishness.

"Go inside," she echoed, and nodded.

"You know: Ellen has to take her hypertension pills. I don't like to leave it to Angela. Angela doesn't run on a schedule and so she tends to forget."

Portia must only be here to manage the others, Susan realized as they picked their way along the flagstones—or to ensure, rather, that Angela did not mismanage them . . . she must see that as her duty, watching over the frailer ones.

Herself, she was seeing how all those years had been, falling behind her in ripples, fading. In a rush she heard what Hal had said to her on the telephone from Belize. He was sorry for forgetting her, he said, so taken up with Casey, and he regretted that, regretted leaving her alone. It was true that she had often been alone, but not always; and she had left him too, obviously, for the theater of other men and the straining distraction of vanity. But that wasn't what gripped her now, that wasn't a new recognition. She had left the children also, when she turned from teaching to the coldness and orderliness of what she did now, the procedural neutrality of office work. She had decided to be anonymous in her public life and flagrant in privacy—anonymous except to the few people she selected. She chose the sly exhibitionism of her new slut vocation and turned away from the openness that she used to have, once, with children.

Not their openness but her own. That was what was missing.

She had left them behind because she was a coward. It was clear. Only a fool could have missed it.

She had missed it herself and so she must be a fool—or if not a fool, then a person without self-awareness, though she'd always flattered herself otherwise. But there it was: she had looked at her little first graders and seen Casey and seen, after childhood, everything else that would happen to them. Everything that could, and would, and never—not even at the furthest limit of possibility—the single thing that should, that they should remain this way forever, the way of being children, the way of eagerness, sweetness and hope. The hope she used to have for them, the warm hope you had to have for each child once you had a child yourself, was lifted like a thin veil and replaced with cold certainty: they would feel pain and die, some of them before they even found out who they were. Others would soldier on and meet defeat in everything they did, the joy of that first thrill of life falling away, disintegrating. She saw them in their futures, pitted and bowed down.

This was what Hal had known, how she had been captured by dread. He hadn't known the other part, how she pursued a certain state of being known—sex as a form of fame, wanting to be instilled in other people's memories. She'd wanted to make herself stay with them, an image in a great hall of figures. She'd thought she would live more that way. But Hal had known she was running, in the end he'd seen: in the fell swoop of the accident she'd been gripped with a fear of children, of them and for them. The sadness of the future had dazzled her. She turned her face away.

But at least they could have the present, its heat and light. Weightlessness! The lightness of now, the infinity. The children had no past, so all they had was in front of them. Not far in front but right in front, now. You could get a glimpse of it yourself—what it was to be unencumbered. She wanted to be there with them.

Then she would have the past in her house and the present in her work—she could dispense with the future, she could stop wishing for what she'd never have.

•

For some minutes she rested with the old women around her, while outside in the backyard the backhoe ground and creaked and, in reverse, emitted a harsh warning beep that went on and on and penetrated the eardrums. She sat a few feet from their card table on a couch, in a daze until Angela came over and arranged herself on the cushions nearby. It was Oksana's day off and Susan had said they could do without a sub, knowing the ladies would be there. Now they'd taken Ellen Humboldt aside and were holding a glass of water at the ready, prying her assortment of pills out of a long white-plastic tray whose compartments were marked with the beginning letters of the days of the week.

"There are small elevators that are quite affordable," started Angela. "You can order the whole thing, they put it together at the factory. I saw it in a brochure. Or they also have the kind that lift wheelchairs. They put them right on the rail of the staircase."

"We don't need an elevator," said Susan distractedly.

"Well, you see," said Angela, "I'd like Ellie to live with me. And she really wants to. You know, her son has a new girlfriend. Most nights she's all alone."

Susan turned and looked into her face. Angela was smiling uncertainly, as though she knew the request was outlandish.

"But Angela," said Susan gently, "you're not even living here permanently yourself."

"My son could pay for it. He's very generous. And Casey could use it too, when she visits."

"You do understand," said Susan again, "you're staying here with me just until they get back from Malaysia. Right?"

Angela gazed at her, wounded. Her eyes shone.

"As far as I know, that is," went on Susan, to soften the impression.

"I like it so much here," said Angela.

"Thank you," and Susan put her hand out to pat the woman's arm. "But I'm not quite ready to discuss major renovations. Ellie looks to me like she may need real care. More than we can give her. With nurses and doctors. You know, medical help on standby in case of emergencies. Don't you think?"

"She doesn't *want* that," said Angela. "She doesn't want that at all."

"I'll tell you what. Why don't we move you down the hall for now. OK? We can put you both in the same room, together. We'll set up some screens up around your beds, however you want them. The music room, maybe. Then she won't have to navigate the stairs and you can look after her."

And Oksana would look after both of them.

"The music room," mused Angela. "Does it have lamps? We like to read our books in the evening. We eat cookies and drink tea and I read to her before we go to sleep. Because she can only read the large print."

"It's a pretty spacious room," said Susan. "And you'd have that whole wing of the house to yourself at night."

"Can we have tents to sleep in?"

"Tents?"

"Pink tents make a nice light inside them. We could have lamps under there. And cushions. It's the Arabian Nights," said Angela.

They were girls in a fairy tale—children again, listening to stories. That was how Angela saw herself with Ellen. The novels about angels coming down to earth were only the beginning. Together, as they faded out, they could step onto those sweeping dunes, they could look up at white palaces and minarets, flying carpets, clouds that bore horses with wings. They would move among the genies and camels and the thieves, the women in veils, reflecting pools and curtains of brocade.

Storytime: to sit and listen and let the years pass. How many years had it been? Five was the school district's limit, she thought she remembered. It had been longer than that now. But before she could teach again she would have to call the teaching commission, renew her credentials, maybe work for a while at a small private school.

"Ladies? I'm going to drive Ellen up to the drugstore to refill her Adalat prescription," said Portia.

"Wait, wait. Will you come back tonight, Ellie?" asked Angela eagerly, and rose from beside Susan.

Susan watched as they walked the oldest one slowly down the hall to the door—all five of them, long skirts swaying gently. The dog called Macho trotted at their heels.

Then she composed a letter to send to Casey and to T. She was resigning from working for him, now that they were family, now that his business had changed, now that he had become a foreign traveler and a philanthropist. She was happy for both of them, she wrote, she loved what they were doing. Or the idea of it, because truthfully, she wrote, she didn't really understand what it was they were doing, she failed to understand the venture's actual content. The "non-timber forest products," the "sustainable community-based harvest models," frankly it was pretty much Greek to her. In her mind's eye she only saw brown men with loincloths, looking quite good. She saw women who had never heard of brassieres tapping latex out of big trees.

Despite her lack of comprehension she liked the gesture, she wrote. She liked the idea of the shower that hung from a branch and was heated by the sun, she liked the all-terrain wheelchair, she even liked the non-timber forest products that stopped you from having to cut down the trees; but there was no room for her in all of that. There was no reason for her to go into the office anymore, to draw a paycheck for sitting at an empty desk and staring at the unruly stacks of his boxes—boxes whose documents were no longer relevant anyway. She was alone in the shell of what had once been his company, and she was turning the light off, locking the door behind her, and leaving.

She was still his mother-in-law, she wrote jokily, so he had better be nice to her. She hoped all was going well in Borneo. She hoped there were no more frightening incidents of violence. Here in the city, she was digging up her yard. She was fending off lawsuits with moderate success. Her house was turning into a retirement home, though it still retained its displays of ferocity. Old people roamed the halls, forgetting everything. The old people forgot their lives, but still they kept on living them.

•

None of the others were in the house when the backhoe driver came to get her, beckoning but not saying much, wiping his dripping brow with the back of his forearm and swigging from a large bottle of orange soda. It was the end of the afternoon.

She followed him out the French doors in the back, through

the pool enclosure, down the path to the grove. She saw the yellow of the digger first and then a waist-high mound of dirt piled up beyond. Then she was at the hole, standing a couple of feet back because the edge obviously wasn't stable—the soft, dug-up earth gave under her foot when she put her weight on it. She couldn't see in: only a small round of darkness behind the hill of soil.

"But what is it?"

"It's a tunnel. It's got a ladder going down."

She peered over, her stomach turning in a quick thrill.

"But no—no manhole shaft? No metal tube that goes down? That's what Portia said there'd be."

"No metal tube, no. The cover was just sitting there on some cement."

"Huh."

"Can't see how deep it is right now, " he went on. "Too late in the day. The sun's low."

"Then we should wait till tomorrow to go in?"

He fished in a baggy pants pocket for what turned out to be a soft pack of Camels, so badly crumpled the cigarettes should be broken.

"We need to get the dirt back a ways from the opening, make sure it's not going to fall in and collapse the thing. I can't vouch for how safe it is even after we do that, though. That shit's not my deal. You need to get some kind of professional in to reinforce it or test it or whatever before anyone tries to go in there."

"But can you at least move the dirt out of the way now? So you don't have to come back? Or is it already too dark for that?"

He flicked his lighter and lit up and she asked him for one, leaned in close so he could light it for her. After they both inhaled he shrugged and then nodded and blew out his smoke. "We got another forty-five minutes easy."

She watched as he stubbed out his cigarette and climbed back into the digger. He pulled a lever and crunched a gear or two and the yellow arm behind the cab rose off the ground: JCB, read the black letters on the side. It was a claw, though she didn't know if that was the official name. She went back to the house as he started rolling, got herself a bottle of beer from the refrigerator and brought it out to drink while she watched. She looked down at the dirt, at the tracks the backhoe left in the loose piles and in the sparse grass that was flattened beneath the tires; she looked up at the light in the canopy of the trees.

It was a light she'd seen a hundred times before—a light she knew from cinematography as well as from life, a certain familiar watery flutter of sun through high-up openings in the leaves. The way it slanted down, the way it wavered through the blur of green, conferred a sense of a life unmoving yet slowly filtering memories—waiting, existing without a sign of change in the long, semi-bright moment before dark.

•

When he drove the backhoe away and her front gates closed behind him it was dusk.

Jim wasn't coming; he had stayed late at work and she would see him later at the restaurant—a famous, touristy place where the Chinese food was bland and greasy but the good tables had an unparalleled view, on a verandah high on a hillside, overlooking the valley.

She scrounged around in the kitchen drawers till she found a flashlight with live batteries and took it out to the hole in the yard. The soil had been smoothed back and she stood a few inches from the edge, pointing the flashlight down into the hole. She saw the metal rungs of the ladder and could make out, on the walls of the tunnel, a pattern of brickwork. She didn't think it was deep; she thought she could make out the bottom, a dim, flat floor.

If the bricks collapsed, no one would know where she was. She stood still, hesitating.

In front, headlights scoped around and then cut off as a car turned into the drive. It was someone who had the gate remote. She stood with her flashlight pointed at the house, listening. A couple of car doors slammed faintly.

The old ones had returned.

They left Angela with Ellen Humboldt in the kitchen, heating up microwave dinners: chicken with small cubes of carrot, Susan noticed, which resembled the rehydrated food of astronauts or recalled the gray airplane upholstery of economy flights to Pittsburgh. Angela had once been a good cook but these days she was catering to Ellen, who preferred to eat small portions of highly processed frozen entrees. Portia and the gray lady came outside with Susan—the gray lady whose name, she realized, had been told to her enough times now that she could never ask again. She would have to listen slyly to the others until she caught it.

"So where do you think it could lead?" asked Portia, carrying her own flashlight.

There were footlights along the path, but once they came to the end of the flagstones and into the dark of the trees they needed the spots of light at their feet.

"Maybe down to an old cellar, at least," said Susan. "On the original plans there was a basement and a wine cellar. But it's so far from the house, Jim says there's no way."

"It would be better to wait till morning," said Portia.

"I'm just going to take a quick look," said Susan. "That's all. Just to see what it is. Then I'll come up the ladder again."

She knelt next to the hole, her flashlight in a back pocket, as the lades focused their beams on the first rung of the ladder. She stretched a foot back and felt for the bar.

"What if the ladder's unstable?" asked Portia. "You could fall down and break your neck."

"It's not that deep," said Susan. "Maybe twelve feet. Maybe fourteen."

She looked up at their faces, relieved to see that the gray lady was nodding.

"Hold on to my hand till you get down a ways," said Portia, and reached out to Susan, who grabbed it.

"Here goes," she said, and put her weight on the top rung. It held; it was solid. Down to the second, the third, the fourth, until she could let go of Portia's hand and grab the top rung with both of her hands. Their flashlight spots glanced off the bricks, into her face when she looked up, blinking, and then away again. A few seconds later she felt hard ground beneath the leading foot, stepped onto it and switched on her own flashlight.

"Concrete floor," she called up as she turned. Her magnified voice echoed.

"What do you see?" asked Portia.

"A door," she said. She stood in a kind of simple well, nothing to see but the bricks around her, the cement beneath her feet and the gray of the door.

It was metal, with a key lock. She felt a sinking disappointment but reached out anyway and grabbed the knob—gritty with dust, but it turned without stopping and she felt the mechanism click. She pulled it toward her and it gave; cold air swept in. Ahead there was a hallway with the same concrete floor and brick walls. The end of it was too dark to see, but it seemed to lead back toward the house.

"Give me five minutes," she yelled, turning her face up so that the old ladies were sure to hear.

"I warn you, after that it's 911," said Portia. "Because we're not standing here all night, and I'm certainly not coming down."

Susan pointed her beam at the narrow hallway's ceiling: a naked bulb with a dangling cord. That meant it was wired. She reached up and pulled: nothing.

Maybe the bulb was out, she thought, and kept walking.

The hallway turned and she faced another door—nothing but that. It was just like the first and like the first it opened. She pulled it all the way back until it scraped the wall beside her and stopped; she stepped in. And here she was, in her own basement.

It was a gray, industrial space, almost clinical. There were old pipes along the ceiling, dusty and utterly dry, bearing no beads of moisture; there was the same gray cement floor, stretched out from where she was standing. In rows stretching along the far walls, and then spaced neatly between them like library stacks, were banks of metal cabinets that looked like high school lockers, and between them aisles with enough space to walk. There was the thick smell of mothballs and also something else—a chemical scent she couldn't identify.

It was surprisingly dry. She scoped her flashlight around again, looking for another lightbulb, and finally saw a switch on the wall. After she flicked it there was a pause, then a series of clicks and flickers and the overhead fluorescents went on, long bulbs in the ceiling, mostly out of sight beyond the tops of the cabinets. They cast a sickly, clinical light. She turned off her own. Other than the closed cabinets everywhere she noticed only one other element: sacks marked with printed words, lying along the tops of the cabinets and piled on the floor at their ends. She leaned down to the pile nearest her and read the words on the bags: SILICA GEL MIXTURE. DESICCANT.

Desiccant, she thought. Desiccant?

She heard someone call, then—it must be Portia. She propped the basement door open quickly with a bag of the silica so the light would fall into the hallway, then ran back along the hall.

"I'm fine, I'm fine. No 911 needed," she called up from the bottom of the well. "It's a basement. It's just a basement. But there's a lot of storage space and I want to check it out."

"I'm curious," came Portia's voice. Flashlight beams shone into Susan's face.

"Relax, get on with your evening," said Susan. "I'll give you a full report. Go inside and have dinner, don't wait outside in the dark. Really—it's just a basement. Concrete and brick and there are lights that work. The walls aren't going to fall in on me."

She waited till they took their flashlights and left, then went back down the hallway. In the morning, she was thinking, she'd bring Jim down and he could help her look for the connection between the basement and the main house—there must have once been a door, must have once been a passage between them. It made no sense, this isolation.

The metal cabinets were of all different widths, she saw, some tall and thin like lockers, others as wide as a walk-in closet, and all closed tightly, though she could see no locks. When she pulled at the handle on the first locker she felt another pull against her, as though the door was vacuum-sealed. But the handle moved down, there was a pop, and the door was open.

She thought at first it was a fur coat. But it was simply a fur— beautiful, striped—or maybe more like a hide, not as thick as a fur, coarser and more like horsehair. Striped horsehair, golden-blond and white.

She pulled it out gently—it was fastened inside somehow, maybe hanging from a hook or something—and saw it had a mane, and even the mane was striped. Moving up from the mane, it had ears, eyelashes and eyelids. It had a face. It was a whole skin, maybe—a whole beast, minus the architecture. On the inside of the door a sticker bore careful notations in ballpoint block letters: *Africa Mammals 2.1.6.11. Damaged. Equus quagga quagga. South Africa native. Collection. Zoological specimen, Artis Magistra, Amsterdam. @ 1883. In wild, @ 1870s.*

She let the hide fall back into its closet. You couldn't mount it, she thought, at this point—she suspected it was too late for that, though she was no expert. Maybe her uncle had kept it because of its monetary value. An antique skin had to be worth something—possibly even for DNA study, if he had known about that, although he'd never struck her as much of a scholar.

She counted the doors, moving back through the room—dozens of separate compartments, hundreds even. She would open a couple more before she went upstairs. Possibly these were the spillovers from his collection, the skins that were substandard and therefore not fit to mount.

She was near the back, standing in front of one of the larger compartments; it had double doors, two metal handles that met in the middle. She took one in each hand and wrenched them downward. It took a minute, but then the seal broke, they too came open and she stood back.

It was a wolf, already mounted. A gray wolf, it looked like to her. It stood with its front paws close together, its head raised, as if listening. The mouth was shut; it did not look fierce at all, merely attentive, even faithful.

She turned to look at the right-hand door, where another white sticker read *North America Mammals 1.1.7.01. Newfoundland wolf, Canis lupus beothucus. Canada native. Extermination. Wild specimen, @ 1911.* It was a kind of wolf she hadn't heard of, she thought. But she couldn't leave it here: she would have it moved upstairs. The next cabinet took her by surprise: a huge penguin-like bird, black on its back and white on its stomach, standing on a fake rock. It was almost three feet tall, and had big, webbed feet and atrophied-looking wings. *North America, Europe Birds. 1.2.1.02. Great auk, Pinguinus impennis. Iceland native. Collection. Zoo specimen, @ 1844.*

The great auks were extinct—had been for a long time. She had read about it in one of the old man's natural history books, a thick one in the library with lithographs or pen-and-ink drawings, she didn't know which. She'd trailed her fingers over them for their minute details and the fineness of the lines. She found it while she was looking up another bird, looking up *albatross.* She'd wanted to know what kind of scenery an albatross would need, to order a fix on an albatross mount, and then she came to *auk* and read the auks' story and it was impossible to forget. Auks mated for life; they did not know how to fly and walked very slowly, so they were easily taken. Around the middle of the nineteenth century the last known pair in existence was found incubating a single egg on a rock in Iceland. Both the adults were quickly dispatched by strangling and their only egg was crushed beneath a boot.

The auks had been known to be on their way out, down to that one last, isolated colony, and collectors had wanted them for the skins.

Had the wolf and the quagga also vanished?

She crossed the room and opened another cabinet at random— a small, square one at eye level. She saw what looked like a mouse. *South America Mammals. 3.1.8.06. Darwin's rice rat, Nesoryzomys darwini. Galápagos native. Competition by nonnatives. @ 1929.*

Beside it, in another square compartment, was a brown frog with yellow spots sitting on a large plastic leaf, which looked, like most of the amphibian mounts in the old man's collection, as though it had been shellacked. *South America Amphibians. 3.3.7.14. Long-snouted jambato, Atelopus longirostris. Ecuador native. Uncertain; disease, weather warming. @ 1989.*

She turned and went to another wall, opened another small locker and this time found a bird: *Asia Birds. 5.2.2.08. Bonin Islands grosbeak, Chaunoproctus ferreorostris. Japan native. Habitat destruction by nonnatives. Zoo specimen, @ 1827.*

She stopped and looked around her—the many closed doors beneath the fluorescent tubes, the few she'd left standing open with their mounts visible within. The bags of silica gel must be to keep them from molding, though it wouldn't work forever. Maybe they were already gathering mildew, breeding the larvae of beetles and moths beneath their wings or claws . . . they should be moved, she should move them as soon as she could. She wondered what T. would say, with his interest in rare animal species. All of these were extinct, obviously; the dates would have to be when they disappeared.

In a dark back alcove off the main room, past what looked like a disused furnace, she saw a big glass case. There were no fluorescents on that section of ceiling and it was too dim to see; but maybe the case had its own light. She walked over and looked around on the wall for a switch, but couldn't find one and impatiently turned on her flashlight instead.

Inside the case there was no backdrop—no diorama at all, only a bare plywood floor and an oversized bird skeleton. It was brown and ancient, not the usual clean white of bones, and its bill had a bulbous, rounded end. From head to foot the skeleton was easily the size of the great auk and looked like a dinosaur to her, maybe a kind of bird dinosaur, but the sticker on the side read

Raphus cucullatus. Dodo. Competition by nonnatives, some collection. Mauritius @ 1688–1715.

That was all.

It had to be: the old man's legacy.

•

Upstairs the women drew near her when she went into the kitchen—Portia and the gray one, at least, who hovered close at her elbows and plied her with questions. Angela and Ellen stayed seated at the table, forking up their frozen meals out of cardboard boxes with the lids peeled back; Oksana had come back and was counting pills into piles on the counter.

"It's just a regular basement with a lot of closet space," she told them. "And more skins for taxidermy."

"Good lord," said Portia.

"Talk about overkill," said the gray lady, in a small chirp of a voice.

"I think these might be valuable, though," said Susan. "I think maybe a university or something might even want them. Maybe they could be donated."

"Dear, aren't you late for the meeting with your lawyer friend?" asked Angela—as though Jim didn't, for all intents and purposes, live in the same house with them. With Angela what was familiar frequently became strange, the near withdrew into the far distance and then came close again. She moved a cube of carrot around with her fork.

Susan had almost forgotten, she realized, after the basement. It was late but she could still go to meet him.

"Thanks for everything," she told Portia, and took the back stairs up to her bedroom to change her clothes. In fact she felt cut off and subdued. She couldn't say anything to the old women, she was not qualified to tell them about the basement's contents. She was marginal in all this and they were even further away from the matter: they had nothing to do with it. She couldn't bear to say the wrong thing about it, disturb the truth with a false statement. She didn't know what the legacy was, if it was important or run-of-the-mill, whether its specimens were real or reconstructed, contraband or legal. For all she knew they had been stolen in the first place. Best to move on, best to close off the subject of the mounts in the rooms beneath to casual discussion and quietly bring in her own natural history expert.

Best to leave out what purported to be the skeleton of a dodo.

10

When they got back she'd had too much wine—Jim had driven them home—and she collapsed on the bed, useless for sex. He kneeled at the end of the bed and took off her shoes for her, slipped off her skirt and lay down beside her as she pulled the sheet over herself, groaning.

"Ice water?" she asked, pathetically. "Please?"

"Sure," said Jim, and heaved himself off the bed again. "I'll brave the geriatrics."

"Aren't they asleep?"

"Some of them are nocturnally active."

He didn't come back immediately and soon she felt too dizzy lying down. To make her head stop spinning she stood up and went to the bathroom sink, where she splashed water on her face.

She found some aspirin in the medicine cabinet and swallowed three tablets with tepid water drunk messily from the tap. She thought of the shaft walled in bricks, the shaft that struck right down into the ground, and now it seemed to be imbued with a mysterious and magnetic attraction . . . down into the earth, down below, into the caverns that for years had known no footfalls but her own. She thought of the stainless steel rungs of the ladder, which she had descended with care and with deliberation as though she were an explorer, a miner, a sailor on a submarine. When she descended the rungs of a ladder she had a direct, secret and linear purpose: she would open the doors. She would go down there now and open all the doors.

She expected to run into Jim on the way out of the house, take him with her down into the well. But she cruised through the empty, well-lit kitchen and did not see him, cruised out to the back, clutching her flashlight, stumbling awkwardly over pieces of ground in the dark. Still she often felt she was floating, elevated—no doubt due to the fact that she was so far from sober. Barefoot, she had to pick her way over the flagstones, not wanting to step into the cracks between them, not wanting to feel the hard nubbins of rock on the tender soles of her feet. She had never had the benefit of tough feet, never formed calluses on the balls of her feet or the back edges of the heels or the big toes.

"Never got the tough feet," she said aloud, sloppy.

At the shaft she told herself to be extra careful, reminded herself she was loaded and this would be a perfect time to break her neck, crumpled and wasted at the bottom of a brick-lined well. She held the flashlight in her teeth—it barely fit, and biting

down on it made her jaw ache—and descended with the uneven-
ness of her own heavy breathing filling her ears. She almost lost
her footing twice, her bare feet slick on the metal.

Then she was down, through the door, along the hall and into
the locker room, where she turned on the light and staggered to
the first bank of cabinets.

Open them, she thought, open, open, open.

The first was a gazelle, the second some kind of warthog, then
a pygmy hippopotamus. In a bank of smaller boxes there was a
bear's head, a mouse, a bat labeled FLYING FOX. A kind of cat with
huge ears—a serval subspecies, according to the sticker—and the
head of something cow-like, almost like a longhorn but thinner,
labeled HARTEBEEST. Then reptiles: a skink, a tortoise, a big boa.
All the stickers had dates on them, all of the species had expired,
some as far back as the early nineteenth century. A duck, an owl,
a parakeet. Pigeon, starling, dove; coot, petrel, warbler.

Then she was past Africa and into Europe: a Caspian tiger,
a Caucasian moose, an elk, an ibex, a lynx, a hare, a dormouse.
Two lizards, a raven, a glass tray of insects labeled PERRIN'S CAVE
BEETLE and TOBIAS CADDISFLY. Past Europe to Oceania: wallabies
from Australia, rats, long-eared bats, one kangaroo. From New
Zealand some birds—shorebirds with long, straw-thin legs, a
bunch of tiny wrens, a tray of snails, a gecko. Then she was in
Asia and the doors opened to a leopard, a pig, a Japanese sea lion,
an ostrich. The sea lion she stopped and stared at—its brown
hide faded to gold and then back, and its head, much like a seal's,
was graceful with huge black eyes and long black whiskers.

Her head was still spinning and she wished she'd brought
more water. Water, water and more water—she needed it—

but she couldn't stand to retreat now. She had to open all the doors. North America next, where there were still a lot of closed cabinets—first the birds, far more of them than she'd known were lost, bright-colored tropicals, macaws and parrots and parakeets. Then reptiles, iguanas and salamanders, frogs and fish—chubs and trout and dace and shiners. The cabinets of small mammals—a shrew, a vole, a fox, a gopher, a pygmy rabbit, a skunk. Then she was throwing open the big doors to a bighorn sheep, a bison, a monk seal, a jaguar . . .

She was tired already, she realized. Too many doors. Closed and open. The old man had been far more methodical down here than he had been with the more pedestrian collection in the house above. She stood with her ears ringing, her bare feet cold against the cement floor, her eyes smarting, her thoughts muddled. She was looking back at the door she'd come in through, all the way open against the wall, and saw something protruding from behind it on the wall—a picture frame, it looked like. She crossed the room and closed the door.

It was a framed map of the basement, a floor plan with each bank of cabinets labeled by continent and taxon. *South America Mammals* or *Asia Reptiles*, for all of the continents. At the top of the plan were the black words, in old-fashioned type, GLOBAL HOLOCENE EXTINCTIONS. @ 1800–2000. At the bottom, THE LEGACY COLLECTION. A PROJECT OF HUNTERS CLUB INTERNATIONAL. But it wasn't 2000 yet, she thought ploddingly. He had been looking forward to his completion date, but then had died before he could finish.

Upstairs was also a map somewhat like this; she had tried in vain to impose a neat order on the collection . . . the story of the auks, she thought. Of how the skins were acquired . . . the question of whether they were murdered for the sake of their own history, murdered in order to become mementos of themselves.

Why did he have to be dead? The old man was dead just like his specimens, but not as nicely preserved and she could ask him nothing. Still she wanted to know about all of this. She wanted to know where he had gotten his bestiary. She leaned in and looked at the map again: there was a piece she thought she had missed, a large square on the corner of the footprint. It appeared to be a room she hadn't noticed, a room that maybe wasn't here. There was no label on it. The square was blank, with only a notch in one side for a door. She turned around, orienting herself. It should be past the dodo case, she thought, the door to the room, and checked the floor plan again to make sure. If it was here at all.

She walked back, past the glass, past the yellow-brown rib cage of the bird. What if that skeleton was fake, she thought—a movie prop from a back lot somewhere or an ostrich or something—and all of this some kind of hoax? Possible. The old man was so inscrutable. In the semidarkness she could see planks propped up against the wall, two-by-fours. She reached up and moved them aside. And there it was: a thin white door in the sheetrock, unfinished. Not even a knob yet, only a hole cut near the edge, where a future knob was meant to go . . . she hooked two fingers into the hole and pulled, and the door wobbled and came off entirely. It wasn't on hinges, even, just sitting there. She set it aside.

Black then, in front of her: a whole separate room. She took a step and fumbled inside to the left, then the right for a switch, and finally she found one. More clicking fluorescents, and she was in. She thought it was empty at first, until she noticed the walls were divided into squares—cabinets, all of them. Drawers. Square white drawers from the floors to the ceilings, like a morgue in a crime procedural, except there was no refrigeration. She assumed the drawers in morgues were refrigerated. Weren't they? Toe tags, people's lips blue? She'd never been to a morgue.

The drawers in this room, like the metal cabinets in the other, were unmarked on the outside. She approached the first one on her right, at eye level, with hesitation. It took her a minute, and then she pulled it open.

Bones, old-looking—maybe a chimpanzee or gorilla, something large and anthropoid, not all connected and not complete, but neatly arranged where they should be. There was only half of one leg, and the skull was far back in the drawer. She could make out a jawbone.

She didn't want to look closely at the skull. The skull was excessive. But then—the sockets of her eyes shot with pain suddenly, her headache returning to prominence—despite herself she opened the drawer beneath: another set of similar bones.

But these had scraps of clothing on them. She saw the foot bones and the shins.

And the drawer above. Filthy, stained-looking and ancient brown bandages: the remnants of some kind of mummification process. She'd seen one long ago on exhibit, though mostly she remembered the pharaoh's gold coffin with his headpiece of blue stripes. But this was no monarch. More reminiscent of those glassed-in scenes of Indians, old-fashioned displays from before the days of political correctness—the colonial superiority, the cruelty of patronage. Women in beaded headbands sitting and grinding corn on concave stones near a campfire, or women weaving with their papooses on their backs, a scene from a made-up history.

She looked for a label now, found she was looking, inevitably. And it was there, on the inside of the drawer's front panel, hard to make out at first.

Haush tribeswoman. Tierra del Fuego, Argentina. Extermination, measles, smallpox. @ 1925.

The label in the middle drawer, which held a smaller skeleton, read *Chono youth, T del F, Argentina. Early 20th c.* The bottom drawer, with a label printed on a dot-matrix printer, as though it was more recent: *Yaghan man, "Domingo," T del F, Argentina. Measles, other diseases, prob. introduced by missionaries. @ 1960.*

The headache came in waves—maybe the aspirin would dull it once it was all the way into her system. She sank down to the floor, her back against the closed drawers. Her knees were raised in front of her and she studied them. If she dropped her knees to the cold floor and her legs stuck out straight she would be a parallel set of bones . . . it made no sense, she thought: he had his club, they had their animal trophies; his club hadn't hunted these dead people, the members of vanished tribes. It was as though the old man had changed his angle at the end of his life, suddenly. Almost—though she would never know, she thought, self-pitying—as though he had veered from his hunting trajectory, from his celebration of killing, into this plain and sad little corner. An unfinished room of people's bones.

The room had a melancholy spareness, the end of a long fight, a battlefield desolate with the flattened—the now so modest!—remains of the dead. Above the dry winter grasses rose the pen-

nants of friends and enemies alike, shredded and flapping in
the wind.

•

Someone was saying her name; she must have nodded off. A
ghost of the old man, maybe, or one of the victims in those far-
off tribes, killed with measles, killed by the passion of the emis-
saries of Christ.

But no: it was only Jim. He was calling down from a hole in
the roof of the earth. The hole in the world. He called down to
her from the sky.

She got up slowly, not without some twinges of joint ache,
and went through the animal room again, aware of the spectacle
of their dead beauty on both sides of her as she walked, dreamily. She followed his voice toward the brick well, surrounded by
the derelict loveliness. Then the half-light of the open door was
behind her. She blinked and fumbled with her flashlight.

"Susan," he was saying, insistently. "Are you down there?"

She found the switch, felt the plastic ridges under her thumb
and pushed it, raising the light shakily until it captured his legs—
his legs at the edge of the opening. The bottom of his shirt. He
wasn't bending down, rather he was standing. He wore pants.

Of course he wore pants. A man often did.

She liked, come to think of it, the idea of men who didn't
wear pants—Scotland men. Scottishers, Scotch. Was that what
they called them? Scots, that was it. Also men in parts of Asia,
including monks, possibly. And certain Arabs. They wore djel-
labas, for instance. Bless them, bless them, bless all those skirt-

wearing men. Truthfully, the skirts looked good on them. There was nothing feminine about a skirt. Not necessarily. If more of the men, over the course of history, had worn skirts . . . but she, of course, had never been on the battlefield. She and the others of her kind were always far away—the tragedy elapsed and people like her, for much of history, remained on the sidelines. Men slew each other, they slew the animals, went slaying and slaying. Women were mostly witnesses. They were not innocent—it wasn't that simple, not by a long shot—more like accessories to the crime, if not the principal offenders. They saw killing ravage all things beneath the sun and were the silent partner in it. You didn't want to kill, you had no interest in killing—your very genes went against it. Possibly your hormones. Again, the molecules that governed you. But you were also far too weak to stop it. Your weakness was your crime.

Not weaker than the men, per se, just differently weak. The wanting to be liked, avoidance of conflict . . . you were profoundly and eternally guilty of this terrible weakness, this moral as well as physical weakness, the fear of being hurt, of being injured, of being embarrassed. You were crippled by the guilt of being who you were. Guilty of being yourself.

The self-help books urged you to be yourself, and yet, as it turned out, being yourself was the crime to end all crimes.

"Susan! You down there drunk? All by yourself?"

Drunk yes, but not alone.

She turned and looked back to the rectangle of light, past which the corpses lay in state. If there were ghosts here they were the ghosts of men, not of the animals, men hovering over the artifacts of their prey. They had no interest in her, none at

all. Rather it was for her to be interested in them. The ghosts of
men, in this case the ghosts of killers, because that was part of
the atmosphere of institutions . . . a museum held, in its perfect,
orderly, austere glass cases, not only the presence of the artifacts
but the invisible presence of those who had hunted them, those
who had dug them up or even stolen them. The unknown or the
dead people—no, their desire, that was the presence that hovered
there, their deep wanting, part of the sacred air.

When she was married and slept around she'd lived in the
desire of men, in all that ambient wanting, where once she felt
noticed. Now she lived in the aftermath of what they wanted,
among the phantoms of men's desire—not the same men, but
men all the same. It was the feeling you had after a feast, the feeling that came after gluttony and was part regret over the feckless-
ness of the party—the wantonness, the excess. A memory of the
white-draped tables, heaped high with many varieties of sugar
and of flesh. The madness, the sumptuous feast.

The men gave their tragedy to everyone else—handed it
out like a gift. They gave it to the mammals, the birds and the
amphibians. They handed it to whole species of trees, to the
oceans and the forests, where her daughter had gone; handed it to
the far-flung people who had fewer possessions. Beside them, as
they handed it out, stood the wives, hostesses at the gathering—
arranging the tables, placing the silver and linen, the fruit and the
soup tureens. So gracious, nodding and smiling. Smoothing it all.

Her little girl lived with animals now—the ones who were
still alive, though the condition, of course, was fleeting. But she
herself existed in a kind of permanent sculpture, a kind of monu-
ment. When it came to the animals' bodies, or what remained of

them in the mounts, you couldn't exactly call them the dead—or at least, they were a version of the dead that had, in the end, almost nothing to do with who or what the animals once had been. She would tell Jim, though his interest in taxidermy was limited. To say the least. She would reach out to him. I love you, Jim. And I was a slut back then but I loved my husband too. Now he's gone—gone into other molecules. The binding is released, the molecules have not held. The molecules let him go. Now I'm with you, but I'm also with him and I always will be. I'm staying with both of you. We are the memory of others, we are the memory of ourselves.

"No, no, not by myself at all," she called, though her voice was a mumble.

Jim! The dead have sent their bodies down to be with us—the ones with fur, the ones with skin, the ones with scales and hides and feathers. Some of them even have skeletons. They're more beautiful than we are—golden, orange, an iridescent green, scarlet, the blue of tropical water, the blue of skies, the blue of violets. Lions and peacocks, auks and bears. The deep brown of comfort and hibernation. White like the snow. Their faces are so *different*, as different from each other as the faces of people are. But they're not people and they never were; the people tracked them and killed them, then flayed off the skins. I was here the whole time, forgetting everything beyond my field of view. On rare occasions I caught sight of them, but still I never moved.

Jim, listen. I'm so drunk, I'm so drunk. Once God glorified us and made us burst with love—but love of ourselves, in most cases, is all that it turned out to be. And then our human sacrifice. Our sacrifice of everything. But museums are capacious, they can contain both God and molecules, even our passion for ourselves that brought smallpox to baby Indians. I never knew the old man and I never knew his friends; all I knew was keys moving on a piano, a liver-spotted hand and maybe a croquet mallet. We'll keep the stuffed animals, OK Jim? I know you don't like them but indulge me. We'll have them here with us, figures from history, figures that once roamed beyond Pasadena, beyond Palos Verdes, where your rich ex-wife lives whom you will always love. Beyond the inland empire. Both of us love the gone ones, you and I, we live with them still, we always will, but Jim I welcome it. And I don't care who made all this, Jehovah or Darwin—Jim? I really don't give a fuck. My point is, it'll never come back again.

I'll look at them every day, I'll touch them with my hands, I'll listen as they make no sounds, to the ringing stretch of their silence. I'll look at their details for as long as I live—the fur and feathers, the beaks, the bones and shimmering tails. I even like their eyes, made out of colored glass to look like the real ones. I'll walk through the rooms and you can come with me. Here's our ticket; now let's go in. Let's walk along the velvet rope and never touch the specimens. Stay with me, Jim. There's still some time. We'll keep each other company. Stay in these rooms for years and years, live on forever in a glorious museum.

—